# EDUCATING SADIE

ALAYNE SMITH

EDUCATING SADIE



This is a work of fiction.

Cactus Moon Publications, LLC
1305 W. 7th Street, Tempe, AZ 85281
www.cactusmoonpublishing.com

First Edition

ISBN 978-0-9996965-8-3

For Ruth

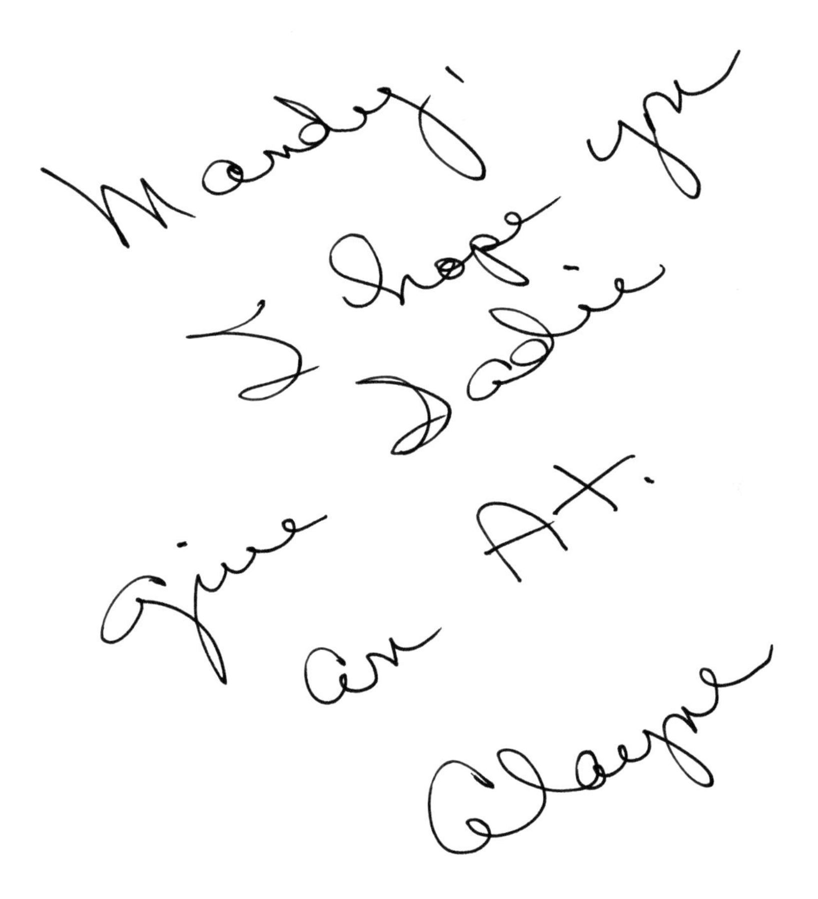

## Acknowledgments

I love the name, Sadie. It's a family name. The Sadie in this novel and the Sadie in our family were strong, intelligent women—the similarity stops there. Our Sadie was married to my warm, caring brother. We were blessed to have her in our lives.

We are a family of teachers—my great-grandfather, my grandmother, my mother, myself, and now our son, Jeff. My maternal grandmother taught in a schoolroom much like Amanda's. It is a noble profession.

I'm grateful to my publisher, Lily Woodmansee of Cactus Moon Publications, who publishes beautiful books. Thank you for publishing *Ellen and the Three Predictions* and *Educating Sadie.*

My editor, Dawn Richerson, is a magician with words. Thank you, Dawn, for everything.

I owe a great deal to Connie Corley and Mary Grace Holder, beta readers who changed *Educating Sadie* for the better.

I am overwhelmed by the support of my friends. Love and gratitude to each of you fantastic women.

A huge thank you to L.C.'s brother, Gene, and his wife, Sharron, for all their help with story ideas, book festivals, and all the other support they've given Ellen and Sadie.

Gaineswood is a National Historic Landmark located in Demopolis, Alabama, and L. C., Sharron, and I spent a wonderful afternoon at Gaineswood with Carolyn Bell and Paige Smith. I love that Gaineswood played a role in *Educating Sadie.*

My husband, L.C., has given me advice when I'm stuck in the telling of my story, edited my books, and has pushed the sale of my first novel, *Ellen and the Three Predictions,* across three states. He's a force!

Our Smith family—L.C, Jeff, Katie, Doug, Christy—is a wonderful family, and I'm thankful to be a part of you.

*Educating Sadie* was a finalist in the William Faulkner - William Wisdom Creative Writing Competition.

Early October 1892

# First Chapter

## Open House at Marshall School

The full weight of her body balanced on the tips of her toes, Amanda Sarah Oglesby, stands before the empty blackboard, straining as she writes, "Education is not preparation for life; education is life itself. John Dewey." The flaky chalk flows across a board that should be black but is instead a ghostly gray, shadowed by the erasures of the many teachers and students who have stood here before her. She takes three steps back and looks up at the quote, then nods with satisfaction. She wants the children and their parents, so many of them poor sharecroppers, to understand the importance of an education. Amanda knows a good education can transport her students anywhere they want to go. She wants to inspire her students to reach further in their pursuits—most importantly, an education.

Everything is in order for Amanda's debut as a first-year teacher. Tonight is open house in Marshall, Alabama. Wandering to the window, Amanda notices a tall, willowy woman walking up the street toward the school. She is attractive and well-scrubbed, but it's obvious from her flour sack dress and bare feet that she's probably poor. The school seems to be her destination even though she has no child in tow. Amanda is curious about this woman, and she watches her for a moment.

Turning away from the window, Amanda takes in the scarred desks with scrolled, cast-iron sides lining the classroom. Each wood-topped desk comes with an attached wooden bench in front that flips up and down. Here, the children will take soon take their seats. On the wall, Amanda has hung maps of Alabama, the United States, and the world—huge maps that hang low so even the smallest student can trace the outline of a state or point to the capital of a European country. Everything is ready.

Amanda is proud to be the lone schoolteacher in Marshall, Alabama. The white clapboard building with a cedar-shingled roof hints at the history inside. Amanda sniffs the faint smell of cedar wafting down from the roof and into the room. It reminds her of the cedar tree at her parent's home at Christmastime.

By far the most noteworthy feature of the old school is the louvered belfry atop the schoolhouse. You can squint through the louvered slats and get just a peak of the old brass bell hanging inside. Inside the front door to the schoolhouse, the rope for ringing the bell snakes down from the ceiling and is securely tied to an oversized black iron hook.

Amanda releases the rope from the oversized hook and wraps it around her small right arm. She grasps the rope with both hands and tugs as hard as she can to ring the bell until she's sure that its clanging is heard throughout Marshall. She stands perfectly still, closes her eyes, and listens to the chatter and laughter of the parents and children of Marshall as they begin to make their way to the schoolhouse for the Saturday night open house. She hears giggles from two small girls, followed by their mother's sharp, "Stop that."

"Lord, give me strength," Amanda mutters under her breath.

Walking back to the window, Amanda notices the tall woman in the flour sack dress has stopped on the sidewalk to the school. Amanda feels the woman is hesitant to enter the school building.

Mr. Pitts, the township school superintendent and owner of Pitts General Mercantile, is the first one through the door. Walking to the window beside Amanda, he too notices the woman in the flour sack dress.

"I'm watching the lady without a child in tow. I think she's coming to open house, but she seems hesitant," says Amanda.

"That's Sadie Wiggins. She's a local sharecropper's wife. She's an interesting one, all right. I haven't had a lot of contact with Sadie, but my first impression is that she's very bright. I hesitate to say this, but I think her husband, Harley, may be abusing her. People in the store talk and I can't help but hear.

"I can't stand to think of any woman in that situation. I hope she comes on in for the open house. Maybe we can help her, Mr. Pitts."

Turning to face Mr. Pitts, Amanda says, "I hear people talk, too, and much of the talk is about the excellent job you and the trustees are doing for education."

In a rural world, away from the uniformity of other state schools, Mr. Pitts and two other trustees set the standards for the Marshall school, standards that would be considered high when compared to other rural counties in the state. Mr. Pitt's only reimbursement for his role as a trustee is to pay no poll taxes and to receive an exemption from jury duty.

Amanda turns as a tall, bony lady with a small boy in tow steps into the classroom.

"Step lively there, Randy. Pick up your feet!" she says to the boy.

Mr. Pitts says, "Oh, Mrs. Peevy, let me introduce you to Miss Amanda Oglesby, our new schoolteacher. And Amanda, this fine young man is Randy. He's all of six years old."

Amanda nods in the direction of Mrs. Peevy, then kneels in front of the boy. "So nice to meet you, Randy." Her voice is filled with a warmth that naturally puts both mother and child at ease. "I'm glad that you are in my class." She smiles at Randy, who is wearing clean, worn overalls and a red and blue plaid shirt that has that stiff look of newness. In all likelihood, it has been saved just for today.

Randy's face turns red as a fall apple, and he slides behind his mother.

"Randy Peevy, you stand up straight and welcome Miss Amanda," says Mrs. Peevy.

Still standing behind his mother, Randy looks up wide-eyed and grins sheepishly. "Welcome, Miss Amanda."

Amanda can almost hear the dripping as her heart melts. This shy, snaggletooth child is charming.

They are interrupted by a raggedy-looking older boy who tears through the schoolroom door and races around the classroom until he notices Amanda out of the corner of his eye. He stomps over, looks her up and down, and says, "If you're the teacher, you sure are short."

All of five feet five inches, Amanda doesn't need this rude boy telling her she's short. "And who are you?" Amanda asks.

"I'm Burt Hester, and I'm the meanest boy in Marshall."

"How do you know you're the meanest boy in Marshall?"

"I know because my daddy tells me I am—every day."

A rough-looking man who Amanda assumes is Mr. Hester walks in and apologizes. "I'm sorry, Miss Schoolteacher. I can't do nothing with Burt since his mama died." Amanda wants to tell him that he might try not telling the boy he's mean. She bites her lip.

Mr. Pitts interjects, "Miss Amanda, this is Mr. Hester. Burt is fourteen and is the youngest of Mr. Hester's children. His wife died last April of consumption."

"I'm sorry to hear about your wife, Mr. Hester. I assure you I'll do all I can to help Burt."

"Thank you, Miss Amanda. I shore appreciate anything you can do with the boy."

Like a breath of fresh air, Mr. and Mrs. Fox come in with their daughter, Ann. Mr. Fox owns the local bank, and Mrs. Fox stays home with ten-year-old Ann. Before Amanda can introduce herself, Ann pipes up.

"You must be Miss Amanda. I'm so, so, so glad you're here! You sure are pretty. I love your long hair and the way you twist it on your head. Miss Amanda. I'm gonna be your best pupil."

"Delighted to meet you, Ann." Amanda turns and looks at Burt who is making gagging noises about Ann's comment. She gives him a severe look of disapproval before turning back to address Mr. Fox.

"I'll be into the bank to open an account next week, Mr. Fox,"

"Ask for me, Miss Amanda. I'll assist you personally." During this entire time, Mrs. Fox has remained silent. Amanda turns to her and smiles. Mrs. Fox smiles back. Though no words pass between them, Amanda feels assured that Mrs. Fox will be one of the supportive parents at Marshall School.

More children and parents jam into the schoolroom and, out of the corner of her eye, Amanda sees Miss Sophie struggling to get up the steps. She's the widow that Amanda is boarding with, and she is wearing a traditional bell-shaped skirt that hugs her ample hips and flares down to a wide hem. Tonight, her skirt is a bright, shiny red and she's topped it with a white, high-necked blouse and leg-o'-mutton sleeves. It's her hat, made of crushed black satin with an outstandingly large ostrich feather that dips down over Miss Sophie's eyes, that completes the look. With every labored step Miss Sophie takes, the feather bounces. Amanda feels a deep affinity for Miss Sophie and is touched that she came out tonight to show her support.

Amanda sees Mr. Pitts help Miss Sophie up to the last step and turns her attention from Miss Sophie to Sadie, who has entered the schoolhouse and seems out of place somehow.

"Hello there," Amanda says. "I'm glad that you could come tonight…?" She leaves the statement hanging with the inflection of an open-ended question, hoping the guest will introduce herself.

The young woman picks up on Amanda's query and replies softly, "I'm Sadie Wiggins. I don't have children, but I wanted to see what it would be like to be in a schoolroom. I hope that's all right."

"Of course. You're more than welcome. Do you live locally?"

"Yes, ma'am. Harley—that's my husband—and I are sharecroppers on Mr. Owens land. She adds with pride, "We own our own mule and plow. Mr. Owens gives us the seed. We do the plowing and planting. I guess there are worse ways to live. But there's so much more to living than plowing the land. I dream of reading books and traveling to Rome and Egypt and the Greek

Isles. Through the books, of course. I could never really go to those places."

Her voice trails off as she reaches up to the United States map hanging on the wall, idly tracing the Mississippi River with her right forefinger. Amanda notices the sleeve of her homemade dress fall back to reveal an ugly mark on her upper arm. The mark looks like large purple and black fingers as if someone had grabbed her upper arm and squeezed it brutally. Amanda is shocked, yet she doesn't want Sadie to know that she noticed. Her husband is abusing this beautiful woman.

"Thank you for talking with me, Miss Amanda."

"You feel welcome to come anytime, Sadie. I'd love to share my learning with you, and maybe we can learn together."

Before Sadie can respond, Mr. Pitts urges everyone to come into the adjacent classroom and take their seats. Marshall Schoolhouse has two rooms—one where Amanda will teach the students and another room lined with chairs facing a stage at the front of the room. The townspeople make their way to the chairs.

Mr. Pitts jumps onto the low stage and speaks in a loud voice, "Good evening. It's my pleasure to introduce our new teacher, Miss Amanda Oglesby from Demopolis, Alabama. Miss Amanda is a first-year teacher, but she has already made a name for herself at Livingston Normal School. First in her class, and that's a fact. Julia Tutwiler herself assured me that we're getting the best."

Much to Amanda's dismay, Mr. Pitts continues his lofty introduction. "While many teachers are prepared to do little more than teach the basic reading, arithmetic, and spelling, our Amanda has finished high school and two years of college. Besides studying the theory and practice of teaching, Amanda's studies included botany, chemistry, geology, Greek, Latin, mathematics, philosophy, and political economy. I'm proud to announce that in our schools—yes, I include the colored school—we're moving away from memorization and strict discipline to a child-centered method of teaching. Miss Amanda Oglesby is going to lead the charge in Marshall for a better education for all our children."

*Lead the charge? My goodness!* Amanda stands to address those gathered for the open house. She smiles at the group and thanks to them for coming. "I'm here to answer your questions, so please see me after the meeting. I'll stay as long as you have questions."

# Second Chapter

## Miss Sophie Gives a Tour

Miss Sophie patiently waits as Amanda straightens the room and, one by one, turns down each of the gas lanterns lining the wall of the old schoolhouse.

"You made quite an impression on the folks of Marshall, Amanda. Being off to a good start is nice. But I have to tell you; there's more to life than teaching." She pauses then picks right up. "You need a man. Now I recommend Leonard Staple. He works at the mercantile store, has never been married, and doesn't drink. Why don't I invite him over to the boarding house for dinner?"

"Miss Sophie, I don't need a man right now. All I want to get this school year off to a good start."

"Now Amanda, every young woman needs a man. Me, I'm too old, but I'm going to see that you are fixed up with a suitable young man. Mark my words."

Amanda grabs Miss Sophie's arm and catches a whiff of lavender as they begin their descent down the steps of the old schoolhouse. "You know what I need from you, Miss Sophie? I need a tour of the town. Can we do that on the way back to the boarding house?"

"Certainly, child."

At that moment, Miss Sophie's spaniel, Harold, ambles up and licks Amanda's ankle. She bends down to scratch his head and the silky ears that almost drag the sidewalk. Amanda says, "Come on, Harold. Miss Sophie is gonna give us a tour."

The two walk arm in arm down Walnut Street, then turn left to begin the walk down Main Street. Gas streetlights line the street filled with the buildings that make life go 'round in the peaceful town of Marshall, Alabama.

Here, Miss Sophie begins the tour in earnest. "Well, Amanda, on the left is Clifford King's law office. I know you'll meet him soon. He's one of the three school trustees, though I'm not certain I saw him tonight. And here on the right is the train depot and post office all rolled into one. Elizabeth Fuller, who boards with me, has been depot agent for the Southern Railroad for five years, and her father was depot agent before her. They wanted her to be postmistress as well. She said she'd agree to it if they'd put the train depot and post office in the same building. And voila! They did.

"When do I get to meet Elizabeth, Miss Sophie?"

"I imagine she'll be there when we get in tonight. You should get along with her. She's not too much older than you."

Miss Sophie continues, "Next is the jail on the left. We're lucky to have Sheriff Winfield as our sheriff. Things are pretty quiet here in Marshall, thanks to him. Now, see that empty lot across the street? Clifford King is trying to build a Knights of Pythias building there—no success yet."

"What are Knights of Pythias?" asks Amanda.

"You'll have to ask Clifford. I think its purpose is to bring peace and understanding after that Reconstruction mess, but I'm not sure really." Miss Sophie is distracted by Harold. "Harold, come back here. He always has to sniff around that old empty lot."

Amanda says, "Marshall Bank and Trust. That must be Mr. Fox's bank there on the left."

"Yes, and the largest store in Marshall, Pitt's General Merchandise, is across the street from the bank. Most popular place in Marshall—along with J. H. Sprig's Grocery."

"My gosh, Miss Sophie. Look at that mansion across the street. Looks very grand, especially mixed in with all these businesses."

"Oh child, that's Mable Todd's mansion. She lets her husband, Theodore, live there, too. Avoid her like the plague. She's a racist, a born-with-a-silver-spoon-in-her-mouth woman. You do want to avoid her if you can. Fortunately, she has not spawned any little Mables."

They continue down the sidewalk to Miss Sophie's boarding house. "Miss Maggie, the doctor's widow, lives across the street from me, and she fancies herself a rebel. She's modeling herself after her relative, Dr. Fedelia Harris Reid, who organized the Wisconsin Florence Nightengale Union during the Civil War. Dr. Reid tended to soldiers in the field and the hospitals wearing bloomers. Maggie's pretty much doing the same—wearing bloomers and tending to the ailing. Enough about Maggie—the churches, Methodist and Baptist, are further down the street. The roundabout is after the churches, where you'll see a statue of Mildren Pickens, Marshall's famous liberator of women. And that's that, young lady."

Amanda leans over and kisses Miss Sophie's cheek. "Thank you for supporting me tonight, and thank you for the tour. I'm lucky to be boarding with you."

"Come on in, child. I'll put the tea on and serve us some apple crumb cake."

"Sounds wonderful, Miss Sophie."

When they enter the kitchen, Sister Sarah, who Amanda met when unpacking this morning, is sitting at the table with her tea. Sister Sarah is a psychic. Amanda has never known a psychic before. Sister Sarah could be Miss Sophie's duplicate—same bell-shaped skirt, same white blouse with leg-o'-mutton sleeves, and same shape with ample hips and an even more ample bosom. Sister Sarah is distinguished by the delicate scent of orange flower perfume she wears. That and her hair. Whereas Miss Sophie's riotous red curls are piled up on top of her head, escaping any kind of order, Sister Sarah's smooth, brown French twist is refined and understated.

"Amanda," she drawls. "Charmed to see you again. You must let me read you."

At that moment, a young woman who can only be Elizabeth floats into the kitchen. What a stunning girl. Dressed in her light blue, high-waisted dress with its silk ribbon at the waist, she makes quite the picture. Any woman would want that creamy skin and dark brunette hair that hangs to her waist.

"You must be Amanda," says Elizabeth. "I've been dying for you to get here. We need another young person for Miss Sophie to spoil. She's making me rotten."

Amanda laughs. "Nice to meet you, Elizabeth. You're the postmistress and the depot agent?"

"Yes, I'm doing my best to keep the trains running and the mail flowing through Marshall."

"I'm impressed. That can't be easy."

"Well, I learned a lot about the Southern Railroad from my father. I am trying my best with the mail. The folks here in Marshall are pretty forgiving about my mistakes."

"I'm glad to hear that. I hope they're that forgiving about my teaching. Speaking of teaching, if you'll forgive me, I'm going to head upstairs. I need to think about that first day of school on Monday. I'll have the apple crumb cake later if that's all right."

"Of course. Good night, child. Sleep tight," says Miss Sophie.

"Thank you again for the tour, Miss Sophie. And I love that you came to the school tonight. See you in the morning."

# Third Chapter

## The First Day of School

Amanda looks out over the group of twenty-three students in her charge and smiles. “Welcome to the first day of school. We’ll open our day with a prayer. Please stand.” She waits as the students, with varying degrees of grace, get out of their desks and stand. They bow their heads.

Amanda offers up a short prayer, “Lord, guide us through this day of learning. Let us be ever mindful that we are your children. Amen.”

“Amen.” The chorus of students echoes through the room.

“Now, please place your right hand over your heart.” She walks around the front rows showing the youngest students where their hearts are. Amanda recites the new Pledge of Allegiance, published just last month, "I pledge allegiance to my Flag and the Republic for which it stands, one nation, indivisible, with liberty and justice for all."

She then divides the students into smaller groups. The oldest six students sit in the desks on the back row. On their slates, they will work through both algebra and geometry problems that Amanda has written on the blackboard. This process helps Amanda know where to start their instruction.

Amanda assigns the middle group of students, which includes Ann Fox, the poem "I Wandered Lonely as a Cloud" by Wordsworth to memorize and recite. Students have one hour to prepare. As she moves to the front of the room, Amanda hears the mumbling coming from the middle group as they begin to recite. Amanda recites the last lines to herself, "And then my heart with pleasure fills, and dances with the daffodils."

The youngest students, including Randy, are sitting patiently with their slates and chalk ready on their desks as Amanda reaches them. These students are called "Abecedarians," because they've yet to learn the ABCs, which Amanda has written in upper case letters on the blackboard. She starts with the letter A and sings a little song about all the objects that start with the letter A. Amanda then asks the students to form the letter A on their slates.

Amanda asks Ann Fox to come up and work with the youngest students while she returns to check on the most advanced students in the back. She works out the difficult algebra problems on the board and discusses them with the older children. Amanda is surprised that Burt Hester has quite the aptitude for algebra. Before moving to the middle group for recitation, Amanda asks Burt to see her after class. He bristles.

"I see that you are good at algebra. I have some fun problems that you might want to take home with you." The surly look slides off Burt's face, replaced with one of mouth-wide-open shock. She smiles at Burt. "You don't have to take the problems. I think you'd like them, though. I'll have them for you after school." Burt nods his head.

After hearing many recitations of "I Wandered Lonely as a Cloud," Amanda announces that it's time for nooning—lunch and recess. Half the students walk home for lunch, and the remaining students reach under their desks to bring out a variety of metal lunch buckets. Some are lard buckets, and some are tin syrup cans. All repurposed for lunch pails. Amanda hears the lids popping and smells the aromas as students bring out their lunches.

She sniffs in the sulfur smell of cooked cabbage—a little like rotten eggs—and the salty, smoky scent of cooked ham. Amanda brings out her lunch: cheese, bread, and the apple crumb cake from Miss Sophie's kitchen. She and the students, comfortable with each other, eat until they have finished their lunch. Students clean up, close their lunch buckets, and slide them back under the desks.

"Time to go out for recess. I'll be out in the schoolyard if you need me. When you hear the bell, it's time to come in."

"Let's play London Bridge," yells Ann, skipping down the steps.

"I don't wanna play that," sulks Burt.

"Aw, come on Burt. You can choose the game tomorrow."

"Still don't want to play this sissy game, but OK," says Burt.

Amanda watches as two of the older children join hands high to form the bridge. The other players march under the bridge, each holding the waist of the player in front. All the players sing the familiar words together, "London Bridge is falling down, falling down, falling down. London Bridge is falling down, my fair lady."

As they sing, "…my fair lady," the older children forming the bridge drop their arms to capture Randy. He just grins—such a good sport. He is out of the game.

Amanda rings the bell to bring the students back in from recess. As they enter the schoolroom, she herds all the children into the other classroom. She's arranged the chairs in a big circle but invites the students to sit on the floor at her feet if they want to. "Students, you don't know I grew up in Demopolis, Alabama. My parents, Mr. and Mrs. Oglesby, still live there, and they write at least one letter a week."

Amanda takes a letter out of her deep pocket. "This is the last letter I received from my mother, and I'm going to read you part of it. Before I read to you, I want to show you the parts of the letter. Amanda digs down into her pockets and brings out enough letters for all students, including the Abecedarians. She passes one letter to each student.

"OK, open your letters." Amanda waits patiently until the rustling sounds of paper sliding out of envelopes is over. "Everyone is holding a letter. Look at the top right corner. What do you see?"

"The address," shouts one student.

"A date," shouts another.

"That's right," says Amanda. "That part of the letter is called the Heading."

"What's next?" asks Amanda.

"Dear Amanda," says Ann proudly.

"That's correct. That's called the Greeting. So, we know two parts of a letter: The Heading and the Greeting. There are three more. Everything that my mother has written to me about the news from home is called the Body of a letter. What do you see next?"

"Love," says Burt, blinking his eyes in an exaggerated manner.

"That's right, or you could write, sincerely or fondly. That's called the Closing. The fifth part of the letter is the signature or the signed name of the person who wrote the letter."

Amanda continues, "So, five parts to a letter—Heading, Greeting, Body, Closing, and Signature. Don't worry if you don't remember all these. I'll be reading letters to you from time to time, and we'll talk about these five parts each time."

"Now, let's talk about my mother and father. They live right in town in a large, white house right on the Tombigbee River. Several cousins live with them—it's a big house. One of the cousins is named Donald, and Donald doesn't do right. I want to show you a picture of Donald so you can see him in your mind when I read about him. Amanda passes around a picture of a freckle-faced, skinny boy wearing overalls and no shirt. He's holding a Rhode Island Red Rooster. The image has captured the concentration on Donald's scrunched-up face as he tries to hold on to the rooster.

"Here's what my mother wrote about Donald yesterday. Get comfortable, settle in, and let's hear what Donald has done now."

Amanda reads aloud the words her mother has written:

*2 Washington Street*
*Demopolis, Alabama*
*10 October 1892*

*Dear Amanda,*

*Today your cousin Lily baked three coconut pies and placed them on the kitchen windowsill to cool. She went outside to do the laundry and was upset when she returned to the kitchen to see that one of the pies was missing—only two pies sat on the window sill when she came back in the house. Cousin Lily asked your father about the pies.*

*"Lily, I haven't been in the kitchen all day," your father replied.*

*Then Cousin Lily asked Cousin Ed about the pies.*

*"Lily, I haven't been in the kitchen all day," he answered.*

*Cousin Lily was perplexed—she just didn't understand who could have taken her pies. Then she spotted Donald and his dog, Davy, playing in the backyard. Now, as you may remember, Davy, named for Davy Crockett, is a shaggy, black and white dog with few redeeming graces. He and Donald make quite the pair.*

*Lily marched out the back door to the spot where Donald is playing. "Donald, did you steal my coconut pie?" she demanded.*

*"No ma'am, Cousin Lily. Donald doesn't steal."*

*At this point, Lily placed her hands on her hips, leaned toward Donald, and huffed, "Then you tell me why you have coconut pie on your face." Lily turns and looks at Davy. "And why that mutt has coconut pie on his nose."*

*"Well, Cousin Lily, you can go ahead and thank me. You see, Davy was smelling that coconut pie on the window sill and accidentally knocked it to the ground."*

*"I knew it—I knew you and that mutt were responsible. And why on earth should I thank you?"*

*"Because Davy and me cleaned that pie right off the ground for you. That's why."*

After collecting the letters, Amanda dismisses the students for the day, reminding them to take their lunch pails with them. She is pleased to hear the students laughing about Donald and his dog, Davy, as they leave the schoolhouse.

# Fourth Chapter

## An Occurrence at Mr. Pitt's Store

On the way home from school, Amanda pops into Pitt's General Mercantile. Mr. Pitt's store is divided from front to back by a lengthy wood and glass display case. Everything on the left side of the case is for men. Everything on the right side of the store is for women. Women can buy hats, bolts of fabric, and almost anything they need to maintain a well-run home.

Mr. Pitts is crouched down placing feathery hats inside the display case but stands as he sees Amanda enter the store. "Amanda, how was the first day?"

"Oh, Mr. Pitts, it was glorious."

"I'm so glad—bodes well for the school year." Mr. Pitts looks over Amanda's shoulder and asks, "Amanda, have you met Sadie Wiggins?"

Amanda turns to see Sadie standing across the store. "Yes, I met Sadie at the open house. How are you, Sadie?"

Before Sadie can answer, the door to the store is thrown open. An angry, sour-looking man strides into the mercantile. Amanda shrinks away. The man reeks of urine, old sweat, and tobacco. His overalls look like they've never been washed and his face hasn't seen a razor in months, but it's the fingernails that grab Amanda's attention. So disgusting. They are long, broken, and crusted with dirt.

The man growls, "Give me foin pour mon cheval."

"I'm sorry, Zackery. I don't understand you," says Mr. Pitts

The man shouts even louder, "Foin pours mon cheval." He seems to think raising his voice will make him more understandable.

Mr. Pitts leans forward over the counter, "I just don't understand you, man."

"It's French, but I can't make it out," says Amanda.

Sadie crosses the store and stands near the display case. "He wants hay for his horse, Mr. Pitts."

We turn our heads to stare at Sadie. How does a sharecropper's wife in the heart of Alabama know French? As if hearing the unspoken question, Sadie says, "My father was French. I learned to speak French and English growing up."

Zackery turns to Sadie and sneers, "I don't need help from no femme. Worthless—tous."

Amanda says, "I'd think you would appreciate Sadie's help."

"And who are you?"

Mr. Pitts interjects, "This is our new schoolteacher, Zackery."

"Kids ain't gonna learn from no femme. Ignorant bitches, all of 'em."

Everyone was so focused on Zackery; no one notices Miss Maggie creep up on him until the six-inch barrel of her Smith and Wesson revolver presses against his thick neck.

"Hold it right there, Mr. Aucoin. That is no way to talk to ladies. You need to leave right now."

Zackery Aucoin's face is so red and puffed out; it looks like it's going to explode right there in the store. He turns and walks back toward the door with Miss Maggie matching him step for step, holding that revolver against his neck all the way.

"You ain't seen the last of me," Aucoin snarls when they reach the front door.

"For today we have," Miss Maggie responds. She turns and walks back toward Mr. Pitts.

"Well, Miss Maggie. You continue to amaze me," says Mr. Pitts.

"No lady should be exposed to that kind of language," says Miss Maggie.

Amanda can only stare at this five-foot, nine-inch lady who has obvious disdain for the corsets and stiff petticoats that most women wear. She's just as Miss Sophie described her. Her baggy bloomer trousers reach her ankles and have frills of lace at the cuff. She misses being pretty with a nose that's a tad too large for her face. Haphazardly parted in the middle, her brunette hair gathers in a bun at the back of her head, and strands of hair are carelessly falling around her forehead and temples. She jams the gun in her purse and turns to look Amanda in the eye.

"You, obviously, are the new teacher, since I know every other female in town," says Miss Maggie. "Nice to meet you."

She then turns to Mr. Pitts, "Herbert, we have to do something about that Zackery Aucoin. He's an abomination, for sure. I've never seen a body so lacking in social graces."

"I agree," says Mr. Pitts. "But imagine what life is like for his family. You know he has a wife and a small daughter living out in the woods outside of town. I worry about them."

"Well, if he keeps up this behavior someone's gonna shoot him," adds Miss Maggie. Slightly disoriented, she looks around the store as if to find something. "Oh yes, I remember why I came in. Betty Ann Jems is in labor. Do you have any of those cloth diapers? Wanna take those with me. Makes a nice gift."

Mr. Pitts nods. "I'll get them and wrap them up for you, Miss Maggie."

Miss Maggie turns back to Sadie, "How's your husband, Sadie? Farming good?"

"We're struggling but thankful that we have food in our mouths," she says.

"Aren't we all," says Miss Maggie.

Mr. Pitts hands the diapers to Miss Maggie. "I'll put these on your account, Maggie."

"Thank you, Herbert. Nice to meet you, Amanda. I'm off."

After Miss Maggie walks out the door, Mr. Pitts says, "Well, Amanda. You've just met the infamous Miss Maggie Langford, widow of Dr. Langford. In some ways, seems she tries to fill in for him. She delivers most of the babies around here. Even does house calls for simple ailments. She also has more money than she knows what to do with. She's quite the phenomenon around Marshall. You'll see a lot of her, Amanda. She and Miss Sophie are close friends."

As Mr. Pitts turns back to his task of putting hats in the display case, Amanda smiles at Sadie. "I'm impressed that you speak French, Sadie."

"And I'm impressed that you are a teacher at such a young age, Miss Amanda," replies Sadie. "All my life, I've always wanted to learn. There's so much out there to learn. If I could read better and if I had access to books..."

Sadie's passion touches Amanda. "I'll help you, Sadie, and maybe you can teach me a little French. I could share what I learn with my students."

Sadie raises her hands in surprise to cover her mouth. Amanda notices the same dark purple bruise still there on her upper arm. Sadie notices where Amanda is looking and moves quickly to lower her arm and pull down her sleeve. Amanda stares at Sadie, and Sadie slowly shakes her head.

"Sadie, you said your husband is a sharecropper?"

"Yes, ma'am."

"Do you have children?"

"No children, Miss Amanda. I keep house in the mornings and work in the fields with Harley in the afternoon. That's my life."

"Well, Sadie, I'm so glad we ran into each other. I think we can journey to miraculous places together. That's what education does for us."

Amanda swings her bags down to the floor and bends over to rummage around. She pulls out a book, smiles, and hands it to Sadie.

"I'm lending you this children's book by Nathaniel Hawthorne, *Greek Myths: A Wonder Book for Girls and Boys.* Read it and, when you finish it, we'll meet to talk about it."

Sadie takes the book and holds it flat against her chest. "Are you sure I can take it, Miss Amanda?"

"Yes, Sadie. I want you to. Remember we'll talk about it after you read it."

Sadie's eyes sparkle. "I'm so excited, Miss Amanda." She smiles at Amanda.

Amanda picks up her bag and smiles back.

# Fifth Chapter

## All Aboard

"All aboard," Amanda shouts. Her students have been finishing up their early morning exercises and turn to the front of the class where Amanda is standing when they hear her unusual welcome this morning.

"All aboard," Amanda shouts again. "We're going on a train ride this morning." All Amanda's students stare at her, their mouths hanging open.

"Well, get up. Let's go get on the train." Amanda leads the students into the next room where she has lined up chairs two by two. The chairs snake through the room.

Amanda pulls out a train engineer's hat and waves it, asking, "Who wants to be the engineer?"

Most of the students stare at Amanda. Not Burt. He volunteers right away. "I'll be the engineer."

"Fine, Burt. Here's your cap. Please put it on. You are going to drive us to a place called Cahawba."

"Ca…where?" asks Burt.

"That's Cahawba, the site of the first permanent state capital in Alabama," says Amanda. "So blow the whistle Burt, and we'll all pretend we're on a magical train ride to Cahawba."

Burt goes into action. He makes a whistling sound with his mouth. "Whoo, whoo," says Burt as he pumps his hand up and down.

"It's magical?" asks Randy.

"We just pretending, Randy. I'm going to tell you about Cahawba on our pretend ride and then I'll have a surprise for you."

'Now, about Cahawba being the first state capital, the state of Alabama was formed in 1819, and people in the state needed a capital where they could conduct the state's business. They chose a site in the wilderness where Alabama and the Cahawba Rivers come together."

"Where is that, Miss Amanda?" one of the students asks.

"It's near Selma—not too far from Marshall."

Burt asks, "When do I stop the train, Miss Amanda?"

"You can stop now, Burt. We're here." Amanda continues, "The capital was up and running by 1820. Now here's the surprise. Amanda points across the room as she says, "I have borrowed my father's magic lantern."

"It's a magic lantern?" interrupts Sue.

"Not really, but I can use it to show pictures of Old Cahawba," Amanda answers as she lights an oil lamp behind the lantern. A picture of a stately mansion appears on the wall. "This is the Crocheron house built around 1843. The Crocheron family was from New York, and they built Alabama's first statehouse. They owned and operated a mercantile store in Cahawba. R.C. Crocheron built the mansion for his wife.

Amanda changes the glass plate. "This is St. Luke's Episcopal Church. She changes the plate again, "And this is a picture of the rivers. What were the names of the two rivers that merged where they built Cahawba? Do any of you remember?"

"Alabama and Cahawba," shouts Burt.

"Good for you, Burt," says Amanda.

"Unfortunately, Cahawba did not remain the capital for long. Mosquitos spread fever, giving Cahawba the reputation of being unhealthy. Because it was situated near the two rivers, it was prone to flooding. The capitol building itself never flooded, and no records were ever damaged, but the state legislature moved the capital to Tuscaloosa in 1826."

"Cahawba thrived as cotton became a prosperous business in Alabama. Paddlewheel steamboats would take on thousands of bales of cotton at Cahawba. Then came the Civil War. The Union blockaded the shipments of cotton, and Cahawba was no longer a prosperous town."

"This last slide is of the Cahawba Military Prison developed from a cotton warehouse located in the middle of town. By the end of the war, it housed over 3,000 Union soldiers as prisoners."

Amanda reaches to turn off the magic lantern. "That's the end of our visit to Cahawba. Burt, will you drive us back to school?"

Burt places the engineer's hat on his head and grins.

On the pretend ride back to school, Amanda asks, "Does anyone know where the capital is today?"

Amanda hears shouts of "Montgomery," "Birmingham," and "Tuscaloosa."

"Montgomery is the correct answer. It became the capital of our state in 1846."

"Are we gonna take more train rides, Miss Amanda?" The question comes from the back of the room.

"I like them," says another student.

"Of course. I have the next one all planned, but it's a surprise. You'll have to wait until later in the month. OK, this is the end of the line. Burt, you were an excellent engineer. Thank you for driving today."

Burt turns red. "Gosh, Miss Amanda."

# Late October 1892

# Sixth Chapter

## Amanda and Elizabeth Take Charge

The frost is here. That means you cover your tender plants with bed sheets, and you have plenty of wood chopped and stored, ready for burning. It also means it's time for the Fall Carnival, an annual tradition in the town of Marshall. Because Amanda is the new teacher, she has to plan the carnival by default. But she won't plan alone. She's cagey enough to rope Elizabeth into taking charge with her.

"So, Elizabeth, what do you usually do at the Fall Carnival?"

"Well, there's cakewalks, fortune tellers, storytelling, pie-eating contests, and pumpkin carving contests. The little ones can bob for apples and Go Fish."

"The cakewalks will take up a lot of room," says Amanda. "We'll need to hold that in the extra classroom. Why don't we do those early on and have dancing in that room to finish out the night?"

"I like that idea," Elizabeth says. "What kind of dancing? Square dancing might be fun."

"That sounds great. Know anyone who can call a square dance? And we'll need a musician," says Amanda.

"Believe it or not, Clifford King can call a square dance. I'm sure he can round up a fiddle player."

"Let's do that. We could have storytelling in this room between the cakewalk and the dance," says Amanda.

"Yes, we need to get Miss Griffen to tell her ghost stories, too. We could line the kids up on the stage in the room and have a costume judging with prizes," says Elizabeth.

"Wonderful. So that room is taken care of," says Amanda. "First, cakewalks. Then storytelling followed by the costume contest. We'll end the night with square dancing."

Elizabeth and Amanda turn toward the door to Miss Sophie's kitchen when they hear it creak open. Sister Sarah slips into the room. "You two look thick as thieves!" she says. "What are you plotting?"

"We are planning the Marshall Fall Carnival," says Amanda.

Sister Sarah claps her hands in front of her face. "Delightful, girls. I love the festival."

"Are you willing to tell fortunes again, Sister Sarah?" asks Elizabeth.

"Of course, darling girl. I'd love to, but you know I don't tell fortunes at the carnival. I don't want to alienate the population. So it's 'You will marry a handsome, wealthy man' or 'You will travel to far places.' That kind of thing. It's all for fun, after all."

"Sounds perfect, Sister Sarah," says Amanda. "Thank you for helping out."

"My pleasure, girls. Well, I'm off to the mercantile store. See you two darlings later."

# Seventh Chapter

## Amanda Meets Reuben Lee

As the strains of "The Old Rugged Cross" fade away, Amanda picks up her Bible and grabs her fringed green silk shawl just before it slithers onto the church floor. She sees Mr. Pitts making a beeline for her pew and waits for him to reach her.

Mr. Pitts smiles. "Wait up there, Amanda. I have someone for you to meet. He's just outside."

Amanda returns his smile. "Sure, Mr. Pitts. Who is this person I need to meet?"

"Patience, girl."

Mr. Pitts crosses the worn planks of the Marshall Methodist Church and heads down the gray concrete steps. Amanda follows close behind, noticing that colored and whites gather in separate groups outside the church.

"Mr. Pitts, have the colored Methodists and the white Methodists always gone to church together here in Marshall?"

"Well, at one time, the coloreds had a church. Lightning struck it. I think that was back in 1852. The church burned to the ground. Since then, the coloreds have attended the white church— sitting up in the balcony section."

"That's terrible, Mr. Pitts. Don't you think they want their own church?"

"Money, child. It all boils down to money."

"Amanda, I want you to meet Mr. Reuben Lee. He teaches over at the colored school."

Amanda takes in the tall, slim man standing before her. Mr. Lee is impeccably dressed in a gray suit with black pinstripes. His starched white shirt and red bow tie add to the classy image he presents to the world. When he talks, his voice sounds like molasses pouring out of a pitcher.

"I'm so pleased to meet you, Miss Amanda."

"Well, I'm pleased to meet you, too. We have a lot to talk about, being the only two teachers in town. How many students do you have this year?"

"Fifteen. I'd have a lot less if it weren't for Mr. Pitts and the trustees. You know, most towns in Alabama allot only a small percentage of tax revenues for colored schools. In some towns, coloreds don't send their children to school because, when they do, they are required to contribute to the teacher's salary. They can't afford it."

Amanda is surprised by Mr. Lee's information. "It's different in Marshall?"

"Yes, Miss Amanda, it is. Mr. Pitts sees to it that my parents pay nothing to send their children to school. He and the trustees pay my salary outright. I wouldn't want to take it if it came from the parents."

"Mr. Lee, you may have a southern name, but you don't have a southern accent. May I ask where you are from?"

"Of course. I'm from New Hope, Pennsylvania."

"I have to ask—how did you choose Marshall?"

"My grandfather was from this area. I always wanted to visit. I have relatives living here, and they told me the town needed a teacher. My wife was willing, so we moved here last summer."

"Your wife sounds like a brave lady. I want to meet her."

"I'll make sure that happens, Miss Amanda. Louise would love to meet you."

"Has she adapted to life in Alabama?"

"To a degree. Louise misses the library back home. Louise is always happiest when she has a book in her hands."

"We don't have a library here? Guess I haven't been here long enough to notice."

"No, we don't. I would love to have a library at the school so the children can check out books. And, of course, a library for the adults would be wonderful."

"You know, Mr. Lee, we might be able to do something about a library in our schools. I'll bet the church would let us sponsor a drive. We could collect old books and money for ordering new books."

"Miss Amanda, the parents of my children don't have books in their homes. And they sure don't have the money to help with the library."

"I'm sorry, Mr. Lee. Are most of the parents sharecroppers?"

"Some are yardmen, cooks, and housekeepers. They work for a place to stay, food, and a couple of dollars a month pay. But yes, most are sharecroppers. You'll see their board and batten cabins dotting the farm roads around here. They do the plowing, chopping, hoeing, and picking of cotton."

"Do they get to sell the cotton and keep the money?"

"Half the bales of cotton go to the landlord."

"That sounds like a lot."

"It is, but most landowners give them the land, seed, fertilizer, a mule, and a plow. The tenants provide the labor. So, I think you can see they don't have extra money for a library."

"Well, Mr. Lee, let's see what we can do. I'll talk to Mr. Pitts and Preacher Sprague. Maybe they'll make an announcement next Sunday."

"You know, I'd love to see my students checking out *Treasure Island* or *Kidnapped* and taking those classics home to read. It's sure nice to meet you, Miss Amanda. I think you'll stir things up around here." Mr. Lee smiles and tips his hat.

"Nice to meet you, too. You wait," says Amanda. "Our students will be checking out books from our school libraries in no time."

# Eighth Chapter

## Aucoin Causes a Stir

Miss Sophie sits rocking in her rocking chair in the front parlor, preparing her Sunday School lesson. She glances up over her half-rim glasses and stares out the window. She's shocked to see Zackary Aucoin walking down the sidewalk. He's walking straight for her house. This is a different Zackery Aucoin. Today he is wearing clean overalls and a worn, but clean, pale blue shirt. His hair is slicked back with hair wax. There's so much wax in his hair, a monsoon could blow through town, and not a hair on Aucoin's head would move.

"Oh, Lord," Miss Sophie thinks aloud. "He's walking up the front walk."

Miss Sophie sits very still, waiting for him to reach her door. She watches his approach through the large window pane at the top half of the door. When he reaches the door, he will twist the bronze knob just below the window pane to ring the doorbell.

"Surely I'm imagining this. Zackery Aucoin is not on my front porch."

No sooner were these words out of Miss Sophie's mouth than she hears the clanking, ringing sound of her antique doorbell. There's no denying it now. Zackery Aucoin is turning the doorbell on her front porch.

*Courage, Sophie. See what the scoundrel wants.* She takes her time walking from the parlor to the front door, hoping he'll change his mind and go away.

More clanking and ringing.

Miss Sophie reaches the front door, throws back her shoulders and inhales for courage, then opens the door.

"Bonjour, Miss Sophie. Bonjour."

'Good morning, Mr. Aucoin."

"May I come in, Miss Sophie?" He nods his head toward the inside of her house.

"Entrer dans la maison?"

"No, no, Mr. Aucoin. We'll talk right here."

"Well, Miss Sophie. I've practiced in English and hope I get this right."

Zackery shuffles around a bit on the porch, looking at his feet, not sure of himself. He looks up tentatively. "I think you're a fine-looking lady… a bit thick through the hip but a fine-looking lady."

*Oh, Lord ! Where could this conversation possibly be going?*

"Since Ruby gave birth to Emme, she doesn't want me to touch her. Fights me like a she-devil. A man can't get no relief like that."

Sophie gasps.

"Why are you telling me this, Mr. Aucoin? I'm highly offended, and, honestly, I have no right to hear about your personal problems."

"Oh, but you do, Miss Sophie. I've picked you to take Ruby's place."

Sophie stands there, stunned.

"We don't have to—uh, forniquer today. I can come back in a couple of days."

Miss Sophie rolls the word *forniquer* around in her head, then says it aloud, "Forniquer."

*My sweet Jesus. Does the fool mean fornicate?*

Miss Sophie picks up the watering can beside the front door and holds it in front of her like a shield. "Mr. Aucoin. It's time for you to leave my porch. Right now. I'll bean you with this watering can if you don't leave right now."

Miss Sophie raises the can high above her head so she can slam it down on Zackery's head. Zackery holds both hands out in front of him and slowly backs down the steps.

"I'll be back, Miss. Sophie. Je vais retourner." He turns to walk down the front walk.

Miss Sophie can't help herself. She throws her right arm back over her shoulder and, with all the strength she can summon, hurls the watering can forward. It hits Zackery Aucoin square in the back.

He turns and looks at her with an evil-eye squint and says, "You'll regret that, Miss Sophie. And you *will* take Ruby's place."

# Ninth Chapter

## David Henry Callander Comes to Church

Amanda opens her eyes and raises her arms to stretch, stretching so high that the iron headboard clangs against the wall. She laughs out loud and settles back into the squishy mattress. Today is Sunday, and she can't lounge around in bed too long. She already smells ham and bacon frying downstairs in the kitchen — time for her to get up and get ready for church.

Amanda walks to the armoire and, using both arms, swings open the double doors. She looks at the selection of dresses. Pretty minimal. Most of her clothes are still at her parents' home in Demopolis. She pulls out a blue ankle-length dress. She loves the scooped neck and long sleeves tipped with lace that whispers across her wrists. She moves to the walnut chest of drawers and pulls on the worn wooden knobs to open the drawers. Out comes a chemise, drawers, and two petticoats. These make her skirt stand out. And they keep her warm.

After layering these undergarments on her small body, she slides the blue dress over her head. Looking in the mirror, she's not dissatisfied with what she sees. A petite girl—correction, a petite woman—looks back at her. Her long, light brown hair with a touch of honey hangs loosely around her shoulders, curling just a little. Her nose is perfect on her face. Her eyes are October-sky blue, but then there are her ears. Too large for her face and no, they won't lie flat. They stand out from her head. If she's doesn't fluff her hair, they tend to peek through. Amanda smiles at the reflection in the mirror and sticks out her tongue. She can hear her mother, "It's inner beauty that counts, Amanda."

When Amanda walks into the kitchen, she is surprised to see Miss Maggie there. She and Miss Sophie are locked deep in conversation. They don't hear her come in and don't look up.

"You stop this sniveling, Sophie. I'll kill the bastard if he so much as touches you."

"Is everything OK?" Both Miss Sophie and Miss Maggie turn to look at Amanda as she stands in the doorway.

Miss Maggie speaks first. "It's that darn Zackery Aucoin. He was bothering Miss Sophie yesterday."

"Child, how pretty you look," says Miss Sophie. "Come, come–– have some breakfast before it gets cold." It's obvious she doesn't want to discuss Zackery Aucoin in front of Amanda.

Amanda slides out a chair, sits down, and scoots the chair closer to the table. Helping herself to sausages and eggs, she says, "Miss Sophie. You tell me if there's anything I can do."

"Well, child, you can walk to church with me this morning."

***

Amanda follows Miss Sophie down the aisle of the Marshall Methodist Church. Miss Sophie has recovered from her former doldrums and stops to speak with nearly everyone—right and left––as she moves down the aisle. At the sixth row from the front, on the left, Miss Sophie turns into the row and sits down. Sixth row on the left. It's Miss Sophie's seat. No one else would dare sit there.

As the two take their seats, Amanda turns to look around the sanctuary. She makes eye contact with a tall man sitting directly across the aisle. He's not handsome in the traditional sense, she thinks, but he certainly is memorable. The man smiles, and from the corner of her eye, she sees him wink at her. A wink? In church?

Amanda turns her attention back to Miss Sophie, who prepares to open her Bible to the topic of today's lesson on charity. Preacher Sprague booms, "Now turn your Bible to 1 Corinthians 13:13." There's a rustling of thin paper as church members turn their King James Bibles to Corinthians. "And now abideth faith, hope, charity, these three; but the greatest of these is charity." Preacher Sprague opens his sermon.

After the benediction, Miss Sophie and Amanda stand to leave the pew. Amanda spots Miss Maggie on the back row. She knows they will move in her direction and diverts her gaze to the man across the aisle, who is now in deep conversation with Mr. Pitts.

When the two reach Miss Maggie, there are hugs all around, even though the three had met over breakfast hours earlier. Preacher Sprague is standing in the church doorway and strikes up a conversation with Miss Sophie. *Now's my chance.*

"Miss Maggie, who's that gentleman talking to Mr. Pitts?"

"Oh my, girl. You have a good eye. That's Henry David Callander, richest plantation owner around."

"Oh, really. Where is Mr. Callander's plantation?"

"Outside Marshall. It's called Callander. Of course, Callander is the family name: they say it's named for a relative's home in Scotland. It's quite something. The 1,200 acres are made up of rich soil that grows anything. There's a grist mill, a commissary, a syrup mill, a sawmill, a blacksmith shop, even a cotton gin. The Linley River runs on the border of the property and, where cotton is not planted, it's as green as the land in Scotland must be." Miss Sophie finally takes a break. "You interested in that Callander boy?"

"No, ma'am. I had not seen Mr. Callander before and just wondered who he was."

Miss Maggie looks at her with a small, tight frown right between her eyebrows, like she doesn't believe her.

# Tenth Chapter

## The Face in the Window

"All aboard." The students jump up out of their seats at Amanda's call, ready for their imaginary train ride.

"Where are we traveling to today, Miss Amanda?"

"Oh, since it's near Halloween, we're going to a spooky place––Carrollton, Alabama."

"What makes that town so spooky? Doesn't sound spooky."

"Well, hop on the train, and you'll find out. I think we'll let Burt be the engineer again. He's had some experience."

Burt beams as Miss Amanda hands him the engineer's cap. He climbs aboard the front seat, ready to drive the train to Carrollton.

"Let's begin our journey, Burt," says Amanda.

"Whoo, whoo," says Burt.

"Now children, Carrollton is in Pickens County, Alabama, located in the western part of Alabama. It's named for General Andrew Pickens, who fought in the Revolutionary War. Carrollton is the county seat. Who knows what that means—to be the county seat?"

Randy says, "Does it mean where the most people in the county sit?"

"That's a good guess, Randy, but it means that's where they conduct the business of the county. Now, on with our story.

Carrollton County had a courthouse that was burned in 1865 by Wilson's Raiders during the Civil War. Wilson's Raiders were Union troops led by General James H. Wilson."

"They were Yankees," yelled Burt.

"Yes, they were. The people of Pickens County didn't give up when their courthouse burned to the ground. They built another courthouse, and, you know, in 1876 that new courthouse burned to the ground, too."

"Did the Yankees do it, Miss Amanda?"

"No, the Civil War ended in 1865. The citizens blamed the fire on a man named Henry Wells. We do not know that he was guilty. We do know, upon hearing he was blamed for the fire, that he hid out on the third floor of the courthouse."

"How much further, Miss Amanda?"

"You can stop the train, Burt. We're there now." Amanda gets up and walks to the magic lantern, still set up from the last train ride. An image of the Carrollton courthouse appears on the wall.

"Look carefully, children. Find the top window of the courthouse. It's the only window at the very top of the building."

"I see it!"

"I do, too."

"That's the window where Henry Wells was standing, looking out at the men below. There was a group of men milling around the grounds of the courthouse, looking for Mr. Wells. Now, let me tell you, children, they were not going to invite him to supper. They wanted to hang him."

"Because they thought he set the courthouse on fire?"

"Yes, but that's not the spooky part of the story. While Henry Wells is looking out the window, down on the crowd, lightning strikes the window. You won't believe this—lightning engraved the face of Henry Wells on the windowpane."

"Really, Miss Amanda?"

Using the magic lantern, Amanda brings up a shot of the window. Right there on one of the panes is the ghostly image of Henry Wells.

"That's Henry Wells, Miss Amanda?"

"How scary!"

"He looks terrified."

"Now you want to hear the scary part?" Miss Amanda asks.

"Yes, tell us the scary part."

"I don't want to know; I'm scared enough."

"Don't be a ninny. Tell us, Miss Amanda."

"Well, my daddy told me that they have changed that window pane and the face comes back every time."

"It's still there, Miss Amanda?"

If you went to Carrollton today, you could see the face in the window. It will be there forever."

# Eleventh Chapter

## Mable Todd Donates to the Library

Amanda wakes up to the barking of hounds—hundreds of hounds. It sounds like hundreds, anyway, and they are just outside her window. She rolls out of bed and peeks around the window frame. She doesn't want anyone who might be out there with the howling pack to see her.

She sees lawyer King and eight to ten other men, all seated on horses. Each man seems to have at least three hounds, circling the horses and baying. Opening her window to hear their muted conversation, she can tell the men are talking about fox hunting. Poor fox—with that hoard after him.

It must be somewhere around seven o'clock in the morning, but sleeping is not an option, so Amanda gets up to dress for the day. She barely brushes her hair and skips adding the light red lip balm she wears daily. She's in a hurry. Today, she will begin organizing the donated library books. Mr. Pitts is sending over at least one bookcase, and Amanda can't wait to set up the new library.

***

Amanda is standing outside the school, watching the students play Red Rover. "Red Rover, Red Rover, send Ann right over." The object is to pick the weakest spot in the chain and try to break through the barrier.

There are two lines of students, holding hands, facing each other. Amanda watches as Ann runs as fast as she can toward the line of students who are forming a human chain. When Ann hits the chain between two of the smaller children, they hold on for dear life. Surprisingly, Ann does not break them apart.

"Sit down, Ann."

"Yeah. You're out, Ann."

Amanda yells, "Ann, come sit on the steps with me. We'll watch together."

Ann shuffles over to sit down on the steps by Amanda. They watch as Burt breaks through the line easily and takes a student back to his line with him.

"Look, Miss Amanda. It's Mrs. Mable Todd."

Amanda looks up to see a well-dressed lady laboring up the walk to the school. She is trying to hold a large stack of books without dropping them. Amanda has time to check out Mrs. Todd before she reaches the steps. Mrs. Todd is sporting a Settin' Hen on the top of her head. Amanda can barely hold back the grin as she visualizes an actual fluffy hen perched on Mrs. Todd's forehead.

"Well, someone could get up off those steps and help me," the woman says.

Amanda immediately jumps to her feet, brushes off the back of her skirt, and reaches for the books. "Oh, I'm so sorry. I'm Amanda Oglesby, the teacher. So nice to meet you, Mrs. . ."

"I'm Mable Todd. I live in the Todd House on Main Street. When I heard you were forming a library, I wanted to help. Of course, we have a library at home."

"Oh, how fortunate you are, Mrs. Todd. Imagine having your own library."

"Yes, we are fortunate. That doesn't stop me from doing my Christian duty."

"Oh, you are to be commended for that, Mrs. Todd."

"Well, I will tell you right now, my Christian duty only goes so far. Please see that you put none of these books in that colored school."

"Ma'am?"

"I'm sure you heard me. None of these books go to that colored school."

To hide her shock, Amanda deals with the task of getting the books transferred from Mrs. Todd's arms to her own.

"Ann, here. Please take a few of these for me into the schoolroom."

Amanda composes herself and turns to Mrs. Todd. "Well, thank you so much for your donation, Mrs. Todd." Amanda takes note of the books that she hands Ann. "I see that you have donated the finest books we've received to date. History books, the geography of Europe, poems of Henry Wadsworth Longfellow. Excellent, Mrs. Todd. Excellent."

Mrs. Todd preens. She turns to walk back down the path to the school and looks back over her shoulder. "One always has to do one's Christian duty."

Ann and Amanda carry the books into the school room and put them down on the school floor next to other stacks lining the wall.

"Oh Ann, I'm so excited. We're going to have a real library."

"You certainly are, young lady. Do you think some of the older boys can help me get these bookcases inside?" Mr. Pitts is standing on the top step, right outside the front door.

Amanda walks over and peers out the door to see a wagon drawn by two mules who take this moment to announce their presence by braying loudly. Ann comes to stand beside her. "Miss Amanda, look at our bookcases."

Four highly polished walnut bookcases are standing in the back of the wagon. They are the most beautiful things Amanda has seen lately. Two pieces of bowed, carved wood adorn each side of the bookcases. Amanda can't wait to polish them and fill them with books. She can have a fiction, two nonfiction, and a reference bookcase.

"Burt, can you and the older boys come help Mr. Pitts bring the bookcases in?"

"Yes, ma'am."

"We're putting them in the empty schoolroom—on the long wall to the right."

Mr. Pitts and the older boys unload all four bookcases from the wagon and line them on the wall, just as Amanda had requested. The sun shining through the western windows hits the bookcases and Amanda gasps. How wonderful! Later, when the shelves are full of books, Amanda can add a few small tables with chairs. Oh, it's the Marshall Library—it's real.

"Thank you, Mr. Pitts. You are so thoughtful to do this for us."

"It's for all of us, Amanda. I may come to check out that book on Crazy Horse that I see on top of that stack." He winks at Amanda and smiles.

She smiles back. What a wonderful man to be in charge of the Marshall schools.

"I have to get to the store, Miss Amanda. I'll be back to see the library soon."

Amanda follows Mr. Pitts to the front door as he leaves. She sees the heavy rope hanging by the door and has an idea. She wraps the rope around her arm and tugs as hard as she can. The bells rings and rings. You can hear it all over Marshall.

The students playing in the schoolyard run to the front door to be followed by some of the townspeople.

"What's the matter?"

"The bell doesn't ring in the middle of the afternoon, Miss Amanda."

"Never heard it do that before."

Amanda is pleased to see most of the townspeople headed to the school to discover why the bell rang but realizes that many of them are concerned.

"Please. There's nothing to worry about. I didn't mean to alarm you. It's just that the bookcases for the library have arrived, as have the books. If we can work together, we can put our library together this afternoon."

"Oh, glad to know nothing's wrong."

"Yes, we'll help."

"How thrilling."

"I can help, too?" asks Randy.

"You can all help."

"I have already divided the books between Mr. Lee's school and our school, so all the books in the empty room that from now on will be called the library are ours. I've spent weekends placing cards and pockets in each book. Each pocket has spaces to mark the date the book is to be returned. Each card has the author and the title of the book. There are spaces for the borrowers' signatures on the card."

"Oh, Miss Amanda. It is a library."

"I'll need Mrs. Peevy to be in charge of the non-fiction section, Mr. King to be in charge of reference, and Pastor Sprague, will you be in charge of fiction?"

"I'll be delighted, Miss Amanda," says the pastor.

"I cataloged the books as they came in, and I'm afraid they're all mixed up."

"How can we help, Miss Amanda?" asks Ann.

"Here's how. Burt, will you take the older students and work with Mrs. Peevy in nonfiction. I'll need you to search the stacks of books for books with a number on them like this. We are using a new system called the Dewey Decimal System."

Amanda holds up a book of poetry with an 800 classification on it.

"All these books come back to Mrs. Peevy except the ones with the word Reference above the number. Once you have gathered all the books, you can all work together to put them in order in the last two bookcases."

"And me, Miss Amanda?" asks Ann.

"Ann, you'll work with your group to help Mr. King. Remember, you and your group are looking for all the books with Reference on the spine."

"Umm—that leaves the Abecedarians. Randy, will you and your group help Pastor Sprague? Remember, you bring him any book with Fic on the spine."

"Here's a book with 900 on the spine."

"And here's 600."

"Here are six books by Louisa May Alcott labeled Fic."

"This reference book is too heavy. Someone else needs to carry it to Lawyer King."

All at the same time. Amanda is hearing all this at the same time. It's chaos. It's wonderful!

"We're through Miss Amanda," yells Randy.

"We're through, too," says Ann.

"We've been through," says Burt.

Everyone stands back and looks at the shelves. The books are lined up in order. Well, for the most part, in order. Amanda sees a 599.7 on the shelf before 597. She smiles, then she laughs. A library at Marshall School. Wonderful!

She feels someone tugging on her sleeve—tugging so hard she jerks to the right. Looking down, she sees Ann.

"Miss Amanda, all the books are on the shelves except the ones Mrs. Mabel Todd brought today. They don't have cards and pockets or labels."

Amanda frowns, wrinkles forming between her eyebrows. Then her eyes twinkle as her mouth turns up into a huge smile. "You know, Ann. I think that we'll give those books to Mr. Lee at the colored school."

Ann draws in her breath and places both hands over her mouth.

Amanda laughs at the shock on Ann's face. "It's my Christian duty," she states.

## Twelfth Chapter

### Sister Sarah Lifts the Table

"Miss Sophie, I can't eat another bite. Your banana pie looks yummy, but I can't do it—not after meatloaf, fried okra, mashed potatoes, stewed tomatoes, and pole beans."

"That's all right. I'll save some for your lunch tomorrow. Oh, and Amanda, I want to tell you that I have the perfect beau for you. Walter Brown."

"But I don't want a man, Miss Sophie."

"Sure you do, and Walter Brown is a fine catch. He's a lawyer over in Greenville. He has three children—lost his wife in 1890—but they are lovely children, just lovely."

"Miss Sophie, I appreciate your help in this department, I do, but—"

"Good. Leave it to me. You'll be on the front cover of the *Selma Times-Journal.* Such a beautiful bride you'll make."

"Not yet, Miss Sophie. I. Do. Not. Want. To. Meet. a. Man. Not now, Miss Sophie." Amanda pats Miss Sophie's hand to take the sting out of her words. "I'll let you know when I'm ready, Miss Sophie." Softening, she looks up and smiles at Miss Sophie.

"All right, Amanda. We'll do it your way for now."

Sister Sarah squirms backward in her chair and straightens her shoulders in a way that signals an important pronouncement will follow. “Tonight is important," says Sister Sarah. "I feel someone trying to break through from the other side.”

Sophie says, “Not tonight, Sarah.”

“But it may be a message from your dear departed, Sophie.”

“Patience was a virtue of my ‘dear departed.’ Certainly, he’ll be willing to wait.”

Miss Sophie sees the question written on Amanda's face and turns toward her. "Sarah claims to be able to talk to the dead.”

Sister Sarah protests. “Claims to? Claims to? You know we talked to your Jack last month.”

“Well, Amanda is not ready to talk with the dead. Why don’t we go into the front parlor, and you can do that nice table trick?”

“What table trick, Miss Sophie?” Amanda asks.

“Sister Sarah can lift a table off the floor by concentrating on it.”

Sarah grumbles, “Fine. Let’s go to the parlor.”

At that moment, the dining room door swings open, and Elizabeth walks in. “I’m sorry I missed dinner, Miss Sophie.”

“That’s all right, Elizabeth. Join us. You’re just in time. We’re going to the front parlor, and Sister Sarah is going to lift the table.”

“That’s because they won’t participate in a full-blown séance," Sister Sarah says. “Maybe you’re interested, Elizabeth. Isn’t there someone who has passed over that you would like to contact?”

“No, no, Sister. That’s a little scary for me. But I will watch you lift the table. I’ve heard about table lifting but never seen it.”

“Then lead the way to the parlor, Miss Sophie.”

All four walk in tandem down the wide, front hall to the main parlor located at the front of the house. Miss Sophie removes a lamp, a Dresden figurine, and crocheted doilies from a small, circular table and moves it to the middle of the parlor floor.

"Thank you, Sophie. Now choose a chair and pull up to the table." Amanda slides a pink, floral fauteuil chair to the table for Miss Sophie. "Take this chair, Miss Sophie. Elizabeth and I can get the ladder-back chairs."

Sister Sarah drags a heavy, upholstered chair to the table for herself and sits down. She begins her talk. "I can feel the energy in the room tonight. Sister Sarah and Amanda place both hands on the table at the same time. Elizabeth hesitantly places her small hands on the table to join Sister Sarah's and Amanda's, and Miss Sophie adds her plump hands—plump hands that have a wide, gold wedding band on the left hand and an elegant ring composed of an emerald surrounded by diamonds on her right.

"Now, everyone," says Sister Sarah, "spread your fingers out into a fan and touch your little fingers to the persons on both sides of you."

Amanda feels the feather-like touch of Elizabeth's finger on her left and the forceful touch of Sister Sarah on her right.

"Now, everyone close your eyes and clear your mind of all daily affairs. If we want the table to lift, we have to concentrate."

Amanda squeezes her eyes shut. She tries to clear her mind. She hears the sound of a neighbor trimming the hedges next door and children running down the street yelling, "Can't catch me." She hears a bumblebee droning outside the open window, and she inhales the sweet smell of honeysuckle. Gradually, she tunes out the external noises. She peeks to her right: Sister Sarah has her head bowed and appears to be asleep. Wait! Did the table move?

Yes, Amanda feels a slight lifting of the table. Elizabeth felt it, too. Amanda hears her gasp. Slowly, the table rises off the floor, the womens' hands rising with it. Just as slowly, the table lowers back down to the floor.

They sit there with eyes wide open. Not a word is said. Sister Sarah slowly rises from her chair, pushing back from the table. She stands, straightens her shoulders, turns her body, and walks out of the room with the bearing of a queen.

After what seems an eternity, Miss Sophie breaks the silence. "Sometimes I think Sister Sarah has one foot in another world."

# Thirteenth Chapter

## Sadie Interprets the Story of Pandora

Arriving early for school, Amanda is pleased to see the attractive sharecropper's wife sitting on the front steps of the school—the one she first met at open house.

"Sadie, hello. Are you waiting for me?"

"Oh, yes, Miss Amanda. I heard about the new library."

"Of course! You want to see it. Follow me." Amanda pushes open the heavy schoolroom door and walks into the classroom.

"I have to tell you Sadie—I'm so impressed with the way you communicated with Mr. Aucoin at the mercantile store. Speaking French is no easy task."

Placing her books on the teacher's desk, she turns back to Sadie, "Let's see what you think, Sadie. The library is in the next room."

Sadie steps through the doorway into the next room as if she is stepping into another world. The four bookshelves, almost full, immediately catch her eye. "Sacre bleu."

"It is wonderful, having all these books to read. Sadie, you know these books are not just for the schoolchildren. They're for you to check out as well."

"I won't take one today. I still have to return the book of Greek myths by Mr. Hawthorne."

"Have you finished it?"

"Almost. I read slowly, but I know I'll get faster. I have hope—you know that was what was left in the jar, Miss Amanda."

"The jar?"

"Yes, Pandora's jar."

"Oh, of course. I remember the story of Pandora. I thought she opened a box."

"According to Mr. Hawthorne, she opened a jar that released all the evils into the world. Do you think that's when men like Harley and Mr. Aucoin were created, Miss Amanda?"

Amanda gets very still. How does she answer this bright young woman who is abused by her husband in her own home?

She pauses for just a moment, then asks, "Harley gave you that mark I saw earlier on your arm?"

"Yes, ma'am. I'm not supposed to talk about it. But I know it's wrong. It's not normal for a man to be so brutish."

"He hurts you often?"

"Not too much, if I'm smart."

"Why did he hurt you this last time?"

"I corrected his grammar. I just told him not to say, 'He cotched the mule outside the fence.' He caught the mule, I told him, not cotched the mule."

"He hurt you because of that?"

"Yes, ma'am. Harley turned beet red in the face and grabbed my arm. I thought that he was going to squeeze my arm off. I don't correct his grammar anymore, Miss Amanda."

"Oh, Sadie. I hurt for you. Have you ever told the sheriff?"

"I think Harley would kill me if I did."

Sadie quickly shifted their conversation back to the story of Pandora. "You know, Miss Amanda, I think the story of Pandora asks a question."

"A question? What question?"

"Why is there evil in this world?"

"Oh," says Amanda, amazed at Sadie's insight into the story.

"But you know what's left in the jar, Miss Amanda?" Sadie does not wait for her answer. "Hope. And I hope, Miss Amanda."

# Fourteenth Chapter

## Getting Ready for Speeches

Amanda watches Sadie walk down the path leading from the school. Sadie passes by the schoolchildren arriving for the school day and speaks to each one.

Once the students settle in their desks, Amanda has an announcement. "Students, our big project next month will involve speeches. Each student will give a one-minute speech."

"A speech, Miss Amanda? I'm afraid to talk in front of folks."

"Yes, a speech, Randy. Speaking in front of others is such an important skill. All educated persons should be able to speak to a group."

"But I don't have anything to say."

"Oh, yes, you do. Class, if you are in Randy's group, you will give a speech about yourself. If you are in the middle group, Ann's group, you will learn about our first president, George Washington, and you will give a short speech about him. And those of you in the older group—you will compare and contrast your life to that of George Washington's. Some of you will talk about food, some about farming, and some about entertaining. We'll decide who's doing what later."

"Where do we find out about George Washington, Miss Amanda?"

"Why, from our library. And from your textbooks. If you are in the older two groups, you'll research first."

Amanda turns to the blackboard and picks up a stick of chalk. "After you research and before you share your talk, you have to write. Now let me show you how easy the written part will be. Each student will have only five parts to his speech."

Amanda writes on the board, *1. Introduce your topic.*

"Students, you want to grab the class's attention in your opening. For example, if you are in the first group and writing a speech to introduce yourself, you could open with, 'I'm Joe Brown. Here's some information about me.' That's one way of doing it. But this is better. 'I'm Joe Brown, and I'm the best first baseman in the whole town of Marshall.' See the difference?"

"What's the next part, Miss Amanda?"

"I told you there are five parts. We have talked about the introduction. Parts two, three, and four are the same. Give a different piece of information in each part. So, this is what we have so far."

1. *Introduce your topic.*
2. *Explain a piece of information.*
3. *Explain a piece of information.*
4. *Explain a piece of information*

"Can you give us an example?"

"Certainly. I'll talk about myself:

*1. When I was a child, I wanted to be a teacher. I am Amanda Oglesby, and I am a teacher in Marshall, Alabama.*

*2. My great-grandfather Oglesby was a teacher. He moved to Demopolis, Alabama, from the state of South Carolina. He taught in Demopolis for twenty-one years.*

*3. My grandmother Shelby was a schoolteacher. She taught in an academy in Mobile until she married at the age of twenty-three.*

*4. I finished high school and attended Livingston Normal School for two years. Normal schools were designed to help teachers become better teachers.*

"I get it, I get it," yelled Ann. "Tell what your speech is going to be about and give three different details about your topic. But what's the fifth step?"

Amanda writes on the board, *5. Write a conclusion that ties everything together.*

Burt speaks for the first time. "That's not so hard, Miss Amanda. We can do that—the writing part, that is. Speaking in front of the class is gonna be harder."

"I tell you what, Burt. We'll set aside some class time every day to practice. And we'll start right now. Who can stand up and talk until I tell you to stop?"

Several students readjust their legs, so they are sitting on their hands. Not one student raises a hand.

"Now, I've talked about myself and how I love to teach. Can one of you stand up and talk?"

"I will," says Ann.

"Thank you, Ann. When I say go, start talking. You can talk about anything. I'll tell you when to stop. Go."

"My mother and I made sugar cookies yesterday. First, we sifted together flour, baking soda, and baking powder. In another bowl, we creamed butter and sugar for a long time. Then we beat in an egg and some vanilla. Then, we added flour and stuff. We rolled dough into little balls that took forever. We baked them for ten minutes. I brought some in my lunch bucket today and. . . ."

"Thank you, Ann. Excellent."

Another student hops up. "I'll do it."

"Good for you, Jimmy. Go ahead."

"Well, we had turnip greens and cornmeal dumplings last night for dinner. I picked those greens for Mama myself. They grow in our backyard garden. Some plantation owners don't let their tenants have gardens—they want all the land planted in cotton. Mr. Callander thinks we all need gardens.

Anyway, I picked the greens and even washed them. They're covered in dirt, ya know. I washed and washed them—uh, those greens. While they were cooking, Mama made big cornmeal dumplings—the size of my fist, they were. She dropped those dumplings in the pot-licker and cooked them 'til they were done. We didn't have no meat; we didn't have enough money to buy meat this week, and Papa tries not to charge at the commissary. Don't matter. Those greens were great."

"Thank you, Jimmy. You're making my mouth water," says Miss Amanda.

"See students; you'll take turns just talking to the class about anything to get used to talking in front of people. Practice will help. Talking to a group is different from writing an essay or a letter. Speaking of letters. . ."

# Fifteenth Chapter

## Another Donald Tale

Amanda removes a letter from her pocket. "I have another letter from my parents. Do you know what that means?"

"Another story about Donald?"

"Yes. For sure."

"Yea."

"I love Donald—and his dog."

"Me, too."

"Well, I'm afraid Donald has done it again. Remember in the last letter he and Davy ate the pie?"

"Yes."

"We do."

"The dog had pie on his face."

Amanda laughs. "You're right, and, you know, he's in trouble again. Here's what my father wrote about Donald:

*Donald wanted to see what it would be like to collect eggs from under a hen. He tippy-toed around the hen house, hushing Davy and making him promise not to bark. Thin wire formed into hexagonal shapes covers the front of the chicken house.*

"Chicken wire on the chicken house, Miss Amanda?"

Amanda looks up and smiles, "Seems appropriate, doesn't it?" She turns back to the letter.

*Donald could see eight hens sitting on fluffy nests made of straw and feathers. Hens pick the feathers from their bodies to form their nests, you know. Donald moves so quietly; those hens don't hear a sound.*

*Donald reaches the door to the hen house, and not a hen has spotted him. Davy is obeying Donald's instructions and is staying very still—not even his tail is wagging. The handle to the hen house is a worn piece of wood with a hole in the middle. A nail is driven through the hole to secure the handle to the frame of the door.*

*Donald turns that handle inch by inch until it is straight up and down. He slowly opens the door and tiptoes inside the hen house. Not a hen has stirred. He sneaks up to the hen at the end of the row. Black feathers cover her, and the feathers on her wings have an iridescent touch of turquoise on them. Her head, topped with the bright red comb, is drooping. Donald slowly—oh, so slowly—slides his hand under the hen. The hen's eyes pop open, and she and Donald are eyeball to eyeball.*

*The hen flies straight up, fluffing her feathers and squawking to beat the band. All the other hens look up and join in. Davy decides to add to the confusion and starts barking as loud as he can. Donald decides he might as well grab an egg or two before he runs. Seeing his intention, that black hen starts pecking Donald on the hand as hard as she can. Donald tries to grab an egg and manages to crush all the eggs in the nest.*

*At that exact moment, your cousin Lily comes around the corner of the hen house. Well, I don't have to tell you how mad she is at Donald.*

*Donald Oglesby, you are a disgrace to the Oglesby name. What are we going to do with you and that mutt of yours?*

*Pumping out his chest, Donald says, "Well, you won't have to worry about me. I'm taking Davy, and we're running overseas to Montana, and we're never coming back."*

Amanda folds the letter and puts it in her pocket. "Now, what's wrong with Donald's last sentence?"

"He's running away, Miss Amanda?"

"So he says, but it's where he's running" Amanda strolls from the front of the classroom to the side of the room with the large maps hanging.

"Burt, do you think you could come up to the map and show the class where Alabama is on the map?"

Burt walks to the map and slides his square-ended finger to the state of Alabama. "Right here, Miss Amanda."

"Good, Burt. Now move your finger to the west and the north. Do you see Montana?"

"Yes, right here?"

"OK students, all of you get up and crowd around the map." The sound of kicked lunch buckets and desk seats being flipped up fills the room. When the children have all gathered around, Amanda says, "Do you see an ocean between Montana and Alabama?"

"No, ma'am."

"Of course not, ma'am."

"Well, now you know where Montana is, and we know Donald and Davy could never go overseas to Montana. You didn't think Donald would teach you geography, did you?"

# Sixteenth Chapter

## The Fall Festival

Amanda taps her toes as strains of music from the banjo and fiddle flow around the townspeople doing the Virginia Reel. Her eye follows the men wearing tapered trousers down to their square-toed shoes with one-inch heels. Their feet are moving so fast, accompanying the women in their flared skirts. Amanda gets a glimpse of ribbons, beads, and rosettes on the swirling petticoats of the women dancers.

"Aren't they beautiful? I always thought I was beautiful when I danced the Virginia Reel," says Miss Sophie.

"Yes, they are beautiful. It looks complicated, though," answers Amanda.

"I agree. And so is that." Miss Sophie nods her head toward the teenagers bobbing for apples.

Amanda laughs as Burt tries to hem an apple up against the side of the water-filled tub. He comes up out of the tub, water streaming down his face and gasping for breath—no apple in his mouth and a look of frustration on his face.

"The children sure have fun with this. In older days, bobbing for apples was a way to find a bride or groom."

"Bobbing for apples? Marriage?"

"Sure. Let me tell you about my grandmother. In her day, there was one apple in the tub, and it represented the man you wanted to marry. If you hemmed up the apple in one try, bit into it, and brought it out of the water, you were meant to marry the man."

"What happened if you couldn't bite the apple the first time?"

"You had a second try. If you succeeded, the man would court you, but his love would fail. Now, if you bit the apple on the third try, love was hopeless."

"So what happened with your grandmother?"

Miss Sophie giggles. "It took her eleven tries to bite the apple and bring it out of the water."

"So her marriage failed?"

"No, they were married for fifty-one years before he died and left this world."

"Oh, Miss Sophie."

"Now Amanda, don't look now, but David Henry Callander just came in the door—alone."

Amanda remembers the tall man who winked at her in church. She tries to keep what she's thinking off her face. She would certainly bob for David Henry's apple. She can't help herself. She blushes.

Feeling a tug on her sleeve, Amanda turns to find Sadie—a very excited Sadie—standing before her.

"Miss Amanda, come with me. They're doing the last cakewalk." Amanda allows Sadie to lead her into the other room where the floor is marked with large numbers, one through twenty, that form a circle.

"Come on, ladies and gents. Stand on a number and take a chance," barks the fiddler.

Following Sadie's lead, Amanda stands on number twenty. Sadie stands behind her on nineteen. The fiddler begins playing "The Sailor's Hornpipe," and Amanda starts moving around the circle with the rest. The music gets faster. Amanda glances back over her shoulder to see Sadie's look of sheer joy. She wonders how Sadie can embrace life so, considering her circumstances.

Faster and faster. The fiddler plays as they walk the circle. Then, all of a sudden, no music—not a sound. Amanda freezes and looks down below her feet. She sees number ten. The fiddler, balancing his fiddle on his knee, reaches into the glass bowl on a stool near him. Ever so carefully, he pulls out one piece of folded paper. Unfolding it, he shouts, "Number ten."

Amanda stands there, staring at her feet. She never wins.

"Number ten," yells the fiddler.

Sadie punches Amanda on the arm. "Miss Amanda, that's you."

She walks up to the fiddler and takes the caramel cake he's holding out to her. Amanda smells the heavenly burnt sugar smell and her mouth waters. She remembers to thank the fiddler and walks back to Sadie with her prize.

"Come on, Sadie. Let's go sit in the classroom and sample this."

Tagging along behind, Sadie says, "But how are we gonna do that, Miss Amanda? No forks."

"Just watch, Sadie." Amanda sits down on the edge of the teacher's desk, scooching back until the back of her knees rubs against the rough wood of the desk. She squeezes her index and middle fingers together and dips them into the soft, creamy caramel. Bringing the fingers out of the cake, she pops them in her mouth.

"Yum, Sadie. You try it."

Following suit, Sadie digs into the cake. She closes her eyes and savors the sweetness.

"Sadie, let's just eat it all."

"Maybe, Miss Amanda. Want to know the French word for cake?"

"Yes, of course."

"Gateau."

"Gah toe?"

"Yes, that's right."

"Let's try some French words for objects in the classroom. I'll share them with the students."

"Yes, I remember that you wanted to do that. First, school is un ecole, and you are un professeur."

"How do you spell those, Sadie?"

Amanda walks to the blackboard and writes the words on the board as Sadie spells them. "Eleve is the word for student." Amanda adds it to the list on the board.

"You might want to give each student a French name, like Adelise or Alfonso."

"Or don't forget David Henri." The booming bass voice comes from the back of the room.

Amanda jerks her head around, hair flying around her head. David Henry Callander stands in the doorway to the classroom.

"We haven't met. I'm David Henry Callander." He takes a few deliberate steps toward her. "I know that you are Amanda Oglesby, the new schoolteacher. May I dance the last dance of the evening with you?"

Amanda sits and stares. He should have asked for an introduction, perhaps from Miss Sophie.

"Go on, Miss Amanda. Dance with him," says Sadie. Amanda notices that Sadie's expression changes to a wistful expression. Has this young lady ever had a handsome man ask her to dance?

Amanda slides off the wooden desk and takes his offered arm.

Looking closely at her, David Henry asks, "Is that caramel cake on your face?"

Amanda would like to sink through the schoolroom floor. Instead, she takes a handkerchief out of her pocket and wipes her mouth clean. She follows him out onto the dance floor as the band begins playing "The Beautiful Blue Danube."

Elizabeth and Amanda had made the courageous decision to include a waltz as the last dance of the evening. The Baptists think that such a dance is the work of the devil—much too daring.

Amanda and David move into the step, slide, step motion of the waltz. They move together smoothly and naturally. Amanda tilts her head back and looks up into his dark brown eyes. He winks at her; she winks back. Very improper!

# Early November 1892

# Seventeenth Chapter

## Culinary Concerns

Amanda looks around the classroom. "Terry, I think it's your turn to ad lib," she says. Terry sits at his desk, hanging his head. He is in Ann's group in school and is very shy. "Surely something is going on at home that you can talk about, Terry."

Terry, with his carrot-colored hair and his worn overalls, looks miserable, but he stands up as Amanda requested.

"All right, Terry. It's easy. Just start talking."

Terry takes a deep breath and starts, "Mama is sick, and we're all worried about her. Miss Maggie says she has pellagra. That she doesn't have enough n-i-a-c-i-n in her diet. I don't know what that means. Miss Maggie says she is gonna bring Mama fish or meat every day to eat. We normally eat cornmeal mush, fatback, greens and, sometimes molasses. All of us kids are having to help out. My job is to sweep the kitchen at night and do the dishes. Thank goodness for Miss Maggie. She's gonna make Mama well."

Terry takes a seat to a silent classroom. No one wants to think about a parent being ill.

"Thank you, Terry, for sharing that with us. I'm sorry to hear that your mother is sick, and I know that you are worried."

"Yes, ma'am."

"Do you think your family would like homemade banana pudding? Miss Sophie is teaching me how to make one. I'll be glad to share it."

"Yes, ma'am."

"Fine, Terry. I'll talk to Miss Sophie this afternoon."

***

Amanda can't get the story of Terry's mother out of her mind. She decides a visit to Miss Maggie would help so, instead of turning right onto the path to Miss Sophie's, she turns left to visit Miss Maggie.

The outside double doors to Miss Maggie's are standing open. The wood-framed screen doors are closed, keeping the bugs out and letting the fresh air come streaming into the impressive old home. Instead of ringing the doorbell, Amanda calls out, "Miss Maggie. Are you there? I need to talk to you."

"Just a moment." Miss Maggie is in the kitchen, making dough for blackberry pie. She dusts her hands together over the flour-covered counter and hurries to the front door.

"Amanda, so good to see you. Come into the kitchen." Amanda follows Miss Maggie's bustling figure down the hall. "Would you like a glass of tea?"

"Yes, ma'am. I'd love a glass."

Miss Maggie takes the tall, stemmed glasses out of the kitchen cabinet and fills them midway with brewed black tea—tea sweetened to the point it makes your teeth itch. Picking pieces of ice from a bowl just brought in from the ice-house, she drops the pieces in the black tea and offers sliced lemons in a bowl that's part of her silver service. Amanda drinks and feels the cold, sweet tea coating her throat on the way down. It's wonderful!

"Miss Maggie, I'm so glad I caught you at home. I'm concerned about the health of our sharecroppers and their families. I understand you're helping Terry Johnson's mother. There's got to be something more we can do."

"What do you have in mind, Amanda?"

"Do you think we could teach a cooking class to the wives—cooking simple things that aren't expensive?"

"That's something to think about, Amanda. There're tons of plants growing around Marshall—edible plants. And some of them can be used to treat different maladies. The wives probably know about some of these plants, but I think a class would be wonderful."

"I like that idea, Miss Maggie. What's an example of one of the healing plants?"

"Elderberries. Jams or jellies made from elderberries have minerals and vitamins, and the berries are used in fruit pies, just like blackberries. They boost the immune and respiratory systems and cure colds. The berries are around in September, and the elderberry flowers are available in the spring. You can make tea or juice out of the flowers if you dry them and steep them in water.

"Oh, that's good, Miss Maggie. Don't you think this kind of class would help?"

"It's a good idea, Amanda. Let's schedule it for a week from Saturday, and you can help me pass the word. I'll see if we can hold it in the kitchen at the Methodist Church."

Amanda gets up out of the kitchen chair and leans over to kiss the feisty Miss Maggie on the cheek. "Thank you, Miss Maggie. The town of Marshall is lucky to have you."

"You, too, Miss Amanda. You, too."

# Eighteenth Chapter

## Sadie's Husband Disappears

Amanda crosses the street from Miss Maggie's to Miss Sophie's. She is surprised to find a young woman sitting on Miss Sophie's steps. Her legs are tucked up under her, and her tan arms are folded on top of each other across her knees. Even though her head is resting on her arms, Amanda can tell that she's crying. As she gets closer, Amanda sees that it's Sadie.

"My goodness, Sadie. What's wrong?" Amanda reaches over to brush the hanging hair off Sadie's face. She keeps crying.

"Sadie, you're scaring me. Are you hurt?"

She shakes her head—she's not hurt.

"Sadie, you've got to talk to me."

"He's gone." Amanda can barely make out what she's saying.

"Who's gone?"

"Harley. Harley's gone, Miss Amanda." Amanda thinks that's the best news she's heard in months. "He hasn't been around in two days. The crops need tending. I've got to take care of the crops. He left—didn't leave me anything."

"Have you eaten, Sadie?"

"Not since yesterday."

Amanda reaches over and grips Sadie's arm, indicating that she needs to stand up.

"Come on, Sadie. Let's go in the kitchen. There's always sweet tea and some leftovers."

Sadie slowly pushes the hair off her face and stands up to follow Amanda into the kitchen. Amanda slices a cold sweet potato and a piece of ham, arranging them on Miss Sophie's everyday china. She hands the plate to Sadie. Sadie slowly eats the leftovers, placing her fork on the plate and chewing between each bite.

"Has Mr. Wiggins ever left before?"

"No ma'am, but he's been threatening to. Tells me I'm not pretty anymore."

Amanda looks at this tall, willowy woman with the straight, blonde hair. Her face is classical with a high nose and strong chin. Her blue eyes reflect her strength and intelligence. Garbed in clothes other than her sack dress, she could have passed for Pandora, the first woman created by the Gods. Pandora, who Sadie understood so well, left hope in the jar. Amanda silently makes a wish that Sadie hangs on to her hope. Secretly, she hopes Harley Wiggins never comes home.

# Nineteenth Chapter

## Miss Maggie Teaches

Sharecroppers wives are filing into the kitchen of the Methodist Church, and Amanda can't help but overhear their chatter.

"That Harley Wiggins is got to be the sorriest man God ever put on this earth."

"You are so right. Do you know Harley disappeared? No one has seen hide nor hair of him."

"I saw Sadie trying to take care of the crops. Maybe if she'd ah been a better wife, Harley wouldn't have left."

The ladies see Amanda at the doorway and stop talking. So, the news of Harley Wiggin's disappearance is out there. Amanda's heart breaks for Sadie. Amanda walks to the front of the kitchen to join Miss Maggie.

"Everything ready, Miss Maggie?"

"Of course, Amanda. I've got leaves from wild violets, rose bushes, and blackberries, all used to make tea. We're going to talk about henbit—how to use it to make salads and soups. Did you know that henbit is in the mint family, and it helps with rheumatism? It's very nutritious and high in iron, vitamins, and fiber."

"How do you know all this, Miss Maggie?"

"I learned most of it from my mother. Then I married Lewis. I loved to go on rounds with him—picked up a lot from him. I sure do miss him, Amanda."

"How long has he been gone, Miss Maggie?"

"Ten years this December."

"I'm so sorry, Miss Maggie."

"That's all right, child. We all have crosses to bear. Speaking of crosses, look at that Sadie Wiggins."

Amanda turns and looks out over the group of women who have come in and seated themselves in the wooden chairs in the church's kitchen. She spots Sadie sitting all alone in the back of the room, and she sees several of the local ladies talking together, looking at Sadie while they talk.

"Miss Maggie, those ladies are awful to Sadie. Watch this."

Amanda strides through the group of gossiping ladies, headed straight toward Sadie. Kneeling on the floor beside her, Amanda says, "Sadie, I need some help up front. Come on up there with me."

Sadie looks up at Amanda. Amanda curses Harley Wiggins under her breath. If those dark bags under her eyes are any indication, Sadie is not getting a wink of sleep. Sadie follows Amanda to the front of the room and sits down beside her as Miss Maggie starts her talk.

"Good morning, ladies. We'll start our morning with a cup of tea. I have prepared teas from bushes that grow right here in Marshall. Sadie, will you help me pass out the cups of tea?"

Sadie is shocked by the request but nods her head that she'll help.

"You know, ladies, it's our duty to help each other." None of the ladies miss the nod Miss Maggie gives to Sadie's back as she passes out cups. "We have enough trouble right here in Marshall, Alabama, without making it harder for people to deal with their problems."

Several ladies hang their heads, and more than a few thank Sadie as she passes out the cups of tea. It appears to Amanda that Miss Maggie is teaching far more than nutrition today.

"Now, let's talk about chickweed. You all know what chickweed is? Grows wild all over Marshall County."

All the ladies in the kitchen nod their heads.

"Some of you know that you can cook it for supper—makes a nice mess of greens. But let me tell you, chickweed is one of the best medicines around. Use it for constipation plus muscle and joint pain. It helps with asthma and helps you lose weight. You can put it right on the skin if you have a boil. Chickweed is the best medicine in Marshall, and it's free, growing on the side of the road."

Amanda tells the ladies about Queen Anne 's lace and how the root can be used just like a carrot. Miss Maggie talks about other things in the area that can help feed the sharecroppers and their families and cure their ailments. She ends by making an announcement.

"Now ladies, I hope what you learned will help feed as well as cure your families, but we're not through yet. I have a huge surprise."

Miss Maggie is squirming with excitement but wants to build the suspense before making her big announcement. Some of you have vegetable gardens; others don't. I am donating a plot of ground behind my house for a town garden. Mr. Pitts says he knows someone who can turn the soil this next week."

"With winter coming, is it too late to plant?"

"We can try growing kale and collards right now. Just think of all the things we can grow this coming summer."

"Where can we get seeds, Miss Maggie?"

"Don't worry about that right now. Come to my house a week from today if you want a row or two to plant. I'll have all the seeds you need right now. And we'll see what we're going to do about the spring planting later on."

"Miss Maggie, how are we gonna keep up with which row is ours?"

"Let's ask Sadie," Amanda suggests, What do you think, Sadie?"

Sadie is shocked. Why would someone care about her opinion? She doesn't want to disappoint Amanda. "Well, Miss Maggie could number the rows right to left. Anyone who planted a row would have to register with Miss Maggie. She would keep a written record of everyone's row number."

Did you ever see a roomful of ladies in jaw-dropping silence? Amanda wonders.

"Thank you, Sadie. I think that's a great idea," says Miss Maggie. "Well, ladies, see you at my house next week."

As the ladies file out of the church, Amanda touches Miss Maggie's arm to get her attention. Leaning over to hug her, Amanda says, "Thank you, Miss Maggie. The town of Marshall is lucky to have you."

"You, too, Miss Amanda. You, too."

They both chuckle over the repeated sentiment and the success of Miss Maggie's first class.

# Twentieth Chapter

## Aucoin Hurts Louise Lee

Reuben Lee's wife, Louise, steps out of Miss Amanda's schoolroom with an armload of books. Rueben Lee, the teacher at the colored school, has reminded Louise that Amanda has novels by the Bronte sisters, books he lacks in his classroom. As Louise steps onto the sidewalk, she collides with none other than Zackery Aucoin. Books fly in all directions, and Aucoin starts cursing. Amanda, hearing the ruckus, walks quickly to the front door of the school.

"Stay out of my way, bitch."

"Sir, I am so sorry I ran into you. I wasn't watching where I was going because I was trying to balance my books."

"Books! What does a colored gal like you need with books? It's for damn sure you can't read."

Shocked at the vitriol she's hearing, Louise stands motionless and stares at Aucoin.

"Speak up, gal. You stealing those books?"

Louise doesn't budge. She stands frozen on the sidewalk. Amanda starts down the steps to help Louise when Aucoin uses both hands to shove Louise to the ground. Thud! Louise's head hits the edge of the concrete curb.

Amanda knows she will never forget that wet sound of Louise's head hitting the ground a second time, this time landing in the pool of blood that formed quickly in the dirt next to the curb. She knows she has never felt such rage. Acting on instinct, Amanda screams at Aucoin, "You awful creature. Look what you've done to her!"

Aucoin lowers his head, spits out a squirt of brown, chewed tobacco. Looking up at Amanda, he says flatly, "Colored people shouldn't be walking on the sidewalks." He walks away before Amanda can answer.

Louise is not moving. Amanda picks up her skirts and tears down Walnut Street to Main Street. Lawyer King is coming out of his law office as Amanda rounds the corner.

"Mr. King. Get help. Get help."

Mr. King gently grabs Amanda's arms. "Slow down, Amanda. Tell me what's wrong."

"That awful Aucoin pushed Louise Lee down. Louise cracked her head, and she's not moving."

"Go back and sit with her, Amanda. I'll get the Sheriff and Miss Maggie."

Amanda, worried about what she'll find, runs back to Louise, who hasn't moved. Amanda can tell that she's breathing. She sits and watches Louise's chest move up and down until Miss Maggie arrives, followed by the sheriff.

"What happened Amanda?"

"That nasty Aucoin did this. Louise accidentally bumped into him on the sidewalk, and Aucoin shoved her—hard."

Sheriff Winfield says, "We'll take care of Aucoin later. Miss Maggie, what do you think we need to do with Mrs. Lee?"

"She needs a hospital, sheriff. The closest one is Selma."

"That's nine miles away, Miss Maggie. Any idea how to get her there?"

"There's no good solution. It's a bumpy ride no matter what we do. I suggest a flatbed wagon. We should make it in under two hours."

The sheriff turns to Amanda. "Somebody's got to tell Reuben Lee. Can you do that, Miss Amanda, while I find a wagon?"

"I'll go get some quilts. Let's pad the wagon as much as we can," says Miss Maggie.

Amanda still hasn't answered the sheriff. She dreads having to tell Reuben Lee about his wife.

The sheriff repeats his request. "Miss Amanda, will you go see Mr. Lee?"

Amanda nods her head.

"He lives right next door to his school. You know where that is?"

Amanda nods again and turns in the direction of Reuben Lee's house. She knows that she needs to get Reuben Lee back to his wife as fast as she can so she starts to run. He'll want to be on that wagon when it starts for Selma.

She's exhausted when she runs up on the porch of Reuben's dogtrot house. Banging on the door, she calls out, "Reuben Lee. Reuben Lee." She hears the creaking sound you hear when someone gets out of a chair, and then footsteps coming to the door.

The door swings open. "Miss Amanda, what are you doing? Are you all right?

Amanda forgets tact and blurts it out. "That awful Aucoin shoved your wife down just because she bumped into him. I saw the whole thing. Louise's head cracked on the cement curb, and she hasn't moved. Oh, hurry Reuben. The sheriff and Miss Maggie are taking Louise to Selma in a flatbed wagon."

Reuben slams shut the door behind him and jumps off the porch to follow Amanda. They arrive back in time to see Miss Maggie and the sheriff carefully placing Louise in the wagon. Reuben jumps in the back to sit near Louise's head.

"Reuben, this is not good," Miss Maggie says, "We don't have any other way to get Louise to the hospital. It's going to be bumpy. Watch her and let me know if she moves or opens her eyes."

"Yes, ma'am. I'm watching my Louise, for sure."

Amanda stands on the sidewalk and watches the wagon roll down Walnut Street. She raises her face to the sky. "God, I know you're there. I know you saw all this. Please hold Louise in your hands. Amen."

Amanda looks down at the Bronte books scattered across the sidewalks. She stoops to pick them up, one by one.

# Twenty-first Chapter

## The Search for Aucoin

Amanda and Miss Sophie are having tea in the kitchen while Amanda tells her all about the incident with Aucoin and Louise Lee. "Miss Sophie, I'll never understand evil people like that Zackery Aucoin. He said outright that colored people have no right to walk on the sidewalk."

"Zackery Aucoin's not the only one who feels that way. Not so much in Marshal but, in our state and across the South, some people want to keep the colored under their heel. They want to keep them segregated."

"But why, Miss Sophie?"

"Well, I think race relations were improving after Reconstruction until those Jim Crow laws were started. Things went downhill from there."

"I've heard of Jim Crow laws, Miss Sophie, but I don't understand what they are. I know that they are not good for colored."

"Jim Crow is a slang term for colored. The whole idea is separate but equal. It's nothing in the world but white supremacy. I think that some white men felt threatened after Reconstruction. They were afraid that colored men would take their jobs."

"Aren't there enough jobs for everyone? Shouldn't the most qualified get the job, no matter what race they are?"

"You are living in a dream world, child. Sure, that's the way it should be, but it is not that way and may never be. Look at Marshall. Even with the wonderful citizens that we have, coloreds sit in the balcony at church, and they have a separate school."

"You are right, Miss Sophie. It's always been that way."

"Well, I hate to say it, but now that those Reconstructionist have gone back up North, things are going to get worse. Two years ago, the Louisiana General Assembly passed a law that made it illegal for colored and whites to ride together on railroads. And just this year the Supreme Court upheld the law passed in Mississippi that denied colored people the vote. Colored men were required to pass literacy tests before they could vote, but those literacy tests involved naming all the vice-presidents of the United States or naming all the Supreme Court justices throughout history."

"That's impossible, Miss Sophie."

"Of course, it is. That's the idea."

During tea, they hear a few yells coming from outside the house getting louder and louder. It sounds like a lot of people.

Amanda runs to the front parlor to look out the floor-to-ceiling windows and is astonished to see a mass of colored men coming down the street with pitchforks and bats. That mass of humanity, dust boiling up around its feet, and the wall of noise coming closer by the minute—terrifying!

Miss Sophie joins Amanda at the window. "Don't you worry, Amanda. You know they are searching for that filthy Aucoin fellow. I hope they find him."

"I'd feel better if the sheriff was here and not on the way to Selma."

Both Miss Sophie and Amanda jump when they hear a knock on their door. "Should we answer it, Miss Sophie?"

"I tell you, child. Those colored men won't hurt us" Miss Sophie swings the door wide.

Mr. Pitts is standing on the porch, hat in hand. "Evening, Miss Sophie. I'm taking it upon myself to tell all the townspeople to stay in their homes."

Amanda speaks up, "Mr. Pitts, what's happening? Should we be worried?"

"You don't have to worry. That Aucoin fellow is the one to be worried. He attacked Reuben Lee's wife. If the colored men catch him, I don't know what they'll do."

"Are there white folks in town that will get involved in this?"

"You mean like the KKK kind of folks?"

"Yes, sir."

"Not so much in Marshall. We have kind of a unique situation here in this town. That doesn't mean there aren't people in the county that will get involved on Aucoin's side."

"That's hard to believe, Mr. Pitts."

The group of coloreds continues down Main Street. Despite what she knows, the pitchforks and bats make them a terrifying sight to Amanda.

Mr. Pitts puts his hat on his head and nods at Miss Sophie. "You ladies take care. I'll let you know when we catch Aucoin." He walks down the front steps and follows the mob down Main Street.

"Miss Sophie, that's a lot of noise coming from down Main Street. Don't you want to know what's happening?"

"You know Mr. Pitts told us to stay inside."

"But don't you want to see for yourself?"

"Oh Lord, what am I doing? Fetch my shawl and get one for yourself. We'll go see."

Miss Sophie and Amanda walk past Mable Todd's mansion to the mercantile store. They see the group of colored men stopped at the jail, but the two can't see over the group to make sense of what's happening.

"Miss Sophie. Miss Amanda. I said you needed to stay in your home." Mr. Pitts is standing in the door of the mercantile store.

"But Mr. Pitts, we want to see what's happening."

"Well, come on up to the second floor of the store. At least you'll be safe up there."

He holds the door open as the two enter the store and move up the wide staircase at the back of the store. They hurry across the second floor to look out the window onto the street.

Amanda sucks in her breath. There on the street is the group of colored men with their pitchforks and bats. Facing them is an equally large group of white men. "Oh no, Miss Sophie. Are they going to fight?"

Mr. Pitts answers for Miss Sophie. "Amanda, you are witnessing a rare event—one you'll tell your children about. Just watch."

Mr. Pitts carefully pushes up to open the window in front of them so that they can hear. Amanda notices that Clifford King and Preacher Sprague are in front of the crowd of white men. She watches as the large, rough hands of the colored man standing in front of the mob tighten around the bat he's holding. He doesn't move the bat, just gets a tight grip on it. He looks like he's ready to use it if he has to.

Mr. Pitts says, "That's William Samuel out in front. He's a sharecropper on Henry David Callander's land."

"He's huge. Shouldn't Mr. King and the preacher be afraid?"

"Or maybe William Samuel should be afraid. Look at the size of some of the white sharecroppers behind the preacher and Mr. King, and they're carrying rifles and shotguns."

It gets quiet down on the street. To Amanda, it seems like hours pass—the two groups faced off on Main Street. When Mr. King finally speaks from below, the group on the second floor of the mercantile can hear every word. "I assume you're looking for Zackery Aucoin?"

"Yes, sir," answers William. "I would appreciate it, Mr. King, if you and your group don't stand in our way."

"What Zackery Aucoin did to Louise Lee is an abomination. We're not here to stand in your way. We're here to help you, man."

William Samuel stands there and stares at Mr. King.

"Do you understand, William? We're here to help you."

William Samuel places the end of the bat down on the ground. He wipes his brow with the back of his hand and smiles at Mr. King. "We appreciate that, Mr. King. We sure do."

"Well, let's get organized. Have anyone been out through the woods to his house?"

No answer. "I'll send ten of our men out to his house. They have guns. How do you think we need to divide up, William?"

"Well, Mr. King, your people probably better search the town. People won't be so scared. We'll divide up. The first half of our group will take the road to Selma; the other half can search toward Thomasville. Does that sound all right?"

"That's a good plan, William Samuel. Preacher, can you stay at the Methodist Church? We'll all report back to you. Will you ring the bell if you catch Aucoin?"

"Be glad to do that, Clifford."

On the second floor of the mercantile, Mr. Pitts turns to Miss Sophie. "You knew that would happen, didn't you?"

"I wasn't sure, but I thought it would happen that way. These are decent people in Marshall. I don't know a soul in this town that would stand up for Zackery Aucoin."

Amanda speaks up, "Mr. Pitts, you are right. I will tell my children this story, and I'll be proud to tell it."

"Good. Thought you might feel that way. Now if we hurry, we can catch Preacher Sprague before he leaves for the church. He can see that you ladies get home safe. I want to join the search."

# Twenty-second Chapter

## Sadie Goes to School

Amanda stops by the mercantile store to see Mr. Pitts on the way home from school and is pleased to see Sadie in the back of the store. Before speaking to Sadie, she asks Mr. Pitts about the search for Aucoin.

"We have searched high and low but so far—no luck," says Mr. Pitts.

"Aucoin has to be punished for what he did to Louise. It's not fair that he gets away with hurting her," says Amanda.

"I agree, and I'll keep you posted, Amanda," says Mr. Pitts. He turns back to the task of restocking the candy jars.

Amanda walks over to Sadie, who is running the blue ribbon from a bonnet through her fingers.

"That's a beautiful bonnet, Sadie. Are you going to buy it?"

"Now Miss Amanda, where would I be getting money to buy this bonnet? I'm barely making it."

"Any word from your husband?"

"Not a word. To tell you the truth, Miss Amanda, it's easier with him gone except for the crops. It's hard to keep up with the crops."

"I want you to think about something, Sadie. If I can get someone to help you in the afternoons with the crops, will you come to school in the mornings?"

"Come to school, Miss Amanda? You want me to come to school?"

"I do, Sadie. You're bright, and there's so much out there for you to learn. I want you to learn higher mathematics, science, as well as great literature."

"But won't I look funny with all those kids?"

"No. My students are a great group. You can work your way up to the advanced group, and you can help me with discipline."

"If you mean it, I'll be there every morning as long as I know my crops will be taken care of."

Amanda gets Mr. Pitt's attention. "Mr. Pitts, you know the farmers and plantation owners around Marshall. Do you think one of them would send a couple of men over in the afternoons to help Sadie with her crops? You know Mr. Wiggins has left Marshall, and Sadie hasn't heard from him."

Mr. Pitts rubs his chin. "I think the best bet is David Henry Callander. Do you want me to ask him?"

Amanda blushes, and Sadie notices.

"Do you want me to ask him, Amanda?"

"Please, Mr. Pitts."

***

Amanda arrives at school early, anticipating Sadie's attendance that day. Looking over that day's lesson plans, she's most concerned about mathematics. She decides to seat Sadie in the middle group by Ann. The lesson today is: does X satisfy an equation? Amanda writes problems on the board, smiling at the students as they file into the classroom. Bringing up the rear is Sadie, her face scrubbed, hair brushed, and wearing a clean dress. The students are curious about Sadie but are polite—no rude comments. Amanda indicates that Sadie is to sit by Ann.

"Class, we have a new member with us today. Our new member is Mrs. Wiggins, and she is going to learn with us. How exciting to have her in our class! Now, let's bow our heads for the morning prayer." Amanda prays the same prayer she prays every morning, "Lord, guide us through this day of learning, and let us be ever mindful that we are your children. Amen."

The Pledge of Allegiance follows the prayer. Amanda walks to the front of the room to give instructions to the youngest group. Then she moves to the back, to give instructions to the oldest group. After accomplishing those two things, she addresses the middle group. "Today we are solving equations and determining if X satisfies the equation."

Amanda turns and adds to the board: 8 + X = 10. "What value of X is a solution to this problem—2 or 4? Write your answer on your slate." Amanda walks down the rows of students looking at their slates. She bends to talk with one student here, another there. When she walks behind Sadie, she is exhilarated to see a 2 written on Sadie's slate. Amanda touches Sadie's shoulder to show her approval and moves on down the row.

***

"I see that all three groups have finished with their assignments, and it's time for another speech. Amanda turns to the most advanced group of students. "Darlene, I see that you are next on the list to compare and contrast your life to George Washington's. What part of Washington's life are you comparing to your own?"

"I have researched the food that he and his family ate. I'm ready, Miss Amanda. Do you want me to come to the front of the classroom?"

"Oh, yes, Darlene. All the students will be listening to your speech." Darlene grimaces at the thought of speaking in front of all those students, but she bravely stands and walks to the front of the room, carrying a basket with her—a basket that smells like cinnamon and sugar. Darlene begins.

*George Washington—you know he was the first president of the United States—owned Mount Vernon, a mansion on the Potomac River. He and his wife Martha had dinner guests almost every day—very unlike our family. We never have guests to dinner—can't even imagine it.*

*For breakfast, George Washington would often eat hoecakes and fish. We never eat fish for breakfast, but we do eat hoecakes. Hoecakes are like pancakes but make them with corn flour, not wheat flour. My daddy said they call them hoecakes because, at one time, they cooked them on a hoe—a hoe stuck in the fire. George Washington's dinner table might have steak and kidney pie, a pie made of beef and beef kidney. You might find green beans and mashed sweet potatoes on the table, just like on our table at home. We don't have steak and kidney pie at home, and I'm glad. Desserts at Mount Vernon included Tipsy Cake and Martha Washington's Whiskey Cake. My mother would never allow alcohol in our house or our food. He also liked cherry pie, and so do we. At our house, we like oatmeal cookies; Mama made some for me to share with you."* Darlene reaches over to grab the basket and starts passing it down the first row. *I was fascinated to learn that George and Martha Washington, who lived one hundred years ago, ate some of the same foods we eat today. Thank you for listening to me.*

Darlene looks to Amanda for approval. Amanda has already begun to clap, and the rest of the class joins in. "What a wonderful way to end the school day. Thank you, Darlene."

While the other students drag their lunch buckets out from under their desks and put on their coats, Sadie sits and waits. After everyone else has left the room, Amanda walks over to Sadie. "Sadie, are you all right?"

"Miss Amanda, I think you are the luckiest human alive, supervising all this learning."

"Thank you, Sadie. You enjoyed it?"

"I can't wait to come back tomorrow. I've got to get home to the crops, but, Miss Amanda, I want you to know you have opened the universe for me."

# Twenty-third Chapter

## The Sheriff Pays a Visit

Amanda, still at school, is working on the next day's lesson plans when she hears someone coming up the steps to the schoolroom. She looks up to find the door filled with the silhouette of a rather large man. As he steps into the room, Amanda notices the star on his vest first; the square-jawed, handsome face, second. "Good afternoon, Miss Amanda."

"Hello, Sheriff Winfield. Is everything all right?"

"Everything's quiet in Marshall today. I would like to pick your brain about the incident involving Louise Lee and Zackery Aucoin."

"Tell me you caught him, sheriff."

"I can't do that, Miss Amanda. No one has seen him since that day he shoved Mrs. Lee."

"He's an awful man, sheriff. The first time I saw him, he was so insulting that Miss Maggie walked him out of the mercantile store with a gun held to his neck."

The sheriff laughed at the image. "I'd have paid good money to see that, Miss Amanda."

"He's the nastiest man alive—I swear he is."

"I couldn't agree more, but I have to tell you I worry about his wife and child."

"Yes, someone mentioned that he had a wife and a child that day in the mercantile store."

"Yes, I met his wife one day. Ruby is her name, and the child is named Emme. They were a pitiful looking pair with worn clothes and shoes. I remember Ruby is cross-eyed. The thought that crossed my mind about Ruby—she looked beaten down."

"And the child? What about Emme? Should she be in school?"

"It's hard to tell, but I think she's still too young for school."

"What kind of life could that be, living alone like that? I heard Aucoin was Cajun. What exactly does that mean?"

"As best I remember, the British conquered a place near Canada called French Acadia; this happened in the early 1700s. The Acadians refused to sign an oath of allegiance to Britain, and many of them migrated to New Orleans. There's a huge Cajun population in Louisiana. How Aucoin got to Marshall, Alabama, is beyond me."

"They probably ran him out of Louisiana."

"You certainly could be right. Now, not that it will help much, can you tell me what you saw that day he shoved Louise Lee?"

"Of course. Louise was leaving the school, her arms piled high with books from our library. She walked onto the sidewalk and accidentally bumped into Zackery Aucoin. Instead of being gracious, he was extremely rude—even asked her if she stole the books. He shoved her, Sheriff Winfield. For no reason, he shoved her."

"Miss Amanda, if this ever comes to trial, will you testify to what you just told me?"

"Yes, sheriff, I'll testify. I've never even been in a courtroom, but I'll certainly testify against Zackery Aucoin."

# Twenty-fourth Chapter

## Amanda and Elizabeth Attend a Concert

"Amanda, you've got to hurry. We're going to miss the buggy going to Selma." Elizabeth wants to be on time to meet Clifford King and his wife, Myrtle. The Kings have invited Amanda and Elizabeth to ride with them in their buggy to attend a concert in Selma. They will all spend the night at the home of Mr. King's brother.

Amanda converses with her image in the floor-length, tilting mirror. Reaching to tilt the mirror back so that she can see her shoes and the curls at the top of her head, she approves of her image. Mother sent the new dress that she's wearing: persimmon-colored with a skirt that's fuller in the back and has a high neckline. Amanda loves the sleeves that fit her lower arms tightly and have a little puff where the sleeve ends at the shoulders. She nods to her image. "You'll do, Amanda Oglesby. You'll do."

Amanda rushes down the stairs to find Elizabeth waiting in the foyer. She's frowning and swinging her embroidered reticule—its drawstring tightly pulled—around and around. "Come on, Elizabeth. Smile. I'm ready, and I think I hear the buggy outside."

Amanda opens the heavy front door and primly walks down the steps and sidewalk, leaving Elizabeth to follow. "Mr. King,

Mrs. King—so good to see you. We can't thank you enough for taking us to the concert."

During the long buggy ride, the foursome talks about the concert. A local group from Selma is performing music from the first act of the comic opera, *The Gondoliers.* Gilbert and Sullivan wrote the music. To make it even better, it's at Sturdivant Hall. Amanda and Elizabeth have discussed Sturdivant Hall and are excited to see the antebellum Greek Revival home.

As the buggy turns on Mabry Street, they get their first glimpse of the mansion rising from the landscape. "It's majestic," says Amanda, awe-struck.

"Did you know Robert. E. Lee's cousin built it?" asks Mrs. King.

Amanda doesn't answer. She tries to take in the house with six Corinthian columns supporting the roof and tall, dark shutters flanking the windows that reach the floor.

"Look at that cantilevered balcony," says Mr. King. Amanda raises her eyes to the balcony that runs the length of the house outside the second floor.

"Mr. King, watch your words. We don't have any idea what cantilevered means."

"Well, Mrs. King, it means fixed at one end or on one side. See, the back side of the balcony is attached to the house. Other than that, it's free-standing."

"Well, thank you for that lesson," says Mrs. King. "Come on. Let's go in."

They walk through the large doorway with sidelights on each side into the L-shaped hallway with the impressive checkered floor. A young girl with blue ribbons in her hair hands them a program and leads them to the drawing room. They find seats halfway up the aisle.

Amanda is looking over the program—"List and Learn" and "From the Sunny Spanish Shore" are up first—when Elizabeth digs her elbow into her ribs. Frowning, Amanda turns to look at Elizabeth, who nods her head to the left.

David Henry Callander is entering the row in front of them. He stops at the chair directly in front of Amanda and turns to check the seat before sitting down. That's when he notices Amanda. He smiles, and his eyes crinkle. "Miss Oglesby, how wonderful to see you this evening. How very wonderful."

Amanda acknowledges David Henry by nodding her head. Elizabeth can't help but notice how flustered Amanda seems even though she continues to study the program. The ensemble begins with the first selection and, looking up, Amanda finds her view blocked by the wide shoulders of David Henry. She explores with her eyes the shape of his head, noticing how his hair touches the top of his collar and how very large his shoulders are. She wonders what it would be like to run her fingers along the back of his neck. Lawdy! She fans herself with her program, prompting Elizabeth to raise her eyebrows.

Midway through selections from the first act, the ensemble breaks for intermission. Amanda and Elizabeth both stand, as does David Henry. "I understand that you are from Demopolis, Miss Amanda?"

"Why yes, that's correct."

"I would love to show you the dining room of this house—There's something there that relates to Demopolis."

He turns to Mr. and Mrs. King. "May I have your permission to show Miss Amanda and Miss Elizabeth the dining room?"

Mrs. King looks up at her husband. "I think it would be proper as long as the three are together."

"I leave these matters to you, dear," says Mr. King

"Would you like to accompany us?" David Henry asks.

"No, thank you. We'll stay here and visit with friends," replies Mr. King.

Curious as to what he means, Amanda and Elizabeth follow him into the dining room.

"Look at the wall behind you; it's a mural of the Vine and Olive Colony."

Amanda is immediately interested. The story of the Frenchmen and their wives who came to Alabama to plant olives and grapes has always fascinated her. In fact, her lesson plans include a trip to the Vine and Olive Colony via the imaginary train.

"Notice the women in the fields in their ball gowns?" asks David Henry. I understand that did not happen, but rumor had it the ladies had no appropriate clothing to wear for working the fields. How unfortunate that they had to do manual labor."

"How I would love for my students to see this. We'll be studying the Vine and Olive Company, and this would be a great visual for them to see."

Elizabeth clears her throat. "Excuse me, but I need to see Mrs. King. I'll see you both back in the drawing room."

Amanda finds herself alone with David Henry. She knows this is not proper. Would her Mother approve? Or Miss Sophie? She looks up to find him staring at her. He moves toward her, and she thinks: *He is going to kiss me, right here in the dining room at Sturdivant Hall.*

She hears the chatter of people in the hall moving back toward the dining room. She thinks: *I don't care.* He bows and, with a sweep of his arm, indicates she is to precede him out of the room. They walk back to the drawing room. Neither speaks.

***

Settling into their room for the night, the two friends finally have a chance to talk through the evening. "Amanda, what happened after I left you and David Henry in the dining room?" asks Elizabeth.

Amanda slides a high-necked, flannel gown over her head. "Absolutely nothing." Her back is to Elizabeth. She turns, looks at Elizabeth, and frowns.

"Confess. What did you want to happen?"

"I thought he was going to kiss me. I wanted him to kiss me."

"Amanda, he was protecting you. If anyone attending the concert had seen you alone with David Henry, it would have hurt your reputation. Kissing him? Mr. Pitts would fire you."

"I know all that. Mr. Callander makes me forget the rules for proper behavior—all that flies right out the window when he's around."

"I see I'm going to have to help you ride herd on all those passionate feelings you have for Mr. Callander."

"Thank you, Elizabeth. Help me keep my actions pure—even if my thoughts aren't." She smiles.

# Late November 1892

# Twenty-fifth Chapter

## Miss Maggie and Miss Sophie Snoop

Amanda and Miss Sophie are enjoying an early morning cup of tea. The topic of discussion is Zackery Aucoin's family. "Miss Sophie, Sheriff Winfield told me that Aucoin has a wife, Ruby, and a young daughter, living on the old Cleghorn place."

"That's what I understand. It must be an awful life for them, living in the woods with only Aucoin for company. How do they live? How does Aucoin support his family?"

"It's rumored that he gets some type of pension—from where I don't know. He also collects scrap metal and sells it over in Selma. Can't be much of a living."

Miss Sophie and Amanda turn as the swinging door to the kitchen opens, and Miss Maggie walks in.

"Hello, Maggie. Amanda and I were talking about Zackery Aucoin's family."

"Now that's a depressing subject. Do you have any of that tea left?"

"Help yourself, Maggie." Miss Maggie gets a teacup from the cupboard and starts preparing her tea.

"Miss Maggie, Miss Sophie—I hate to leave such excellent company, but I have to go teach the children of Marshall."

"Have a good day, dear," says Miss Sophie as she stands up and kisses Amanda's cheek.

After Amanda has closed the front door, Miss Maggie asks, "Well, Sophie, do you think somebody needs to go check on Aucoin's family?"

"By someone, do you mean the two of us, Maggie?"

"Who else will do it? The sheriff, maybe? That would scare the wife to death."

"Oh, Maggie, you're probably right. We'll go."

"Finish your tea. We'll stop by my house before we leave."

An unsuspecting Sophie says, "Fine."

***

Upstairs in her master bedroom, Miss Maggie reaches under the bed and brings out a large, rectangular, flat box. Removing the lid, Miss Maggie removes two pairs of trousers and a couple of long-sleeved cotton shirts.

"What do you think we're doing with those clothes? Taking them as a gift to Aucoin?"

"No, Sophie, we're going to wear them."

"No, we're not."

"Yes, we are."

"Give me one good reason why we should wear men's clothes in public?"

"I'll give you two: it will be easier to get through the undergrowth in the woods, and we won't be recognizable at a distance."

"Well, maybe, but I've never worn trousers in my life. I'm embarrassed."

"Oh, pooh! They're not that different from the bloomers I wear."

"But I don't wear bloomers."

"Well, you should. Bloomers are healthful and, Lord knows, they're more comfortable than that corset you're wearing."

"Just take off that dress and all those petticoats and put on the trousers."

"All right, all right," says Miss Sophie, turning her back to do as Maggie suggested.

When she turns around, Maggie bursts out laughing. She laughs so hard; she can barely talk.

"What?" asks Sophie.

"Look down," gasps Maggie.

Sophie notices that she has not buttoned all the buttons on the trousers. Her undergarments are dangling from the opening. She immediately starts buttoning the trousers, not finding the situation funny.

"Here, this finishes the outfit." Stuffing her hair up under a hat, Maggie pulls the hat down to the tips of her ears and tosses a soft, felt hat to Sophie.

"You do the same, Sophie."

When they are both dressed, they look at each other in the bedroom mirror. Finally, Sophie starts laughing. Maggie joins in and slaps Sophie on the shoulder. "We'd better get going, Mr. Lawrence."

"After you, Mr. Langford."

***

Sophie and Maggie head towards the woods north of town. "Do you know where we're going, Maggie?"

"Of course, I've been to the Cleghorn place hundreds of times. Are you going to let that dog come with us?"

"Harold, you need to stay. Stay here."

They are silent as the two make their way through the woods. They hear squirrels running up and down the rough, dark bark of pine trees. They hear only the crunching sound of fall leaves under their feet. Finally, Sophie speaks, "Being in the woods is a little like being in church. I feel reverent. I look up at the high ceiling of leaves and feel I should fall to my knees. Do you feel that way, Maggie?"

"Shush, Sophie. We don't know where Aucoin is."

After what seems like hours to Sophie, Maggie says, "There's a clearing up ahead. We're close to the Cleghorn house."

Maggie and Sophie creep around the edge of the clearing, spotting the wooden house. "Look, Maggie, There's smoke coming out of the chimney. Let's sneak up and look in the window on the side of the house."

"All right, Sophie, but we have to be quiet." Stooping and running, they make it to the side of the house. Maggie stands on tiptoes and looks in the window. Ruby is seated near the fire with Emme on her lap. She's telling Emme a story. If you didn't know Aucoin lived here, you would admire the familial scene: fire, mother, daughter.

Ruby is telling Emme about her childhood. "And the house where I grew up in Louisiana was a two-story house that had never seen a paintbrush. There was a porch with a swing on the front of the house. That was my favorite place to sit and listen to my mother's stories."

"What stories, Mother?" Emme asked.

"I loved the story about the upstairs bedroom. It was supposed to be the bedroom of my grandfather's first wife, who died not too long after my mother was born. Grandfather married again, and the story goes that every time the new wife went in that bedroom, a vase would fall off the mantle."

"That's scary," says Emme. "Sounds like great-grandmother didn't like the new wife. Do you believe in ghosts, Mother?"

At that point, Sophie feels something wet and cold on her ankle, and she screams. Looking down, she is shocked to see her dog, Harold, licking her ankle. His tail is wagging, which means his whole body is wagging. He's panting, and everything about him says, "Look what I did! I found you." He must have followed them through the woods.

Sophie's scream makes Ruby look toward the window. From her point of view, she sees two men looking in the window. Ruby freezes—afraid to move.

Maggie reaches and grabs the hat off Sophie's head, making Sophie's long hair tumble to her shoulders. Maggie, taking off her hat, yells, "We're women, Ruby. It's Miss Maggie and Miss Sophie from town."

Ruby recovers enough to tell Lucile to get the rifle. "It's behind the bedroom door, Emme. Hurry."

"Please don't shoot us. We won't hurt you," yells Sophie.

Maggie adds, "Will you come to the front door, Ruby? We want to talk."

Emme hands Ruby the rifle. Ruby keeps the rifle in hand as she walks to the front door, pushing Emme behind her.

Sophie and Maggie, hats in hand, walk around to the front door, followed by Harold. Ruby looks courageous—all stocky five feet of her—standing in the front door. Despite the worn clothes, short stature, and a left eye that's turned toward her flat nose, she's the picture of a defiant woman ready to defend her home.

Miss Sophie says, "We apologize for scaring you, Ruby. We didn't want to be recognized, so we dressed as men."

"Yes, Sophie and I wanted to make sure you and Emme were all right. And we want you to know if you ever need anything, you come see one of us. We live across the street from each other at the end of the street by the churches."

She relaxes and puts the rifle in the corner. "That's nice of you to check on us. We have plenty to eat. Aucoin sees to that."

"So Mr. Aucoin is around. I don't see him anywhere," observes Sophie.

"No, but I think I hear him," says Maggie. Both hear the noise of someone or something lumbering through the woods.

"Run, Maggie!"

Sophie tears across the clearing into the woods. Sophie turns when she reaches the woods to see Maggie running with Harold close behind. She hears the loud crack of gunfire and a yelp coming from Harold, who keeps running. Sophie picks him up and runs after Maggie.

"Reviens, connard. Reviens." It's Aucoin, all right.

They don't stop running until they reach Maggie's house. Maggie bends over and gasps for breath. Sophie is terrified for Harold, who is whimpering in her arms. "Maggie, I think Aucoin shot Harold. Help me."

Maggie sees blood on Sophie's hands and moves toward her house. "Bring him in the kitchen. Let me check him out." Maggie walks up the steps to the back door and holds it open for Sophie and Harold.

"Put him on the kitchen table while I get a clean cloth and a bowl of water."

Putting him down, Sophie sees just how much blood is on her hands and her clothes. She is alarmed.

"Hold on, Sophie. Don't think the worst. Let me check him out." Harold whimpers as Maggie washes his side with a warm cloth. "Look, Sophie. It's a graze. That bastard just grazed him. Thank God."

"We have one more reason to take care of Aucoin. Louise and now, Harold."

"Don't you worry, Sophie. Someone will kill the bastard for sure if the law doesn't get him first."

# Twenty-sixth Chapter

## Amanda Visits Louise

"Now what would Louise like to read?" Amanda asks aloud as she slides the tips of her fingers over the rows of fiction books in the school library. *Great Expectations, Little Women, Silas Marner, The Moonstone, The Marble Faun.* Amanda chooses *The Moonstone* and adds the book to the basket of desserts she will take to Louise.

Louise returned to Marshall from the Selma hospital a week ago, and Reuben had assured Amanda that she was ready for visitors. Walking up the steps of the Lee home, Amanda is pleased to see Reuben holding the front door open for her.

"Here, let me take that basket for you, Miss Amanda."

"Thank you, Reuben. How's Louise today?"

"I can tell you she's excited about your visit. Come with me. Hope you don't mind visiting in the bedroom."

"Of course, I don't mind."

"She was up this morning, and it wore her out. She's resting in bed now."

Amanda follows Rueben down a wide hall with clapboard walls, identical to the outside of the house. To the right, Amanda sees a parlor of overstuffed furniture draped with doilies. The doors to the left are closed. The next room on the right is the bedroom. Louise is sitting up in an iron frame bed that's been painted white. A crazy quilt drapes the foot of the bed, its odd-shaped pieces in brown, orange, green catching the eye. There must be five or six pillows behind Louise, all edged with fine crocheting at least four inches long. Louise herself compliments this pretty setting, looking beautiful with her coffee-colored skin against the whitest-of-white pillowcases.

"Miss Amanda, I am so delighted to see you."

"And I'm happy to see you looking so well. I've brought you a book to read and sweets to fatten you and Reuben up. You know There's nothing like Miss Sophie's custard pie."

"Oh, we'll have a tea party."

"I'll go make tea and slice the pie. You ladies visit," says Reuben.

A shadow passes over Louise's countenance before she speaks. "Have they captured Zackery Aucoin?"

"No. But he's still in the area. Miss Sophie swears to it. She won't tell me why she's so sure, but she seems to know he's still around."

"Thinking about him scares me. You know Reuben won't leave me alone? When he teaches, one of his relatives is here in the house—with a gun."

"Good for Rueben. Louise, you just happened to be in the wrong place at the wrong time. I don't think you need to worry about Aucoin bothering you."

"I hope not. Now enough about that. Let's talk about something happy."

"Fine. Tell me about yourself, Louise. Where did you grow up?"

"I grew up in New Hope, just like Reuben."

"Was it a good place to grow up?"

"Goodness, yes. I liked growing up in town but loved all the green around us—so many trees and green pastures stretching forever. There was a huge boulder in the middle of the pasture on the north side of town. After Mother finished with dinner, we'd walk to the boulder and sit. What a show! We'd see deer and bears and wild turkeys. I loved the fan of feathers on the turkey. I thought they seemed dressed up to go someplace fancy."

"It sounds like a wonderful place to live. What did your parents do for a living?"

"My daddy was an undertaker, and my mother stayed home with me—and she cooked. She was the most amazing cook. To this day, I miss her Lally Hoo."

"Lally Hoo?"

"Yes, it is this blackberry concoction. We'd pick blackberries on the edge of the north pasture. Mama would put them in a pot with sugar and water and bring it to a rolling boil. While it was coming to a boil, she'd mix up and roll out dumpling dough. She'd cut the dough into strips, and she let me drop the dumplings into the boiling blackberries. It was the best-tasting dessert ever made. Sometimes Mother would serve it with homemade vanilla ice-cream. So good!

"And your father was an undertaker?"

"Yes, and his father before him. It was a family business passed down for three generations. Boy, could my daddy tell some tales."

"I can just imagine."

"My favorite is the tale about the lady they called Miss Lydia. Miss Lydia turned up on the front steps of the funeral home, dead as a doornail. Not a soul in the whole community knew who she was, so Daddy named her Miss Lydia. His funeral home had a little bowed-out window on the front, and Daddy put a casket in that window, put Miss Lydia up in it, and tilted the casket sideways so everyone coming by the funeral home could look in that window at Miss Lydia. She was dressed in a long, multi-patterned dress and had a blue, straw hat on her head. Daddy embalmed her and put her in the casket dressed just as he found her—hat and all."

"But why did he put her in the window?"

"He hoped someone would identify her."

"And did they?"

"They never did. Finally, Daddy took the casket out of the window and buried the casket—and Miss Lydia—in the graveyard."

"What a tale! And how awful—buried where no one even knows your name."

"I tell you; it's turned into a real ghost tale. None of our folk in New Hope will come anywhere near that window. Some folks say they saw Miss Lydia rise up out of that casket. Some folks say they still do."

"That's spooky, Louise."

"Yes, ma'am. Not many people come to the front of the funeral home. They all go in the back door. They don't want to be anywhere near where Miss Lydia was."

"I love that story. But tell me, Louise, how did you and Reuben meet?"

"He was teaching Sunday school at the church back home, and I was in his class. I tell you that man can teach, and he makes you think about things. Like, if we believe in the Trinity, why does God call Jesus his son?"

"That's deep."

"Yes, ma'am. That's Reuben. He makes you think.'"

"Was it love at first sight, Louise?"

"Reuben says it was; he swears when he saw me walk in the Sunday school room, he knew I was going to be his bride."

"How long before he told you about being the future Mrs. Reuben Lee?"

"About six months, but I had an idea. Us women know these things."

"I agree. I think us women do know—at least I hope so."

"Sounds like something's boiling in the pot, Miss Amanda. Is that right?"

"I'm not positive, but I think so." Amanda blushes, despite being so comfortable being around Louise.

At that point, Reuben comes in the door with a tray of teacups and custard pie served on beautiful china rimmed with small, purple violets and pale green leaves. Reuben puts the tray on top of the dresser. He hands the cups to Amanda and Louise, then pulls a little gate-legged table up beside Amanda. He puts Amanda's pie on the table and places the tray on Louise's lap.

"Aren't you going to eat with us, Reuben?"

"I had a piece of custard pie in the kitchen while you two were talking, but I'll visit with you. How's school, Miss Amanda? Want to share any tips?"

Amanda tells Reuben all about her All Aboard segments of teaching, describing the schoolroom visit to Catawba and the trip to Carrollton to see the face in the window. She tells him all about the Vine and Olive Colony and her plans to take the students on that trip.

"That's so creative. Do you mind if I do that activity with my students?"

"Of course not. I'd be flattered. Do you have any creative ideas that you'd like to share?"

"Sure. My students are making books as an end product of research on the Middle Ages. It's just too hard for my middle group of students to write a research paper. This book is a precursor to the research paper."

"And what's the book like?" asks Amanda.

"The students make it out of brown wrapping paper that Mr. Pitts donated from the mercantile store. The students cut out two rectangular pieces of paper and fold each rectangle in half, which gives them four surfaces to write on. They stack one folded rectangle on top of the second rectangle, giving them an eight-page book. They sew—yes, even the boys—the spines of the paper together to form a book."

"How creative. What do the students write in the books?"

"This is where these books differ from a research paper. Students have five questions to answer while researching. Different students have different questions. Once students have answered the questions, and I'm talking about simple questions and answers, the students prepare their books. The title of the paper with their name goes on the first page of the book. The next five pages contain a written question at the top and the answer to the question below."

"And the seventh and eighth pages?" asks Amanda.

"The seventh page contains a bibliography of resources, and the eighth or back page is usually blank. See how much easier this is, compared to a research paper with paragraphs?"

"Yes, it's a great introduction to research. When students progress to a research paper, they'll be more prepared. May I use this idea?"

"You don't even have to ask. Of course."

"It seems all this talk of education has put Louise to sleep. I'm going to tiptoe out. Please tell her I enjoyed the visit and will bring a new book for her to read soon."

Amanda walks out into the sunny day. She thanks God for Louise's health and for the opportunity to teach in the same town as Reuben.

# Twenty-seventh Chapter

## Etiquette Lessons

“Thanksgiving is almost here, and that means Thanksgiving dinner is almost here. We are going to discuss how to eat properly at the Thanksgiving table.” As Amanda says this, she takes a plate, utensils for eating, and a glass out of a basket.

“Do we have to?” asks Burt.

“Yes, we do,” replies Amanda, as she adds a folded napkin to the place setting. “Now, Miss Sophie has provided me with some leftovers to use in today’s lesson.” Amanda puts a slice of chicken, mashed potatoes, and peas on the plate and fills the glass with water from a lidded jar taken from the basket.

“Before we start this lesson, who can tell me the name of the president of the United States?

“Benjamin Harrison,” says Ann.

“That’s correct, Ann.” Amanda walks behind the desk, pulls out the chair, and sits down.

“We are going to pretend President Harrison has invited our class to Thanksgiving dinner. To accept his invitation, we have to know how to eat properly. We want the people of Marshall to be proud of us.”

She slides her chair to the desk and begins by drinking from the glass of water. Amanda drinks quietly—not a sound is heard. She takes the napkin, unfolds it, and places it in her lap. Sadie is watching intently.

Randy asks, "Don't you tuck it under your chin. You know, at the top of your shirt?"

"Randy, it's good manners to place the napkin in your lap."

"My parents don't have good manners, Miss Amanda." Amanda has no idea how to answer Randy. She certainly can't say that Randy is correct.

She says, "Well, don't forget. We are preparing to eat dinner with President Harrison."

Amanda picks up her knife and fork, cuts a small piece of chicken, places it in her mouth and chews very slowly before swallowing. She places her fork and knife on her plate while she chews.

Sadie asks," Do we always do that, Miss Amanda? Put the fork on the plate while we chew?" She's thinking of her husband at the table with both fork and knife standing up in his hands, ends resting on the table

"It's polite, Sadie. Watch me chew, too. I close my mouth while I chew."

"My Mama says I smack," says Randy.

Amanda laughs. She forks mashed potatoes. "Now watch, children. I have potatoes on my fork. I am going to continue to sit up straight, and I'll bring the fork to my mouth. In other words, don't bend over your plate to feed yourself."

"What about the peas, Miss Amanda? I've seen people put them on a knife. It's hard to get all those peas in your mouth—some of them always fall off the knife.

"Eat the peas with a fork, always. And, by the way, don't pick your teeth at the table. Now, I've finished my meal. I will place my knife and fork side by side in the middle of the plate, and I will push my chair back to rise from the table, leaving the chair where I pushed it."

Ann says, "Miss Amanda, my mother and father will be so pleased with my table manners."

Burt adds, "Miss Amanda, I'm glad we don't eat with President Harrison every day."

# Twenty-eighth Chapter

## Donald, Davy, and the Washhouse

"Now, Sadie and I are going to have a surprise for you the day before Thanksgiving. Remember your manners. They will be important. And don't bring lunch that day."

"What is it, Miss Amanda?"

"Is President Harrison coming?"

"Is it a good surprise?"

"You'll just have to wait and see." Amanda removes a folded letter from her pocket and smoothes it out. "Moving on. I have another letter from my father, and Donald has done it again. Get comfortable, and we'll hear about Donald's latest exploit."

Randy and some of the younger children lie down on the floor, propping themselves up with arms bent at the elbow and heads resting in the palm of their hands. "I just love Donald stories," says Randy.

Amanda starts to read:

*Donald and his dog Davy are playing around the huge, black kettle used to boil water for laundering. Wash day was yesterday, so there's plenty of charred wood under the kettle, which is currently tipped on its side to drain. Donald and Davy are scuffling around on the ground and roll right through all that charred wood. Davy is wallowing in it. Donald knows he's going to be in trouble when he sees his own black hands, and he sees Davy. Every spot on Davy that should be white is now black. He thinks and thinks and heads for the washhouse. Maybe there's something in there that will clean Davy.*

*Donald walks into the wooden washhouse. He smells the clean smell of soap mixed in with the damp smell of wet laundry. Wooden tubs on stands line the left wall of the wash-house, and a long shelf used for sorting clothes is on the right wall. Laundry products are at the end of the long shelf.*

*Donald picks up the soap—it smells so clean—and notices where the women have shaved off pieces to put in the laundry. He picks up a bottle of Mrs. Stewart's Liquid Bluing and reads the label. It guarantees your whites will be whiter. What Donald does not read is that one should not apply bluing to laundry—and presumably not to dogs—unless they have been washed and are wet.*

*Davy has followed Donald into the washhouse and is sniffing around in the corner. Davy unstops the top of the bluing bottle and calls Davy to come to him. Davy, trusting dog that he is, trots over to Donald, who upturns the bottle of bluing over Davy, rubbing it over all the places that were once white. To Donald's consternation, Davy is no longer black. But he's not white either—he's blue!*

*At that moment, Cousin Lily walks in the washhouse, sees Davy, and runs to the big house screaming, "There's a haint in the wash-house—a blue haint! Lordy, help us, I pray." Hearing all the noise Cousin Lily is making, I come out of the house to console her. Donald and Davy choose that moment to make an appearance.*

*After starring at Davy long enough to take in his appearance, I say, "Donald, you explain yourself right this minute."*

*"Why, Davy and I were reenacting the War Between the States. I was a Confederate, and Davy was a blue-bellied Yankee. Of course, Davy lost."*

# Twenty-ninth Chapter

## Sadie Before Marriage

Sadie and Amanda arrive at the schoolhouse early on the day before Thanksgiving to set up the surprise—a Thanksgiving meal for the students with fine china, crystal, and silverware. Sadie and Amanda cover a long table in the extra school room with a tablecloth fit for Mable Todd's dining room table. The cloth is a snowy white damask, and the hem is stitched by hand with tiny, tiny stitches. Amanda and Sadie start setting the napkins that match the tablecloths.

"Sadie, do you mind telling me about your people? Who were your mother and father?"

"I don't mind, Miss Amanda."

"I don't know anything about your past; I just know that you're very smart."

Sadie's face comes to life, and she smiles. "Do you think so, Miss Amanda?"

"I know so, Sadie. You must have had intelligent parents."

"I remember my mother as a beautiful lady—tall and gracious. She took in ironing to help bring in money. My clearest memory is of her ironing long, voile dresses for the Spring Hill ladies of

Mobile. Spring Hill, located on a hill outside the city proper, was an escape for the wealthy from the steamy streets of Mobile.

We spoke French and English because my father's family was French. My father was a lector. That's someone who reads newspapers and books to the factory workers because their jobs were so monotonous. That was his job. Mother would let me walk to the factory some afternoons, and there my father would be, sitting on a platform high above the workers. He read to them most of the time, but sometimes he would talk about his family.

I was there one afternoon and heard him tell about his father, my grandfather, whose relatives date back to the French settlement of Mobile in the 1700s. My grandfather was an itinerant artist. He traveled through Alabama and Mississippi, selling portraits to wealthy plantation owners. When the roads were muddy and grandfather couldn't travel, he would paint portraits of children, men, and women. He would not paint their heads.

Upon arriving at a plantation, the owner could choose a painting he liked, and Grandfather would paint the appropriate head on the painting. Father laughed out loud after telling about a portrait hanging in a home in Tuscaloosa. It's a young boy who is looking in one direction and pointing in another. Grandfather made a mistake and didn't paint the boy facing in the right direction."

"That's fascinating about your father, Sadie. I've never known anyone whose father was a lector. I'm curious. Do you know what books he read to the workers?"

"I remember hearing parts of *The Adventures of Tom Sawyer, Moby Dick,* and *Silas Marner,*" says Sadie.

"Maybe that's where you got your love of reading—from your father," says Amanda.

"Maybe so, but once I married Harley, I had no access to books."

"Please pardon my rudeness, but I don't see who would match you with Harley."

"Matched is the word for it. When I was seventeen, Mother and Father died of Yellow Fever. I was alone—no siblings and no living relatives that I knew. The Wiggins family lived next door. Harley was wild, and his parents thought a wife would calm him down—maybe actually make him a productive human being. They encouraged us to marry. I didn't see any other way out. I married him."

"How did you land in Marshall?"

"Harley is a hothead—constantly causing fights on the streets of Mobile. In one of his fights, the other man died. He had to leave and I with him. His parents knew of Marshall. Harley has an aunt and uncle that live in Thomasville, and they helped us get settled in Marshall."

"Oh, Sadie."

"What choice did I have, Miss Amanda? I couldn't see another choice for me. Anyway, living in Marshall is the best thing that ever happened to me. That's the way I see it."

"Thank you for sharing your story with me, Sadie. And I love Marshall, too. Now, we've got to be ready before those students come through the door."

"Let's hope Miss Sophie and Miss Maggie get here with the food before the students get here."

When Amanda had approached Miss Sophie and Miss Maggie about providing a meal for the students, they immediately agreed. Considering Miss Maggie had invited Miss Sophie and the entire boarding house to her house for Thanksgiving dinner, this was very generous of her to provide dinner for the students as well.

Amanda heard the ladies approaching before she saw them. "Sophie, these children are gonna love this sweet potato casserole."

"Now Maggie, you are just buttering me up. Of course, I'll bring one tomorrow for Thanksgiving."

Miss Maggie is laughing as she comes in the schoolhouse followed by Miss Sophie and two kitchen maids. Each one of the ladies is carrying a box loaded with food. Maggie says, "I have the turkey, Amanda. Let's put it on the table first."

Amanda indicates the large platter she has placed at the end of the table. "Let's put it here; it'll be easier to carve." As Amanda and Miss Maggie struggle to lift the turkey from the box, Miss Sophie and the maids begin putting the rest of the food on the table: dressing, gravy, minced cranberries, greens, peas, and the wonderful sweet potato casserole.

"I have pies back at the house. I'll go get them while the children are eating," says Maggie.

Amanda has asked the students to arrive at noon as there was no regular school today, and she asked that they wear their Sunday clothes. Looking out the window, she is pleased to see Ann coming up the sidewalk in her high-necked blouse and a pleated skirt that swishes below her knees when she walks. Randy follows a few steps behind. He is wearing clean overalls and a pressed, long-sleeved shirt. Randy's hair is parted on the side and slicked over his head—not a hair out of place.

Amanda sees the rest of the students coming toward the school, and she greets them one by one as they come in the door. They are quieter today, unaccustomed to coming to school in their Sunday best. When they are all in the schoolroom, Amanda says, "How wonderful you all look. Now, please follow me into the library."

"Look at all this food."

"A real turkey…"

"Is President Harrison coming?"

Amanda replies, "President Harrison will not be joining us today, but we are going to enjoy a real Thanksgiving meal without him." Once they are all seated, Amanda says, "Please bow your heads for the blessing. Lord, we are thankful for your bountifulness. May we be ever mindful that we are your children. Amen."

After the blessing, the children pass the food and begin to eat. Napkins are placed in laps, forks are placed on plates while chewing, and no peas are eaten off of knives.

# Thirtieth Chapter

## Thanksgiving Day

Lifting a cardboard box off the kitchen counter, Miss Sophie says, "Amanda, could you handle the pecan pies? I'll get the sweet potato casserole and the squash, and we'll be off to Maggie's."

"Yes, ma'am." Amanda picks up the pecan pies, topped with whole pecans arranged in a circular fashion and edged with a perfectly browned crust. She balances one in each hand as she goes down Miss Sophie's front steps and crosses the street to Miss Maggie's.

Miss Maggie's house is a fine example of antebellum architecture. Four Ionic columns—scrolled at the top—line up across the front of Miss Maggie's. Amanda raises her eyes as she passes under the balcony that hangs over the front door. Amanda often looks across the street from her bedroom window and imagines two lovers standing on the balcony—so romantic.

Amanda steps through the front door onto the inlaid oak and mahogany floor. Raising her eyes to the grand, unsupported staircase, she is shocked to see her mother, followed by her father, coming down the stairs.

"Mother. Daddy. You're here. I can't believe it."

Mr. Oglesby says, "Sister, you didn't think we'd let you spend Thanksgiving without us, did you?"

Miss Maggie hears the noise and comes out of the dining room into the hall. "Amanda, you better let me hold those pies so you can give your mother and father a proper hug."

Amanda stands on tip-toe to kiss her father on the cheek and turns to her mother. "Mother, you are looking too beautiful for words." She reaches her arms around her mother and squeezes. A whoosh of air is heard from Rebecca Oglesby as Amanda squeezes as tight as she can.

"I really can't believe you're here. You'll see my schoolroom and meet Elizabeth, and I'll take you to church and, of course, you'll get to know Miss Sophie and Miss Maggie."

Laughingly, Miss Sophie interrupts, "Amanda, please introduce me to your parents."

"Oh, this is the Miss Sophie who is taking such good care of me. Miss Sophie, Rebecca and Milton Oglesby."

"What a delight to meet you, Miss Sophie. Miss Maggie tells us we are staying in your spare room?"

"The room will be ready and waiting for you. I'm delighted that you are here."

"Oh; and wait until you've had breakfast at Miss Sophie's—none like it."

"Something to look forward to," says Amanda's father.

"Ahem. Ahem."

Everyone turns to see who has made this sound. A rather skinny young man with hair parted down the middle and slicked down perfectly stands in the doorway left open by Amanda and Miss Sophie.

Amanda is surprised to see Miss Sophie twitching with excitement. "Oh, Henry, you're here." Henry doesn't seem to match Miss Sophie's enthusiasm. "Henry is a druggist from Thomasville. He just moved up from Mobile where he is friends with my cousin. He's without acquaintances here, so I promised him a wonderful Thanksgiving Day here in Marshall."

Miss Maggie invites everyone to come in the front parlor and, as Miss Sophie passes Amanda, she nods at Henry and winks. Amanda is astounded. Miss Sophie will go to any lengths to find her a husband.

At that moment, Elizabeth and Sister Sarah walk into the parlor, each carrying a dish. "We're so sorry we're late," says Elizabeth. "Sister Sarah had a visitation and couldn't leave for a while."

Mr. Oglesby looks at Amanda with eyebrows squeezing together in a quizzical look. "Father, Sister Sarah is a psychic. She has visitations from people who have moved on from this life." Mrs. Oglesby's mouth forms a perfect "O," but no sound comes out.

"How perfectly charming. So delighted to meet you, Sister Sarah," says Mr. Oglesby.

At that point, Miss Maggie indicates that Thanksgiving dinner is ready, and everyone follows her into the dining room. What a sight! A multi-armed chandelier drops from the ceiling over a dining table that could easily seat twenty people. White tapers rise from silver candlesticks that march the length of the table and the food. My goodness! Turkey, ham, vegetables of every description, cornbread dressing, gravy. The walnut side-board, topped with a mirror supported by an eight-inch wide gold and filigree frame, is loaded with desserts: sweet potato pie, caramel cake, coconut cake plus Miss Sophie's two pecan pies—enough sweets to feed Marshall.

Miss Sophie suggests that Amanda sit by Henry, and she can hardly refuse. She wants to sit with her parents, but they are seating on each side of Miss Maggie at the head of the table. At least Elizabeth is seated on Amanda's left.

"Mr. Oglesby, would you ask the blessing?" says Miss Maggie.

"I'd be delighted. Please bow your heads. Lord, we are truly thankful for the wonderful blessings you have bestowed upon us. Bless this home, hearth, and all within. Amen."

"Amen," says Amanda. As the food passes, she turns her attention to Henry, remembering to be polite.

"What brings you to Thomasville, Mr. Henry?"

He preens as though it is his natural right to monopolize the conversation. "My grandfather settled in Mobile. He liked the Bay. He was a druggist, and he met my grandmother Louise there. They got married and had five children; my father was the youngest. I always thought being the youngest would be the best. Don't you?" Without pausing for Amanda to answer, he continued, "Of course, I'm the oldest. I don't mind that either—"

By the time Henry has finished talking about parents and grandparents, they have finished the soup and are well into the middle of the main course. Amanda glances to Elizabeth for help. She shrugs her shoulders and looks the other way.

"I attended the University of Alabama. You know it's in Tuscaloosa. They have one of the best pharmacy programs in the South. You know, I'm quite upset. I attended a lecture at the university last week that has me very upset. The lecturer opened with a quote from Moliere: *Nearly all men die of their medicines, not of their diseases.* What hogwash! Where would we druggists be if everyone believed that! The lecturer went on and on about humans curing their ills with nutrition, exercise, and human relationships—even had the nerve to state that mercury in our medicine is poisoning us. And would you believe that...

Just as Amanda is about to drive a fork into Henry's tongue to stop this torture, Miss Maggie announces that dessert will be served later in the afternoon and dismisses the guests. Amanda turns to Elizabeth. "Thanks so very much, Elizabeth." Elizabeth is stuffing her napkin against her mouth to keep from laughing out loud.

# Thirty-first Chapter

## The Day After

"You are correct, Amanda. This has to be one of the best breakfasts served in the South," says Amanda's father.

"You are too kind, Milton," says Miss Sophie.

"Not at all. You'll have to share that tomato gravy recipe with Rebecca."

"I'll be delighted to share it."

"Now, Amanda, are you ready to give us that tour?"

"Oh, yes. We'll start with the mercantile store. You can meet Mr. Pitts."

They walk down Main Street to Pitts General Merchandise, impressive in the morning sun with over-tall doors set with beveled glass and its outdoor entryway of tiny octagonal tile with a large black "P" for Pitts centered in the middle of the floor. Mr. Oglesby holds the heavy mercantile store door open to allow Amanda and her mother to enter. Mr. Pitts walks up from the back of the store.

"Amanda, are these your parents? I heard they were in town."

"Mr. Pitts, meet Rebecca and Milton Oglesby of Demopolis."

"So pleased to meet you both. Welcome to Marshall, and I have to tell you your daughter is doing an amazing job in that schoolhouse. She's making a difference here in our community as well."

"It's good to meet you as well, Mr. Pitts. Amanda has told us about the excellent school system that you and the trustees have formed in Marshall," says Mrs. Oglesby.

As her parents are telling Mr. Pitts they will return home Saturday, Amanda notices Sadie in the back of the store and walks over to her. What Amanda couldn't see until she was almost upon her is that Sadie has two children in tow. Amanda takes stock of Sadie's dejected look and the dark red bruise on her left arm.

"Sadie?"

"Miss Amanda."

"What's going on, Sadie?"

"Harley is back, Miss Amanda."

"And the children?

"They belong to Pauline."

"And Pauline is—?"

"The woman Harley brought home with him."

"What do you mean, the woman he brought home?"

"He came home Thanksgiving morning with Pauline and her three children. Says they are living with us from now on. Says I'm to take care of the children, and Pauline will work in the fields with him."

"Oh, Sadie." That's all Amanda can say to this tall, striking woman that she so admires.

"I know, Miss Amanda. You don't have to say a word."

There's a long pause while Amanda tries to take in the picture of Sadie and the two children standing beside her. Tears begin to roll down Sadie's face as Amanda observes her. Finally, Sadie can talk. "Miss Amanda, this is Willis and Eliza. They are old enough to be in school. I'll be bringing them on Monday."

"That's fine, Sadie. And we'll continue your learning as usual. We'll just have two additional students."

Sadie wipes the tears away and struggles to be able to talk. "Miss Amanda, I can't stay in school anymore. The youngest child, Mildred, is just a baby. I have to stay home with her."

The finality of the horrible situation hits Amanda. She wants to join Sadie in crying—crying for this tragic situation. Sadie, a bright light, will not be allowed to shine. She'll be abused and denigrated into taking care of the children of her husband's live-in mistress. The pain that hits Amanda is raw—raw because of the injustice of Sadie's situation.

Amanda can't leave it at that. "Sadie, remember Pandora? Hope Sadie. We'll work something out."

Amanda and her parents say goodbye to Mr. Pitts, and, as they walk down Main Street toward the school, Amanda tries to explain Sadie to her parents.

"That's a haunting story, Amanda. Bless you for helping her with her education. Maybe we can help with the rest. If she gets to the point that she has to leave, send her to Demopolis. We'll take care of her."

"I'm so blessed to have parents like you. I could have been Sadie."

"But you're not. Let's finish this tour at your school, and we'll go back to Miss Sophie's to pack. You can see us off at the station."

"Of course, I will, but let's squeeze everything we can out of the time we have left. And Happy Thanksgiving! Thank you for making my first one in Marshall so special."

## Early December 1892

# Thirty-second Chapter

## Amanda's Dance Card is Full

Dressed to the nines in their ball gowns, Miss Sophie and Amanda step up into the carriage that will take them to the Christmas Ball. Mable Todd always has the Christmas Ball at her home on the first weekend in December. Being invited is quite a coup.

As they settle back against the carriage cushions for the short drive to the Todd mansion, Miss Sophie says, "Oh, child, I love dances! Attending this one always brings back memories of Jack."

"Jack, Miss Sophie?"

"Yes, Jack Lawrence. We were engaged for two years, and we were inseparable—attended dances, soirees, plays. Such wonderful memories."

"That's so romantic, Miss Sophie. How did you meet him?"

"He was courting Maggie, and I met him at this very ball."

"You took Miss Maggie's beau?"

"Incestuous, isn't it? Child, I knew Maggie didn't love Jack. I did."

"And you married?"

"Yes, we married on New Year's Day in 1861. I was eighteen years old. We were only married for three months when the Civil War started. Of course, Jack had to leave."

"What happened, Miss Sophie?"

"Three years into the Civil War Jack was killed at Fort Gaines, and I died with him."

"You died?"

"I thought my life was over. I didn't know how I could live without Jack. My grieving went on for months, and one day in early spring, I noticed the daffodils that pushed up out of the earth with their bright yellow flowers—a new beginning. They seemed so brave and bold, waving in the wind. I had to compare myself to those daffodils. I needed a new beginning, too. The house that we live in now was my Aunt Mamie's; she willed it to me. There was my new beginning."

"You don't seem a sad person to me, Miss Sophie, but that's a very sad tale."

"It is, but you have to move on—a day at a time. I learned that, Amanda. I expect you'll learn that lesson at some point in your life. Life can be damned hard!

"Miss Sophie!"

"Well, it's true child. But tonight, we're going to enjoy ourselves."

Amanda and Miss Sophie alight from the carriage to see the Todd House ablaze with light. They hear strands of "Jeanie with the Light Brown Hair" from the open doors as they walk up the front steps, lined with luminaria. The white bags with flickering candles set the scene for the beautifully decorated mansion.

Seeing Mable Todd and ensemble in the receiving line, Miss Sophie whispers, "I don't like the woman, but let's pay our respects to the hostess. Maybe we won't see her again this evening."

Amanda follows Miss Sophie through the receiving line, expressing her gratitude for being invited to the ball. As they leave the line, they receive a dance card—a small, red, leather book with the outline of a Christmas tree embossed on the front.

Amanda slips the loop of string attached to the dance card over her wrist and turns to watch the quadrille. What a beautiful dance–-danced by four couples. The couples were performing the ladies' chain; opposite women swept past each other to give their left hand to the opposite man, who positioned the lady in place by himself.

Sensing his presence, Amanda looks up into the brown eyes of David Henry Callander. He bows. "May I have the honor of a dance this evening, Miss Oglesby?"

"Of course, Mr. Callander. How delightful to see you again." She removes the dance card from her wrist and passes it to David Henry. Amanda watches as David Henry removes a small pencil from his waistcoat and opens the dance card. He peruses the card and signs in three places before passing the card back to Amanda. Just as Amanda prepares to slide the string on her wrist, she hears a voice from behind her. "Miss Oglesby, may I have the honor of a dance as well?"

Turning to honor the request, Amanda sees David Henry move away out of the corner of her eye. Standing before her, pencil in hand is the immensely boring Mr. Henry from Thanksgiving Day. To refuse him a dance would be an insult to the host and hostess, so Amanda replies, "Of course. How delightful to see you again."

She waits until he returns her card and makes her escape to the powder room. She's dying to see when she'll dance with David Henry. There are four waltzes listed. David Henry has signed his name beside three of them, including the last waltz of the evening. To have signed more than three times would be against society's rules—a vulgarism.

Amanda returns to the ballroom where her dance card rapidly fills up. She moves onto the floor to dance the quadrille with Mr. Pitts, then the first waltz of the evening with Mr. Henry—a stiff, halting affair—and finally a waltz with David Henry.

They dance without a word—one, two, three; one, two, three––gliding around the room. Amanda is keenly aware of David Henry's arm around her waist and the predictable beat of the music. When she looks up, he smiles.

"You are ravishing, Miss Amanda Oglesby."

The music ends too soon.

"Thank you for the honor." David Henry bows and escorts Amanda to where Miss Sophie is sitting with a group of people.

"It's eleven o'clock—time for a small supper, Amanda. Come join us," says Miss Sophie.

Miss Sophie nods to a servant as Amanda sits down. The servant lays a small cloth on the table. Other servants place small desserts, breads, jellies, cheeses, cold meats, and fruits on the table.

"Amanda, you know Clifford and Myrtle King. May I introduce you to Mr. William Little from Livingston?"

"It is an honor to meet you," replies Amanda.

"Mr. Little, please tell Miss Oglesby about 'the thin red line.' I know Amanda would be interested."

"Thank you, Mrs. Lawrence."

He turns to Amanda to repeat the story he has told Miss Sophie and the Kings. "I enrolled in the University of Alabama this fall and am organizing a football team. Our team has a coach, E. B.

Beaumont, and we call ourselves 'the thin red line.' I'm very excited to say that we may play Auburn in February."

"Who are you playing against this year?"

"We have played Birmingham High School. We beat them fifty-six to zero. We'll play four games total this year, meeting with the Birmingham Athletic Club twice."

"I wish you the best of luck, Mr. Little. We will all pull for 'the thin red line.' I'll see to that," says Mr. King.

"Oh listen, it's the last dance of the evening!"

Amanda's heart beats faster as she sees David Henry approaching the table.

"Delighted to see you, Mr. Callander," says Miss Sophie.

"And you as well," replies David Henry. "May I have the honor of dancing the last dance with Miss Oglesby? I'm on her card."

"Certainly, Mr. Callander." David Henry bows and Amanda rises from her chair and takes his hand. The orchestra begins to play "After the Ball."

As they move to the dance floor, David Henry says, "Do you know what this song is about?"

"No," replies Amanda. "I don't."

"It's about a man who saw his sweetheart kissing another man at a ball. He refused to listen to an explanation. Years later, after the lady in question passed away, the man found out that the man was his sweetheart's brother."

"Well, how utterly senseless," declares Amanda.

"I have to agree." It is not Amanda's imagination. David Henry's arm is tighter around her waist, pulling her closer to him as they twirl around the room.

"I haven't taken any young ladies to Callander to meet my parents. I'd like to take you, Amanda."

Amanda blushes. For once, she has no response. The dance ends. David Henry bows.

"Thank you for the honor." As he turns to walk away, Amanda blurts out, "I'd love to meet your parents."

His smile lights his brown eyes. "Then we'll make sure it happens." He turns and walks away, leaving a happy but agitated Amanda—agitated at her boldness. She is happy with all that meeting the parents implies. What a wonderful evening!

# Thirty-third Chapter

## Amanda Hires Sadie

Amanda is surprised to see Sadie sitting on the school steps waiting for her when she arrives this morning. Sadie slowly stands, picks up baby Mildred and settles her on her right hip.

"Miss Amanda, I've brought Willis and Eliza to school."

"So, I see." Amanda squats down, eye-level with Willis and Eliza. "I'm glad you've come to our school. Willis. Eliza." Looking up at Sadie, Amanda asks, "Do you know how old they are, Sadie?"

"No, ma'am. I know neither child can read."

Up to this point, Willis and Eliza have remained quiet. Willis says, "I'm eight, and Liza is seven, almost."

"Thank you, Willis. I'm going to let you and Eliza sit in the section closest to the front. Let me talk to Sadie a minute, and then I'll show you where you can sit. You can go in and look around if you'd like."

"Did they bring lunch, Sadie?"

"No, ma'am. I thought I'd bring it at lunchtime."

Sadie and Amanda watch as the two children walk into the schoolroom. Willis has his arm around Eliza. It's obvious he looks after her.

"Sadie, how are things at home?"

"I take care of the children, the house, and cook. I sleep in the room with the children. I don't talk to Harley or Pauline. I'm a servant, Miss Amanda. Even so, I feel so sorry for Pauline's children, because she is not very motherly."

"Sadie, I have to be honest. I've never heard of a worse situation."

"I'm telling you, Miss Amanda; I will not stay in this situation. I'm biding my time and keeping my mouth shut."

"I have to confess, Sadie. I'm trying to come up with a way you can continue your lessons."

"Thank you."

"I'll see you at lunch, Sadie. Try to get here a little before noon, and we'll talk."

***

"Children, I'd like to say a blessing before we have lunch. Please bow your heads." Amanda watches as all the children bow their heads in unison. "Thank you, Lord, for bringing Willis and Eliza to be with us. Bless this food to the nourishment of our bodies. Amen."

Amanda hears a chorus of amens followed by the scraping sound of lunch buckets sliding out from under desks and the popping sound of lunch buckets opening. The students who go home for lunch pass Sadie as she walks in the door, baby Mildred on her hip and a lunch bucket in her left hand.

"We missed you in class today, Miss Sadie." Amanda watches as the child's comment visibly touches Sadie.

"Come in, Sadie. We had a good morning this morning. Willis and Eliza are working on the letters of the alphabet. You can reinforce their learning at home—point out things that start with an A. "

"I will," says Sadie as she unpacks lunch for Willis and Eliza. She pulls out biscuits, pieces of hard cheese, and two apples.

"Let's sit on the steps while the children are eating." As they settle onto the top step, Sadie puts Mildred in her lap. Amanda asks, "Sadie, would Harley mind your earning some money?"

"I'm sure he probably wouldn't. Why?

"I have an idea. We're gonna be real sneaky, Sadie."

"What? How are we gonna be real sneaky?"

"I'm offering you a job, Sadie. I'm hiring you to clean the schoolhouse at night. Only you're not going to clean. We're going to work on your lessons. Philosophy, mathematics, science, literature."

"Oh my, Miss Amanda, are you sure?"

"Dead sure, Sadie."

"How are you going to pay me? Who's gonna clean the schoolhouse?

"I'm going to clean the schoolhouse, and you don't worry about how I'll pay you. That's my department. I'll take care of it."

"You would do this for me, Miss Amanda?"

"I don't like to see ability wasted, Amanda. You have an aptitude for learning, and I want to see you have the opportunity to do so."

"Don't ever think I don't appreciate you, Miss Amanda. I've never known anyone like you. I'll study real hard. I'll make you proud."

"I know you will, Sadie. I know you will."

# Thirty-fourth Chapter

## Aucoin's Demise

Miss Sophie and Miss Maggie, each carrying baskets full of vegetables, have been checking on the community garden and are nearing the end of Main Street.

"The garden is looking good, except for Sadie's rows. Wonder what's going on there?" says Miss Maggie.

"I noticed the same thing. I'll ask Amanda tonight. Maybe she'll know about Sadie. It's not like Sadie to ignore her garden."

"Good. Ask Amanda," says Miss Maggie.

"Do you want to come over for lunch? I have leftover chicken soup and lemon icebox pie."

"Love to. Give me enough time to put away these vegetables, and I'll be over."

Miss Sophie opens the front door, which is never locked and walks back to the kitchen to put away the vegetables. As she sets the tomatoes out on the kitchen counter to ripen, she hears a sound from upstairs—just a slight noise, but a noise, for sure. Miss Sophie opens the ice box and takes out soup and pie. Another noise. Definitely coming from upstairs. She sets the soup and pie on the counter and tiptoes up the stairs. Walking across the upstairs hall, she hears another sound. Someone is moving around in her bedroom.

Peering through the half-open door, Sophie sees Zackery Aucoin rifling through her jewelry. Almost in the same motion, he lifts Miss Sophie's garnet necklace in the air and turns to look at her.

"Well, well. I've been waiting for you, Miss Sophie."

"What are you doing in my house, in my bedroom?"

"I just told you—waiting for you. I want to see you naked. Now be a good girl. Shuck off those clothes and put this necklace on."

Sophie sputters. Nothing comes out. She's horrified from her head to her toes.

Placing the necklace in his trousers and moving towards Sophie, Aucoin says, "I don't have a lot of time, girl. Get out of those clothes, or I'll take 'em off you."

Sophie can't be sure, but she thinks she hears the front door open. Maggie! Yelling as loudly as she can, Sophie tells him, "Get out of my house, Aucoin."

"Now lady, you don't understand. I told you you're taking Ruby's place." Leering, he makes a circle with the forefinger and thumb on his grimy left hand and, using the forefinger on the right hand, makes a pumping motion—his forefinger moving in and out of the circle.

Before Sophie can utter another word, he's on her. The rancid smell of his unwashed body and sour breath wash over her as he tries to rip her dress off her body.

During the struggle, Maggie comes through loud and clear, "Get off her, you sorry son of a bitch."

Maggie is standing in the doorway, feet apart and gun in hand—aiming at Aucoin's forehead. The scene is frozen. No one moves for a split second. Then with a growl, Aucoin whips a knife out of his boot and rushes toward Maggie. Maggie shoots, hitting him in the dead center of the forehead. Aucoin's body falls back slightly and drops straight down to the floor.

Nothing. Sophie feels nothing: not shock, not fear, not regret for Aucoin as she looks at his dead body. Nothing.

"Sophie. Snap out of it! We've got to think. What to do?"

No response from Sophie.

"Sophie, answer me. Do you want the whole town to know that nasty Aucoin was going to rape you? Worse still, do you want the whole town to know I shot the son of a bitch?"

Sophie doesn't answer. Maggie walks around Aucoin's dead body to Sophie and takes her in her arms. "Sophie. Sophie, girl. It's all right. He's not going to hurt you," Maggie repeats, "He's not going to hurt you." She rubs Sophie's back in a circular motion.

Finally, Sophie starts to cry. Sobbing is more like it — noisy, nose-sniffing sobs. Maggie continues to hold her and rub her back. Finally, Sophie pulls back from Maggie.

"Thank you, Maggie." That's all she says. It's all she needs to say.

"Now, Sophie, we've got to think. What are we going to do with his body?"

Finally, Sophie answers, "You're right about not wanting people to know about this. We've got to move the body for sure. How are we gonna do that, Maggie?"

"An even better question: where are we going to take him when we do move him?"

Maggie paces the floor. Back and forth. Back and forth. Sadie watches. Finally, Maggie blurts out, "I've got it. It's too perfect."

"What Maggie?"

"We're going to move the son of a bitch to the roundabout, right to the base of the Mildren Pickens statue."

"I don't understand, Maggie. Why is that such a good idea?"

"My goodness, Sophie. Don't you remember who Mildren Pickens is?

"Not really. I've passed by that statue for years but haven't paid much attention to it."

"Mildren Pickens is from Marshall. Our most famous resident ever, according to the Marshall Historical Society. They're the ones who are responsible for the statue."

"Really?"

"Yes. Mildren marched on the University of Alabama all by herself—right up to the dean's office. She wanted women admitted to the university, wanted women to vote, wanted women to run for president of this land. Can you imagine any of that? And for sure, she would have hated Zachery Aucoin."

"I vaguely remember something about that. Oh, my goodness. You're right. Miss Pickens would have despised Aucoin. I love the idea, but how are we going to get him there? We have to get him moved, and this mess cleaned up before Sister Sarah comes home. Thank goodness she went to Selma today."

"We'll figure it out. Let's get Aucoin downstairs. It will be easier to move him during the night and easier if he's downstairs," Maggie says. "I'll take the head; you take the feet."

"All right," says Sophie, struggling to pick up his feet by each ankle.

Maggie bends down and grabs the body under the arms. Aucoin's arms flop down to the floor, and his head lolls back against Maggie's stomach. "Ewwww."

They get the body to the bedroom door when Sophie notices that they are leaving a trail of blood. "Stop, Maggie. Put the body down."

"What?"

"Look behind you," says Sophie.

Maggie sees the trail of blood left behind by the body. "Well, what should we do, Sophie?" No answer. Sophie's thinking.

"Maggie, I don't know. I know that Sister Sarah will be back by early afternoon."

"We have to figure something out." Maggie slowly looks around the room and spots Sophie's chemise on the chaise longue. "Hand me that chemise, Sophie."

Sophie puts her hands behind her back. "I will not."

"This is no time for you to be squeamish. Hand me that chemise. I'll tie it around Aucoin's head."

Sophie stands there—not moving.

Maggie drops Aucoin on the floor. "I'll get it myself. Honestly, Sophie." She whips up the chemise from the chaise longue and walks back to the body. Bending down, she lifts the head off the floor and wraps the chemise around Aucoin's head.

"Now, Sophie, can you at least hand me the belt to your robe. On the peg behind the door, in case you've forgotten." Sophie does as Maggie asks and helps her wrap the belt around Aucoin's head and tie it. Making sure to move the head to a clean part of the floor, they survey their work.

"That should work, Sophie. We'll only have to clean your room—not the staircase and the rest of the house." Picking the body up, they move to the top of the stairs. The landing is ten steps down. It's very hard for Sophie especially, since she's moving backward—dragging the body down the steps.

Bump. Bump. Bump.

"This is not working, Sophie. I'll come down and pull with you."

Bump. Bump. Bump. Aucoin's wrapped head pounds each step going down the stairs.

"Pull, Maggie. Only five more steps to go."

Bump. Bump.

Bump. Bump. Bump.

Sophie doubles over to catch her breath after they drag Aucoin to the landing. Maggie is looking down the stairs—fifteen more steps to go. Maggie looks at Sophie.

"The heck with this, Sophie." She bends down and shoves the body. Sophie watches in horror as the body bounces down the stairs, crashing into the wall as it tumbles to the bottom of the stairs.

Maggie runs down the stairs after the body. "Don't just stand there with your thumb in your mouth, Sophie. Help me move this body under the stairwell."

Sophie moves down the remaining steps and walks to Aucoin's feet. Bending down, she picks up the dead man's ankles.

"Oh, wait a minute, Sophie. I've got to open the door." Maggie walks over to the door that closes off the space under the stairs. Turning the wooden handle, she opens the door.

"You can drop him for a minute, Sophie. I didn't know there was so much junk under here."

Moving aside a dressmaker's dummy and a stuffed vulture, both covered with years of dust, Maggie makes room for Aucoin.

"All right, Sophie. Here we go."

With Sophie holding the ankles and Maggie grabbing him under the arms, they lay the body out flat just inside the door.

"Phew," says Sophie. "Good for us. Let's go drink some sherry. We've earned it."

"Sophie, we don't have time to drink. We've got to clean up before Sister Sarah gets home."

"Maggie, you're a tyrant."

"All right, Sophie. Just sit in the parlor and drink. I'll let you explain the blood all over your bedroom. And we haven't even checked the stairs for blood."

"I'm sorry. You're right, Maggie."

Walking up the stairs, both spot the large, bloody stain on the staircase wall. Just one, thank goodness. The landing upstairs is clear, but the bedroom is another story: blood puddled on the hardwood floor and a trail of blood leading from the spot Aucoin dropped to the point Maggie bandaged his head.

"I'll get rags from the linen closet and start on the floor, Maggie. You get the staircase. When you finish that, you might want to clean up yourself." For the first time, Maggie looks at herself. Blood and matter blew back on her body; she doesn't want to think about the matter.

"It's on your face, too. A better idea; go clean yourself up first. Grab one of my house dresses from the peg behind the door. No one can see you like that."

With Maggie cleaned up and the wall and floor cleaned, they look around the bedroom. "We forgot something, Sophie."

"What now?"

"The bullet."

Placing herself in the original firing position, Maggie tries to line up where the bullet might have gone. "Look at the headboard, Sophie. I think it hit your bed."

Sure enough. A round hole is in Miss Sophie's grandmother's bed—a prized possession and family treasure. Sophie wriggles her little finger into the hole and feels the bullet. "It's staying there, Maggie. Years from now, when someone has occasion to inspect this bed, long after I'm gone, they'll make up exciting stories about the bullet in the headboard. In the meantime, cover that hole with pillows."

"I agree with you, Sophie. You know what, I think it's time for that drink."

Walking into the kitchen, Sophie gets two glasses from the cabinet and retrieves the bottle of sherry. She fills the glasses and passes one to Maggie. Just as they take the first sip, they hear Sister Sarah.

"Hello. Miss Sophie, you here?"

Sarah walks into the kitchen and halts. After a moment of looking around, she pauses then says in a serious tone, "Sophie, I'm afraid there's a very disturbing aura in your home today."

***

At three o'clock in the morning, Maggie tiptoes into Sophie's house and waits for her by the staircase. Sophie surprises Maggie by coming in the back door, tiptoeing as well. "I've solved the problem, Maggie. I've got the cart out of the storage shed. We're gonna dump Aucoin in it and pull it behind the Baptist Church to the roundabout.

"Well, aren't you the genius, Sophie?"

Maggie slowly unlocks and pulls open the door to the space under the stairs. After inspecting the body, she exclaims, "Oh my gosh, he's stiff as a board."

Sophie answers, "Stiff or not, we're moving this body tonight. Drag him out, Maggie."

"Well, dang. Let's move this body to the cart right away."

Uh oh. A light. Someone has lit a candle. Maggie and Sophie freeze until the light goes out. "Just someone using the chamber pot" They wait a few more minutes before assuming the positions they were in when they moved the body before. Without further problems, they move the stiff Aucoin across the back porch, down the two steps, and onto the flatbed cart.

"So far, so good," says Sophie. The rectangular wooden cart has two back wheels and no wheels in the front. Two shafts protrude from the front of the cart. Normally, a horse stands between the shafts and pulls the cart. In this case, Sophie and Maggie are the horse.

Sophie walks back between the two shafts and grabs hold. Maggie moves into the space in front of Sophie. Together they pull the cart over the grassy area that extends behind the church to the roundabout. They nearly faint when an owl hoots. Besides the owl, they hear no noises other than the crunching of the wagon wheels over uneven ground.

Thankfully, they reach the roundabout undetected. Looking up into the disdainful eyes of Mildren Pickens, they both shudder.

Maggie says, “We’ve brought you a human sacrifice, Mildren. He was a real woman hater.” They drag Aucoin and lay him at the base of Mildren’s statue.

Sophie hesitates before asking, “Maggie, should we say a prayer for Aucoin’s soul?”

Maggie paces back and forth before finally answering, “Yes, probably so.”

Maggie says, “Let’s bow our heads.” Sophie and Maggie slowly tilt their eyes to the ground.

“Lord, you know the sins of this man. We commit him unto your judgment. Amen.”

“And Lord, forgive us our sin,” says Sophie.

They turn and push the cart toward home.

# Thirty-fifth Chapter

## A Christmas Production

"Miss Amanda, Miss Amanda! Did you hear about the dead body?"

"The sheriff found a dead body at the foot of Miss Pickens's statue!"

"It's Mr. Aucoin, Miss Amanda. Dead as a doornail."

"Whoa! Wait a minute, children. One at a time. Ann, tell me what you know," says Amanda.

"Mr. Aucoin was found dead at the stature of Miss Pickens, just like they said. Everyone's talking about it. Somebody shot him in the head."

"Does anyone know when he was found?" asks Amanda.

"My daddy said the sheriff found him this morning during his morning walk of the town. The sheriff told my daddy that he was shocked speechless. Not often you find a dead body on Main Street. Or anywhere else in Marshall."

"Well, children, I'll see what I can find out after school today. But now, right this minute, we are going to focus on our Christmas play. We will be performing our play for the entire town of Marshall, and you know what that means."

"We have to perform like stars," says Ann.

"Hmmm, well we do have to give an excellent performance," says Amanda. "This year's performance is going to be very different from the plays I was in as a child when we enacted the holy birth of Jesus in the manger with Joseph and Mary and even the animals."

"How will this year be different?" asks Eliza.

"We're going to decorate a Christmas tree. Randy's father has agreed to cut down the perfect cedar tree for our library room. Mr. Pitts is donating wooden blocks from the mercantile store, and you, my dears, are going to decorate the blocks."

"But how is that a play, Miss Amanda?" asks Burt.

"And how do we decorate the blocks?" asks Randy.

"Superb questions, class. Let's start with the first question. It's a play because you will be performing before our audience. Each of you will research a person in the Christmas story, decorate a block to represent that person, and, just before you hang your ornament on the tree, you will tell the audience about your person."

"How do we know who our person is?"

"I have the names of the Christmas story participants on individual pieces of paper. You will draw a name when I pass the bowl. Like drawing names for Christmas gifts, except you'll be drawing a name to research."

Randy raises his hand.

"I haven't forgotten your question, Randy. We'll have a school day to decorate the blocks, and I'm going to provide all sorts of things for you to decorate with—pieces of fur, lace, and fabric, paints, sequins, buttons, rickrack, and ribbons. The name of the person you research must appear on the block, and, if you can find a picture without defacing a library book or any other book, that would be nice. Any more questions, children?"

"I get it," says Burt. "Our Christmas tree will tell the story of Christmas when it's decorated."

"You're right, Burt. Very Good." Amanda turns to her desk and picks up a wooden bowl. "This bowl is for the Abecedarians. Please draw a name as the bowl passes. Many of you will have the same name. Do your research, and we'll determine your speech for the play." The names in this bowl are Mary, Joseph, and Jesus—the most familiar names in the story of the birth of the Christ Child.

"I have the baby Jesus."

"I have Joseph."

"I have Joseph, too."

Removing the second bowl from her desk, Amanda passes the bowl to the middle group. Herod, the Angel of the Lord, Elizabeth, the Shepherds, and the Wise Men are in this bowl.

In the third bowl—Caesar Augustus, Anna, and Simeon.

"Students, I'm going to take the time to write down the name of the person you are researching," says Amanda as she begins walking through the rows of students. Amanda envisions a tree filled with decorative blocks and smiles. The Christmas Story revealed through a Christmas tree. How appropriate!

# Thirty-sixth Chapter

## Early December 1892

## "Aucoin Goes Home"

Amanda is passing by the jail on her way home when she sees a weary-looking mule pulling a wooden wagon. An elderly man and woman are riding high on the wagon's spring seat. What a sad looking couple with pained expressions etched on their faces. "Whoa, mule," says the man, as he pulls back on the reins to stop the wagon in front of the jail.

Sheriff Winfield must have been waiting for the couple as he steps out of the jail, closing the door behind him. "Mr. and Mrs. Aucoin?" asks the sheriff. "I'm Sheriff Winfield."

The man answers, "Yes, sir. We're Zackery's parents. I'm Bill, and this is Thelma. We don't understand. You say someone murdered our boy?"

"I'm sorry to say that's true. I wish I could tell you I've solved the murder, but I can't do that. I was the one that found Zackery, at the end of Main Street. He was shot, and, as best we can tell, had been dead for over twenty hours when I found him.

Mrs. Aucoin speaks for the first time. "Zackery was always in trouble. Seems like from the day he was born he was trouble. We could never make him understand about right and wrong."

Mr. Aucoin says, "He started off hurting the neighbor's cats—drowned one of them when he was six years old. He progressed to breaking into stores and stealing. We finally had to put him in the Mobile Boys' Industrial School. Couldn't keep him at home anymore."

The sheriff says, "I've heard of the Mobile school. I hear it takes boys like your Zackery and turns them around."

"I'm sure it does, in a lot of cases," says Mrs. Aucoin. "We had such high hopes when we put Zackery in the industrial school. Just looking at the place gave us hope. The school was out of Mobile on acreage. Besides the dorm—a three-story brick building—they had classrooms, baseball fields, basketball courts, and all sorts of shops."

"You should see the shops," says Mr. Aucoin. "Those boys could choose between all sorts of vocational programs: printing, carpentry, blacksmithing, bakery, barbering, and sewing.

Mrs. Aucoin adds, "Zackery was in the carpentry program. He helped make beds, tables, chairs, desks—all for the school. I think he enjoyed it. You know he rebuilt the house he and Ruby lived it. Did a real fine job."

Sheriff Winfield says, "I don't have children, but I imagine raising them could be difficult. I have to tell you we had some trouble with your son here in Marshall."

"What kind of trouble?" asks Mr. Aucoin.

"His worst offense was shoving Mrs. Lee down on the sidewalk, for no reason. She accidentally bumped into him. Zackery shoved her so hard she was in the Selma hospital with a concussion."

"It saddens my heart to hear that, sheriff," says Mrs. Aucoin.

"Is there any way that I can help you? Anything I can do to make this easier for you?"

"We brought the wagon so we could take our son home to Louisiana. Do you think that will be a problem?"

"Barring any objections from Ruby, I think that would be fine."

"Did I tell you about the birdhouses, Sheriff Winfield?" asks Mrs. Aucoin.

"No, you didn't."

"Zackery built birdhouses for me. Every year on Mother's Day, he sent me a birdhouse. I wish you could see them. Some look like churches, some like houses, some very modern-looking."

"Thelma hung all those birdhouses together in the woods behind our house. It's a sight to see—all the birds feeding from the houses Zackery built," says Aucoin's father.

"That's where we'll bury our boy, Sheriff. Out there with all those birdhouses."

Sheriff Winfield directs the Aucoin family to the morgue and watches the wagon until it turns the corner of Main Street. He turns to go back into his office and sees Amanda.

"Did you hear all that, Amanda?"

"Yes, sheriff. I did. So terribly sad."

"But you know what I learned from the Aucoin's story, Amanda? I learned that there's good in all people. Even Zackery Aucoin."

# Thirty-seventh Chapter

## Amanda Goes Christmas Shopping

"There's nothing like Christmas shopping in Mobile, Amanda," says Miss Maggie.

"Thank you so much for bringing me, Miss Maggie," says Amanda.

"Shelby's department store is right around the corner. Wait until you see the windows all decorated for Christmas."

As they walk, Miss Maggie and Amanda talk about all the presents they have to buy. "I'm buying for you, Miss Sophie, Elizabeth, Sister Sarah, and Sadie—I want to buy a book for Sadie."

"Well, I can tell you, Miss Sophie likes anything lavender, and I like anything peppermint."

"That helps, Miss Maggie." They round the corner, and Amanda spots the long, smooth plate glass windows. "Oh, look! You're right about the windows. This one is a scene from *Little Women,* the wonderful book about the March children." Jo March, the second oldest of the March girls, is standing in a parlor decorated for Christmas with a shining cedar tree. Garland drapes over the mirror, and Christmas stockings march down the mantle. Mannequins of Amy, Beth, and Meg March gather around Jo. They appear to be having a discussion.

The mannequins fascinate Amanda. They make them of wax with real hair implanted onto their heads. From her position, Amanda can see an undecorated mannequin off to the side. She's surprised to see that the arms and legs are wooden, and the feet are iron.

Miss Maggie says, "Oh, I hope that's the scene where the girls decide to each get Mrs. March something for Christmas, and not get anything for themselves. My favorite scene!"

"I like that scene, too. It reminds me of a lesson my mother taught me: the more you give, the more you receive. Do you think that's right, Miss Maggie?"

"Sure do. Every time I deliver a baby or take a hungry family food, it comes back to me. Someone chops my wood or leaves a fresh-baked pie on my front porch. It's all about sharing God's love, child."

"Do you think Sadie would like *Little Women?"*

"Everyone likes *Little Women.* Sure, she would."

"Good. That's one gift decision made."

"Look at this next window, Amanda. Does that bring out the child in you?"

Amanda stares at the snowy scene in which Santa is driving a red sleigh filled with gifts. But reindeer aren't pulling the sleigh; fat, gray geese with huge red velvet bows tied around their necks and silly expressions on their faces are out in front. Amanda laughs out loud. It's like looking at a single scene from a Broadway play or a canvas painted by an accomplished artist. Amanda falls in love. There's even more magic inside the store with wreaths of greenery over the doors, tiny trains chugging through the snow in the toy department, and twinkling trees scattered all around.

"There's a tea room on the second floor, right near the top of the stairs. I'll meet you there in one hour, Amanda."

"I'll be there, Miss Maggie." Amanda rushes off to the ladies' department to buy sachets of lavender for Miss Sophie and a scarf for Elizabeth. She adds a pure white candle made of paraffin for Sister Sarah and peppermint canes with curved handles for Miss Maggie.

On the way to the tea room, Amanda stops to inspect the gloves. She buys a pair for her mother. The gloves are the color of the pale part of a moss rose. Trying them on, they appear to be a little tight. The gloves will make her mother's hands look smaller. What lady doesn't desire that?

Amanda spots Miss Maggie, who is already seated in the tea room and joins her. "Amanda, if you approve, I'll order for us. And this is my treat."

Amanda reaches over and squeezes Miss Maggie's hand. "Thank you, Miss Maggie."

The waiter brings china plates to their table. The plates are filled with chicken salad, green beans, yeast rolls, and a dish that Amanda does not recognize. She tastes this dish first.

"What is this delightful concoction?"

"Ambrosia. Theirs is famous. They make it with a layer of orange slices, topped with fresh coconut and sugar. Word has it that they crack open a coconut, break it into pieces, and grate it by hand."

"We have to tell Miss Sophie about ambrosia, so she can make it this Christmas season. I'll grate the coconut for her."

Silence for a moment while Amanda and Miss Maggie enjoy the chicken salad with celery in it and the hot, spongy rolls. "You know, Miss Maggie, I can't stop thinking about those magical store windows. Thank you so much for bringing me."

"I remember my mother bringing me to Mobile to shop and remember very well the excitement of seeing the Christmas windows for the first time. Mother told me that the fashion dolls of Europe inspired the mannequins. The dolls were clothed and sent abroad, traveling from country to country to demonstrate the latest fashions. They were so popular and, interestingly, they crossed the border, even in time of war. It's rumored that Marie Antoinette advised her mother and sisters of the latest fashions at Versailles by sending them fashion dolls."

"What a wonderful story, Miss Maggie. And what a wonderful day. No matter what people say about Christmas and commercialism, I'm a fan. Have we seen one thing today that didn't put joy in our hearts? I tell you; I think Jesus would love it all, even the geese. It's about love, joy, and giving, Miss Maggie." Amanda blows a kiss across the table to Miss Maggie and says, "I love you, Miss Maggie."

"I love you, too. Merry Christmas, Amanda."

# Thirty-eighth Chapter

## Amanda Formulates a Plan

Amanda is cleaning up the schoolroom after the children have gone home for the day. She's thinking about Sadie and how the students react to her in the classroom. They like her. It hits her—maybe Sadie could teach. Why not? She's certainly bright enough.

What institution could certify Sadie to teach? Amanda does not know, but she knows the person who has the answers. Closing the schoolhouse door firmly behind her, Amanda heads to the mercantile store. She finds Mr. Pitts unboxing bolts of cloth: flannel, wool, tweed for everyday dresses, and golden silk and burgundy velvet for dress-up.

"Good afternoon, Amanda. What brings you to the store?"

"It's about Sadie, Mr. Pitts. I think she could teach, and I'd love to see her stand on her own two feet."

"It's a sad situation, for sure. We'd all like to see Sadie leave that Wiggins fellow."

"But what about her teaching, Mr. Pitts? Is it possible?"

"Well, I can tell you about the standards developed by the rest of the trustees and me."

"I'd like to see the standards, Mr. Pitts. That way I'll know if my dream for Sadie is attainable."

"Of course, I'll be glad to show you what we've developed. All that material is upstairs. The trustees and I meet up there to conduct school business, and all the school records are there. Follow me."

Mr. Pitts walks to the back of the store and starts up the staircase leading to the second floor. Amanda follows him up, stepping carefully on the narrow, carpeted stairs. She can see the faded image of cabbage roses on the threadbare carpet, and she hears the faintest squeak as she steps up toward the second floor.

"Come in, Amanda, and have a seat while I find what you need."

Amanda is surprised to find a well-appointed room lined with lawyer's bookcases and wooden file cabinets. A large round, cherry table with clawed feet is centered in the room and is surrounded by low-back, leather chairs. She glimpses a small conference room to the right of the office. Amanda slides one of the leather chairs back across the hardwood floor and sits.

"Here we go, Amanda. These are the minimum requirements a teacher in Marshall must have if they have no college education or normal school education. He, or she, must score a minimum of seventy percent on these tests: reading, geography, grammar, arithmetic, and physiology. I can't make an exception for Sadie. She'd have to pass each test with seventy percent accuracy. These exams test knowledge at the level of graduating high school students."

"Are there any other requirements, Mr. Pitts?"

"Yes, we require applicants to take and successfully pass a course on the theory and practice of teaching. One more thing—we require our teachers to sign a contract, agreeing to enroll in

Troy State Normal School with the intent of finishing at least two years of study. Teachers may take courses when our school is not in session. If the teacher shows promise, the trustees and I will pay any tuition required at Troy."

"You know, Mr. Pitts, none of this is impossible for Sadie."

"Just one concern, Amanda. We have a wonderful teacher—you. Why would we need to hire Sadie?"

"I can't answer that, Mr. Pitts. But do the other counties around us have the same requirements?"

"That depends on the individual county. Alabama has no state requirements for teachers, and each county develops its standards."

Amanda stands up and reaches across to shake Mr. Pitt's hand. "Thank you, Mr. Pitts. I think it's possible for Sadie to teach one day if she desires. I think she'd be a natural. And one more thing, Mr. Pitts. Let's keep this conversation a secret."

"Of course, Amanda. My lips are sealed." Mr. Pitt's looks back to smile at Amanda as she follows him out of the upstairs office.

# Thirty-ninth Chapter

## David Henry Extends an Invitation

Amanda walks into the kitchen to find Miss Sophie holding up and fanning what appears to be a hand-written note. "Amanda, we've been invited by David Henry Callander to attend a lecture with him. It's odd. Why do you suppose he sent the invitation to us?"

Amanda blushes and hopes Miss Sophie doesn't notice. "I can't imagine. A lecture?"

"Yes, but it's nothing glamorous, I assure you."

"Miss Sophie, are you going to tell me what this is about?"

"Mable Todd is hosting a lecturer from Bryn Mawr. I believe she's a relative of Mable's."

"And the lecture is about?"

"It appears from Mr. Callander's invitation that it's about the woman's role in society. How dreadful, but I'm sure Mable will turn it into a social event. That's probably why Mr. Callander invited us—for the social part of the evening."

***

David Henry holds out his hand to help Amanda from the carriage. Seeing her safely down, he squeezes her hand. So softly, Amanda thinks she might have imagined it. She quickly looks up.

David Henry looks back with a serious look on his face. Finally, he smiles, then winks.

Miss Sophie is progressing up Mable's front steps and is oblivious to David Henry and Amanda. Mable is standing at the front door and welcomes them. "I'm delighted that you could come tonight. I promise that Matilda's lecture will be fascinating. Come into the front parlor and have a seat. We're just about to start."

A large number of Marshall citizens fill the front parlor. Miss Sophie, David Henry and Amanda file into a row of seats, with David Henry arranging the seating so that he's by Amanda. His lips curl into a tight smile of satisfaction. Amanda sees this before she turns her attention to Mable.

"Ladies and gentlemen, it is with great delight that I introduce to you my cousin from Bryn Mawr, Matilda Shelling. Matilda has been researching the role of women in society. Now we all know how important women are in the home, but Matilda will be sharing her research with us about their importance in our community and beyond."

After applauding politely, the group appears to settle in for what they collectively think will be a boring evening. They couldn't be more wrong.

"Good evening. I thank Cousin Mable for allowing me to speak to you this evening, though I do take umbrage with her reference to women in the home."

Taking in the look of shock on Mable's face, she ignores her and continues. "This summer, I read a book that changed my life. That book was *The Yellow Wallpaper* by Charlotte Perkins Gilman. The husband in *The Yellow Wallpaper* attempts to cure his wife, who suffers from nerves, by prescribing a rest cure. This rest cure removes all intellectual stimulation from the wife's environment because intellectual stimulation is believed to damage a woman physically and psychologically.

Now, learned friends, I hope you find that as ridiculous as I do. I assure you that this book has made me take a deep look at our society. Women, are you taught that your place is in the home? Do you ever consider that you could be a bank president, doctor, or lawyer? Some of you are allowed to teach, but only if you're single. When you get married, most of you must give up your career."

That grabs Amanda's attention! She has never considered that marriage and career could not co-exist. She is seriously disturbed by this woman's comments. Sensing this, David Henry curls his fingers around her hand that has been resting by the side of her body nearest him.

Matilda continues, "And so, I encourage you to take this journey with me. Stand with me. Together, we can change the role of women in society." Matilda starts to sit down but quickly stands up as she remembers, "And just so you know, the lady in *The Yellow Wallpaper* is not healed. She goes insane."

Stunned silence. No applause. Just complete silence.

An embarrassed Mable gets up and walks to the front of the room. She clears her throat several times before speaking.

"We are serving refreshments in the parlor across the hall. Please gather there. We'll share a toast to 1892, a good year for most of us. And Christmas is coming! I'll play our favorite songs on the piano. Come, let's drink a toast and sing."

***

The carriage arrives at Miss Sophie's front door, and David Henry helps Miss Sophie and Amanda down the carriage steps. Miss Sophie says, "Well, David Henry Callander, thank you for a most enlightening evening. I'll leave you two to say goodnight while I go in and get out my mop bucket."

David Henry laughs out loud. "Now, Miss Sophie. Don't hold this evening against me. I just wanted to socialize with you—and Amanda, of course."

"Of course," Miss Sophie replies. "Good evening, David Henry."

David Henry waits until Miss Sophie closes the door before he turns to Amanda. "Amanda, I'm going to kiss you." He puts his arms around Amanda and pulls her to him. He slowly bends his head and kisses Amanda thoroughly.

Before Amanda has a chance to react, he jumps up on the carriage seat and starts to drive away. He drives up the street a few yards and stops. He turns on his seat and says, "Don't worry Amanda. You can still teach after we marry." He drives away without looking back.

Amanda stands there, watching the carriage disappear down the dusty road. Finally, she goes inside and climbs the stairs to her room. She wants to be alone. So much to think about!

Sliding on her old flannel gown, Amanda pulls back the covers on her bed and scooches under the heavy quilts. Time to replay this strange evening. First, there is something there with David Henry. He may even be the one. Amanda hopes so. She feels alive around him. She tingles. She wants him to stay. Is that love?

Second, she loves teaching and never even once has she considered not teaching. It's a noble thing to do. She loves the look in a child's eyes when they understand something new. She puts that look there. It's humbling. It's powerful. Give it up? No. Never.

Amanda visualizes her students bent over their slates. How dare this lady suggest she can't teach after marriage! Amanda curses Miss Matilda Shelling as she pulls the quilt up to her chin and tries to sleep.

# Fortieth Chapter

## Merry Christmas from Donald

Amanda's students are using tracing paper to trace pictures in *Harper's Magazine* and *Life Magazine*. Some students are happily tracing images of the Christmas season that they will hang around the room before parents come to the Christmas pageant. Some students are happily tracing; others are not.

"Miss Amanda, my paper keeps slipping."

"I can't match the lines up after it slips."

Amanda says, "You can do this. I'll help." She walks over to Lydia's desk and slides the tracing paper so that her crooked lines sort of match up.

"Now, the lines match. You trace, and I'll hold your paper still."

Amanda begins to sing, "Good King Wenceslas looked out, on the Feast of Stephen, when the snow lay round about, deep and crisp and even…" A deep peace floats through the air as Amanda sings, and the children trace pictures to be colored later.

Finally, Amanda gets up and walks through the rows of wooden desks. All the students are through tracing except for a few Abecedarians.

"We'll color these tomorrow, and you'll sign yours. Won't your parents love to see these when they come to the play?"

Removing a light-blue envelope from her pocket, Amanda says, "I have a special story to read you. It's about Donald celebrating Christmas. If you are still tracing, keep at it. Just listen while I read Donald's latest adventure."

Amanda drags a chair over in front of the chalkboard, and the students gather around, most sitting on the floor with their legs crossed. Amanda opens the worn envelope and slides the paper out. "I'm looking at the top of the letter," she says. "There are an address and a date. What are these two elements called?"

"The Heading."

"That's right. Next is 'Dear Amanda.' What is that called?"

"The Greeting."

"You are brilliant students. Now let's hear about Donald."

Amanda's mother writes:

*There's always a surprise when Donald is around. This time, it's a wonderful surprise. Donald shared his Christmas gifts with me. I'm honored because no one in the family has an inkling that Donald is giving Christmas gifts. He has picked up unshelled pecans for cousin Lily to use in her baking. They are in a brown paper bag tied with a string that looks like it's been in Donald's pocket for eons.*

*For your father, he has a beautiful red feather from a cardinal. Donald has explained to me that the treasured red feather comes from an old male like your father—his words, not mine. The female cardinal is brown, and the young cardinals are brown, too—only the older male is bright red. I have assured him that Milton will certainly treasure this gift.*

*I'm surprised to see that Donald has a tin of cloves for Jeffery Ellard. When I question him about the cloves, he informs me that they make your breath sweet. Jeffery needs sweet breath because of all the courting he does. I know. I can see you smiling.*

*Donald showed me sweetgum balls wrapped in lace that disappeared from my sewing basket, fragile snakeskins resting on cotton, and multi-colored stones that have been washed smooth in the creek behind the house. Amanda, I have to tell you; after squeezing Donald until he squirms, I tell him he's giving the best gifts ever. I wait until he puts his treasures up and leaves the room. Making sure he's not around, I put my head in my hands and cry—cry that maybe I've lost the meaning of Christmas.*

*Donald's gift to your father makes my gift of an expensive pocket watch look cheap, somehow. After all, it's about love. Donald's thoughtful gifts show that he loves and understands the people in his life. Donald, of all people, has captured the meaning of giving gifts at Christmas.*

# Late December 1892

# Forty-first Chapter

## Sheriff Winfield Has a Clue

Miss Sophie and Miss Maggie are trying on hats at the mercantile store and having quite the fun time doing it. Miss Sophie turns to Maggie. "Now be honest, Maggie. How do I look in this hat?" Sophie is wearing a large-brimmed hat made of black crushed satin; tips of feathers from an unfortunate ostrich adorn it. "Well, Maggie?"

"It will do, but why don't you try this one?"

Maggie hands Sophie a hat made of white felt trimmed with loops of velvet ribbons in a creamy color. Sophie removes the crushed satin hat and, looking in the mirror, adjusts the white hat on her head. Turning around with a smug look on her face—she already knows this one is flattering—Sophie opens her mouth to ask Maggie's opinion.

"Say hello to Sheriff Winfield, Sophie," says Maggie. The sheriff has walked up to the two ladies while Sophie was adjusting the white hat on her head.

Sophie quickly loses the smug look on her face. "Hello, Sheriff Winfield. What brings you into the mercantile store today?"

"Hello, ladies. I'm on the job—investing the murder of Zachery Aucoin."

"You don't say," says Maggie

"Do you have any information on his murder?" asks Sophie.

"Not much to go on. Mighty strange that I found the body at the Pickens statue. The coroner says Aucoin's body was moved for sure, moved after he was murdered."

Miss Sophie shudders, but Miss Maggie asks, "How does the coroner know the body was moved?"

"Something to do with Livor Mortis. I'm not sure I can explain it to you ladies."

Sophie is fanning her face with her right hand. "That's quite all right, Sheriff Winfield. I, for one, can do without that explanation."

"Do you have any other information about Aucoin's death?"

"Yes, I do." Sheriff digs around in his coat pockets for a minute before pulling out a garnet necklace—Miss Sophie's garnet necklace.

"This was found in the left pocket of Aucoin's pants." The sheriff holds the necklace up so that the huge garnet stone swings just the slightest bit.

"I find this stone to be the strangest fact about this case. You wouldn't think Zackery Aucoin would have jewelry like this in his possession. For the life of me, I can't figure this out. I plan to show the necklace around town and hope that someone will know who it belongs to. That would go a long way to help solve this case."

Resting the dangling garnet in the palm of his left hand, Sheriff Winfield allows Maggie then Sophie to get a closer look at the stone. "I don't suppose this necklace looks familiar to either of you ladies?"

Sophie gulps. "No, Sheriff, I've never seen this necklace."

Maggie speaks up with more confidence than Sophie, "It's a garnet, is it Sheriff? It's a very handsome necklace. It must belong to a lady of quality."

"You could be right. But again, why did Zackery have it? That's the question. Well, if you ladies will excuse me, I'll cover the rest of the stores. Maybe someone will know something about the necklace."

As the sheriff turns to walk away, Maggie turns to Sophie and mouths, "Not likely."

Sophie's chin is trembling and tears well up in her eyes.

"Sophie, don't you dare cry. People may be watching." Reaching around Sophie, Maggie picks up a hat to hand to Sophie.

"Here, put this Settin' Hen on your head. You'll feel better."

Sophie takes the hat from Maggie and perches it on the front of her head. Just looking at the frothy pink concoction on her head makes Sophie smile.

"See. I told you. Buy that Settin' Hen, and let's go home for tea."

Sophie says, "Let's go to my house for tea. And I think I'll have it with Evan Williams."

"Evan Williams?"

"Evan Williams Kentucky Bourbon whiskey."

# Forty-second Chapter

## A Play and a Gift

The night of the Christmas play has finally arrived. Sadie is riding herd over the schoolchildren gathered in front of the classroom with their blocks cupped in their hands. Amanda is standing at the front door of the schoolhouse, greeting each parent as they come in the door.

"Ann is so excited about the play tonight," says Mrs. Fox as she steps into the schoolhouse in a cloud of Eau de Cologne.

"I'm excited as well. Come in, and please move to the library. We'll be performing there."

Mr. Hester, Burt's father, is next. "I have to tell you, Miss Amanda, you've worked miracles with my boy. I thank you kindly for all you've done."

"It's my pleasure to work with Burt, Mr. Hester. Did you know he's gifted in mathematics? I'm very proud of Burt."

"Then I'm proud, too."

Mr. Hester seems to be the last of the parents and townspeople who have come to watch the performance. Ann secures the front door and walks toward the group of schoolchildren. "Does everyone have his block?"

"Yes, ma'am."

"I do."

"I have mine."

"Wonderful. Now we are going to perform the play just as we rehearsed this morning. Remember to introduce yourself and tell the audience the name of your biblical character before you hang your block on the tree. Then tell us about your character."

Amanda moves into the library as Sadie lines up the students, blocks in hand, in order of their appearance in the Christmas play. She stands on the small stage. To her right is the perfectly shaped cedar tree, ready to be decorated. Amanda breathes in deeply, taking in the sweet cedar fragrance she always associates with Christmas.

"Welcome to our Christmas play. The class is excited to share the Christmas story with you, and you're in for an unusual evening. We're sharing the story with you in a unique way tonight. I predict you'll love it."

Amanda moves to the bottom of the steps leading to the stage. There are only two steps, but she wants to make sure the children don't trip. Randy Peevy is first. He walks up the steps without Amanda's assistance, turns, and faces the audience. "My name is Randy Peevy." He holds up his block, decorated with pictures and ribbon. "My Christmas block represents Joseph. Joseph married Mary, mother of Jesus. Joseph was originally from Bethlehem." Randy hangs his block ornament on one of the lower branches of the cedar tree and leaves the stage.

Lydia is next. "My name is Lydia." She smiles—a smile so large that the audience is charmed and smiles back. "My block is Mary. Mary is the mother of Jesus. Mothers are very important. Mary is very important." Lydia hangs her block on the tree, walks to the steps and whispers to Amanda, "Did I do all right, Miss Amanda?" More smiles from the audience.

Eliza walks on stage in a clean, starched, pink blouse and a brown pinafore. Amanda thinks that Sadie, not Pauline, dressed Eliza for the play. Eliza holds up her block for all to see. It is covered with lace and feathers. My block is Jesus. Jesus is the child of Mary and Joseph. I have the best block of all because Jesus came to save the world. He is still doing that today. He is saving you and me." Eliza forgot to say her name, but it doesn't matter. She hangs her block on the tree to a round of applause.

The middle group hangs their blocks on the tree—blocks that represent Herod, the Angel of the Lord, Elizabeth, the Shepherds, and the Wise Men. Everything goes well until Terry Johnson hangs his block on the tree. He says Three Wise Guys instead of Three Wise Men. In unison, the audience members clamp their lips together to keep from laughing. The program moves on.

"I am Burt Hester. My block represents Caesar Augustus, who was ruling Rome when Jesus was born. He was the one who issued the decree that a census be taken. Because of his decree, Mary and Joseph traveled to Bethlehem, where Mary gave birth to Jesus in a stable. This decree fulfilled biblical prophecy." Burt carefully hangs his block on the tree. His block is covered with sequins and is painted a golden color. Very royal in appearance.

"I am William Smith." He holds his rick-rack covered block up for all to see. "This block goes on the tree for Simeon—an old man. The Holy Spirit tells Simeon he will not die until he sees the Messiah. Simeon is in the temple in Jerusalem when Joseph and Mary bring Jesus to the temple for the first time. He takes Jesus in his arms and praises God. Simeon knows that Jesus is the promised Messiah. He is now prepared to die."

"I am Anna Simpson. My biblical block represents a lady named Anna, who constantly stays at the temple. Anna is the only woman in the New Testament described as a prophetess. Anna was 84 years old when she understands that Jesus is the savior of mankind. She was the first person to understand the good news." Anna hangs her button-covered block on the tree.

Amanda takes the stage and stretches her right arm, palm up, toward the tree. The audience stands and applauds. Amanda motions for Sadie to herd the children to the front of the room where they take a collective bow.

The parents mill around, greeting neighbors and looking at the ornamental blocks on the tree. Gradually, they put on coats and leave the school building until only Amanda and Sadie are left. Amanda moves to her teacher's desk and removes a Christmas gift wrapped in shiny red paper and adorned with a matching red velvet bow.

"Sadie, thank you so much for your help tonight. You're one of my favorite people, and I have a gift for you." Amanda hands the gift to Sadie.

"But Miss Amanda, I don't have a gift for you." Sadie is obviously upset that she has nothing to offer Amanda.

"Oh, but you do, Sadie."

"I do?"

"I want you to think about teaching. You are a fast learner, the children like you, and you won't always be keeping Pauline's children. That would be my gift from you—promise me you'll think about whether you'd like to teach. Don't think it's impossible. Just think about whether you'd like it or not. Now, open your gift."

Sadie slowly opens the fold, being careful not to tear the pretty red paper.

"It's *Little Women,* and it's about strong women like you, Sadie," Amanda remembers Donald and his perfect gifts. She's chosen the perfect gift for Sadie.

"You think I'm strong, Miss Amanda?"

"Of course, I do. Now, let's close up the schoolhouse and go home."

As they are making their way down the schoolhouse steps, Sadie softly says, "Merry Christmas, Miss Amanda." She proceeds down the steps and on the road toward her home.

# Forty-third Chapter

## A Love Spoon

Amanda sits down at the breakfast table. She always looks forward to eating breakfast with Miss Sophie. As Amanda places the creamy linen napkin in her lap, she reaches for the platter of eggs and sausages. "This looks good, Miss Sophie."

"I tell you what would look good—you with a boyfriend on your arm. You've turned down Leonard Staple and Walter Brown, gentlemen any girl would be lucky to have. But I'm not giving up. I have the perfect boyfriend for you: David Henry Callander."

Amanda pauses; fork halfway to her mouth. She hasn't seen David Henry since the lecture with Mabel Todd's cousin, and she's done her best to forget that kiss.

"And I've invited him to come to tea this very afternoon. You can help. I have some Boston brown bread, and we're going to cut it thin and spread it with soft butter. I've already chopped some peanuts to mix with cream cheese. You can spread the cream cheese at the last minute. We'll have pecan halves mixed with pistachios and bonbons."

"But Miss Sophie—"

"Don't Miss Sophie me. David Henry Callander is the catch of Marshall, and he did invite you to that hideous lecture at Mable's.

Or maybe he invited me; I'm not sure. Anyway, put on your nicest dress for tea. David will be here at three o'clock."

"And if you find yourself alone with him in the parlor, don't forget to use your fan."

"Use my fan?"

"My goodness, Amanda. You are loquacious today. Yes, use your fan—to send David Henry signals."

"Signals?"

"Amanda, what do they teach you girls in Demopolis? I'll be right back." Miss Sophie leaves the room, and Amanda takes a moment to catch her breath.

Miss Sophie returns holding a folding fan, which she quickly opens with a twist of the wrist. The fan is hand painted, showing an English garden at sunrise. "Now, Amanda, you may borrow this fan if you didn't bring one of your own."

"Thank you, but how or why do I signal with it?"

"Let the fan rest on your right cheek to say yes, left cheek to say no. Place the fan near your heart to say, 'I love you.' A half-closed fan pressed to the lips means 'You may kiss me.' Slowly shutting a fully opened fan means 'I wish to marry you.' A closed fan resting on the right eye. . ."

"Miss Sophie, stop. Please stop. I'll never remember all that."

"Well, at least try to remember a few."

"I will, but don't be upset if I tell Mr. Callander I hate him because I held my fan the wrong way."

Miss Sophie reaches over and tucks a strand of hair behind Amanda's right ear. "You'll do just fine, child."

***

"Miss Sophie, you serve the most excellent tea. I'll never eat again."

"Oh, go on David Henry. Now, if you two will excuse me, I need to check on something in the kitchen." Gathering her skirts, Miss Sophie whirls out of the room, leaving David Henry and Amanda facing each other on the settee.

"I'm glad we have a moment alone, Amanda. I have a Christmas gift for you." David Henry reaches into the large pocket of the overcoat thrown over the back of the settee. "I wanted you to open it before Christmas."

Amanda takes the small gift wrapped in glittering gold paper and unties the ribbon. Removing the paper and opening a small box, Amanda finds an intricately carved wooden spoon.

"It is a love spoon. My great-great-great-great grandfather was Welsh. It was their custom to give a love spoon to the lady they wished to court." David Henry reaches over, takes Amanda's left hand, and softly kisses it.

Amanda knows at that moment—this is what she wants. She's wanted this since David Henry winked at her after the church service that day. Scrunching up her brow and trying very hard to remember what Miss Sophie taught her, Amanda places her half-closed fan on her lips.

# Forty-fourth Chapter

## Amanda Goes Home for Christmas

Amanda and Elizabeth stand back as the train bound for Demopolis huffs into the train station, belching clouds of black smoke. The cars on the train are chained together, and, when the train stops, the clanking and clattering are horrific.

Amanda shouts over the noise, "Thank you so much for coming home with me, Elizabeth." She knows that Elizabeth is still not convinced she can leave her responsibilities and celebrate Christmas in Demopolis.

Elizabeth turns back toward the station and shouts, "I promise I'll be right back, Amanda. I want to make sure Jacob understands the train schedules for the next week."

"Elizabeth, you've done that five times."

"I have to make sure, Amanda. You know, you can wait in the ladies waiting room. You don't have to be out here with all this smoke from the train and the men's cigars."

"Oh, but I do. I love the noise, the smell, and standing in the midst of all the people going somewhere."

Elizabeth shakes her head and scurries back to the depot as Amanda watches the porter place a stool at the edge of the last step off the train. Several gentlemen get off the train, tipping their hats to Amanda as they exit.

Amanda hasn't been home since September; she can hardly wait to see her parents and all the cousins and their babies. Even Donald will be a welcome sight. Nettie, the cook, will have made her homemade fried apple pies, the fruitcake she's famous for, and the red velvet cake with its nutty cream cheese frosting. Oh, they'll go to the opera house and the candlelight service at the church on Christmas Eve. Those train wheels can't turn fast enough.

Elizabeth rushes back, nearly out of breath. "I'm here, Amanda. I think Jacob has it, and I'm going to try not to worry about trains arriving late and letters being lost. It's Christmas."

"Allllllllll aboarrrrrrrrd." The conductor, standing on the train steps, is holding onto the train with his left hand, swinging a lantern in his right. Amanda and Elizabeth hurry up the steps and find their seats in the car. Amanda settles back for the trip. She squeezes Elizabeth's hand and says, "We'll be on the white bluffs of Demopolis for Christmas."

***

The Sunday before Christmas, all the Oglesbys meet for Christmas dinner—the Ellards, too. Amanda's mother was an Ellard before she married Amanda's father. The large white Greek Revival house, sitting on the white bluffs of Demopolis, is what they call a four-room-over-four-room.

Like most large houses, it has a wide hall running from front to back on the main floor. Two large rooms are on each side of the hall, and a staircase winds up to the second floor. The ceilings are fourteen feet high. You can tilt your head back and look at the fancy medallions on the ceiling with their scrolled loops and carved flowers. The floor is inlaid with oak and mahogany.

Amanda slides across that same floor to open the front door to her cousin Sidney and his family. They have four children, and Sybil is pregnant, but you will never hear the word "pregnant" murmured in polite society. Sybil is with child. The Oglesby family is a hugging family. Amanda hugs Sidney, Sybil, and all the children.

Picking up the youngest, she invites them into the parlor. She tenderly places her lips on the top of the baby's head and breathes in. Baby Samuel makes a gurgling sound. Amanda smells powder, spit-up, and that sweet baby smell. Such a precious little Oglesby in that long, long gown.

There's so much noise and confusion as the family members hug each other and find places to sit. Sybil takes Samuel out of Amanda's arms and places him on a soft blanket on the floor near the round table in the middle of the room. She reaches down and lifts the leg of the table like she's done it a million times. She scooches the end of Samuel's gown under the table leg and sets the leg down. Samuel, who is crawling, will not be going anywhere.

The doorbell rings again. Elizabeth, already a part of the family, offers to open the door. She gets a glimpse of a man in the sidelights before she swings open the wide white door. Standing on the porch is the most handsome man, not like any man she's ever seen in Marshall. She stands there and stares.

"May I come in?"

Elizabeth recovers, and says, "Certainly. The family is in the front parlor."

The man grins at Elizabeth. "And who are you?"

"I am Elizabeth Fuller, a friend of Amanda."

"Well, I'm Amanda's cousin, Jeffery. On the Ellard side. Jeffery Ellard. Offering his elbow, he says, "Why don't you escort me to the Christmas mess?"

Elizabeth frowns at his use of the word "mess."

Seeing this, Jeffery says, "Just wait. You'll see."

A ten-foot-tall cedar tree dominates the front parlor. The tree is decorated with sugar cookies tied to the tree with red ribbon, dried cranberries threaded together, strung popcorn, and small lit candles. Amanda is sitting under the tree sorting gifts when Jeffery and Elizabeth walk into the room.

Amanda jumps up from the floor as Jeffery reaches her. He picks her up and swings her around. "Cousin, aren't you beautiful."

"Why, Jeffery. A compliment coming from you?"

"You caught me in a weak moment. It is so good to see you. We've missed you."

"You certainly know how to make a lady swoon. It's good to see you, too."

"I may have a surprise for you. Are you still dying to get into Gaineswood?"

"Of course. It's only the most elaborate house in the south."

"Bryan and Mary Alice are living in the Foscue House, and Gaineswood is empty."

"That beautiful home sitting empty?"

"We can go see that beautiful home tomorrow if you like. I have permission from Bryan."

Amanda stands on tip-toe to hug her tall cousin. "Jeffery, you are an outstanding cousin."

Jeffery places one hand on top of the other at his waist and bows. "My pleasure." Looking behind him, he says, "Better run, Amanda. Here comes Uncle Nat."

"Amanda," Nat says in a booming voice. "What's this I hear about you teaching in some backwater town?"

"Hello, Uncle Nat." Amanda prays for fortitude and replies, "Marshall is not a backwater town, Uncle Nat. As for teaching, it's one of life's highest callings. I'm fortunate to be a teacher and blessed to be a very good teacher at that."

"With your background and your family name, you should be here in Demopolis, married and raising children."

"Like Aunt Betty?" Amanda looks across the room to her poor, lackluster aunt, who is married to Uncle Nat. She looks like all the joy has been sucked right out of her through her toes. Amanda feels a twinge of guilt for making a snide remark about her aunt.

Before he can reply, Amanda's father announces, "The George Washington eggnog is ready for consumption." He is very proud of this concoction that includes whiskey, brandy, sherry, and Jamaican rum. This one concoction may be the reasons all the aunts, uncles, and cousins love to come to the Oglesby house to celebrate Christmas.

Once the nog is flowing, Amanda's father settles down in his favorite chair by the fire. As soon as he sits, the children swarm around him.

"Tell us about Rube Burrows, Mr. Milton."

"Yes, Uncle Milt. We wanna hear about the body in Birmingham."

Amanda's mother, Rebecca, says, "Milton, the children won't be quiet until you tell them about Mr. Burrows."

"Fine," says Mr. Oglesby. "First, who can tell me who he was?"

"He was a train robber."

"That's right. What else do you remember?"

"He was arrested and taken to the Linden jail."

"Yes, and that's where the story gets interesting. Rube Burrows was an entertaining fellow, and he had those jail guards thoroughly entertained with his jokes and stories."

"They liked him, Uncle Milton?"

"Yes, they did. When Rube Burrows wasn't shooting people and robbing banks, he was very likable."

"On with the story—around midnight, he said he was hungry, and he had candy and ginger snaps in his grub sack. He'd share with the guards if they'd hand him the sack and untie his hands so he could eat."

"They didn't untie him?"

"Yes, they did. Burrows shared his candy, and the first chance he got, he pulled a gun out of that grub sack, tied up the guards, and walked out of jail."

"He didn't escape though, did he, Uncle Milton?"

"No, he was shot dead in a gun battle on the street outside the jail. The next morning his body was placed in a pine box and loaded on a train that took the body to Birmingham. You know three thousand people came to the station in Birmingham to view that muddy, blood-stained corpse."

Amanda's mother says, "And that's enough about gruesome, dead bodies."

"Yes, and as much as I hate to say it, it's time to pack up and go home," says Sydney.

Everyone scurries around collecting children and belongings and wrapping up before going out into the cold. Amanda's mother and father walk them to the door, saying their goodbyes. Amanda and Elizabeth are right behind them.

Jeffrey says, "And I'll see you two after breakfast. Sleep tight."

Walking back into the parlor, Elizabeth sees what Jeffery means about the Christmas mess because the room is one. But what love was shared in that room this day!

***

"Look Elizabeth. It's Gaineswood—the most glorious antebellum home in the south."

Jeffery laughs out loud. "You can see, Elizabeth, that Amanda is taken with Gaineswood."

The three stand and look at the impressive house that stands like a Greek palace with its columns and porticos. It's sparkling white in the Alabama sun. You can imagine it on a hillside in Greece. It seems to fit there—better than in the Alabama Black Belt.

"OK, ladies. The tour begins here," says Jeffery. "Notice the circle on top of the house; its balustrades form the circle."

"Usually those are square and are called widow's walk, right?" asks Amanda.

"Yes, but this one is round, and the family used it for summer musicals. Locals call it an observation ring."

"Imagine sitting up there on a summer's evening listening to Bach. Magnificent," says Elizabeth.

"Let's go inside," says Jeffery as he walks down the curved walkway to the front door. Amanda and Elizabeth follow him in as he unlocks the door and stands aside for them to enter. Amanda walks up a short set of stairs and turns to her right. "Hurry, Elizabeth. You have to see the dining room."

Soft light falls on the dining table set in the middle of the room—light streams down from the dome set it the ceiling. A cupola made of panes of glass tops the dome. One of the panes opens to allow the hot air to rise up and out of the house during the summer months.

Two large matching sideboards line the right wall of the dining room, and family portraits top each sideboard. Amanda walks slowly down this side of the room, looking at the portraits. She stops in front of the portrait of a middle-aged lady. The lady in the portrait is wearing a low-cut velvet gown that showcases the most amazing garnet necklace. The huge garnet stone hangs on the lady like it was made for her—to adorn her, not the other way around. The lady is the center of interest, not the stone. Smaller garnets dangle from the lady's earlobes. The small golden plate at the bottom of the frame indicates that this lady is named Charlotte Lawrence Whitfield.

The coincidence is too great; this grand lady looks exactly like Miss Sophie Lawrence. The hairstyle is different. This lady's hair is piled high and held in place with a headband. Curls frame the face, on the forehead and above the ears. Amanda feels a slight tingle down her spine. She can't wait for Miss Sophie to explain why the portrait of a lady who looks just like her is hanging in the dining room at Gaineswood.

"Come on, ladies. I'm failing my duties if I don't point out the bust of George Washington in the parlor across the hall. All the better homes have Washington in them. And look at the art glass transoms that depict mythological scenes. You know similar transom windows are in the Capitol in Washington."

Elizabeth says, "I see why you love this house, Amanda. I think I'm falling in love as well."

"Just wait," Jeffrey says. He walks into the drawing room, with its white Corinthian columns and the vis-a-vis mirrors positioned on opposite sides of the room. "These mirrors repeat your image thirteen times. Amanda calls this the ballroom."

"Ballroom—the word sounds so romantic," Amanda says. She twirls around and curtsies to Jeffery. "May I have this dance?"

"After I dance with Elizabeth." Jeffery twirls Elizabeth around the room. It's obvious to Amanda that the flush on Elizabeth's cheeks isn't totally from the dancing. Jeffery finishes the dance and bows low over Elizabeth's hand. "Thank you, madam, for a most pleasurable dance."

Amanda is inspecting the mirrors when she spots a hole in the perfect mirror. "Jeffery, did you know this mirror is damaged?"

"Of course, There's a story there. It seems two men loved the same lady. One of the men and the lady were attending a dance in this ballroom when the other suitor came into the room. Seeing his love dancing with his rival, he pulled out his revolver and fired. Fortunately, he hit the reflection in the mirror, not the living, breathing man."

"Oh my, a lover's triangle and a drama acted out in this very room. I do love this house," says Elizabeth.

"This room was once described as the most splendid room in Alabama, and, as much as I hate to say it, it's time to take you two romantics home."

Elizabeth blushes and says, "Thank you for the tour and the dance. I'll remember both for a long time."

Amanda tilts her head down and raises her eyebrows. "Yes, thank you ever so much Jeffery."

***

Amanda and Elizabeth balance armfuls of Christmas gifts as they take turns hugging Amanda's parents goodbye. The train that will take the girls back to Marshall huffs, clanks, and clatters into the station. "Amanda, you give our regards to Miss Sophie, and thank her for taking such good care of you girls."

"I will, Mother. And Miss Sophie has some explaining to do. Why is a picture of a lady with Miss Sophie's last name—a lady who looks just like Miss Sophie—hanging in the dining room at Gaineswood?"

"I know it's a mystery, but I also know that my Amanda will get to the bottom of it," says Amanda's father.

The conductor, wearing a navy suit with shiny, gold buttons and a gold lapel pin in the shape of a train on the suit lapel, yells "Allllllllll aboarrrrrrrrd." A fabric hat with a shiny, patent leather bill tops his head. The word "Conductor" is written in gold on the front of the hat. Quite the impressive figure!

Hugs are given all around before Amanda and Elizabeth board the train. Father says, "Amanda, we expect a letter from you telling us that you arrived safely in Marshall."

"Promise, Father."

"Thank you for allowing me to share Christmas with you."

"Elizabeth, you're welcome in our home anytime." Winking, Amanda's mother says, "And Elizabeth, I think our Jeffery would be glad to see you as well."

Elizabeth's face lights up like the candles on the Christmas tree. "Thank you, Mrs. Oglesby."

The girls find their seats on the train and settle in, arranging all the Christmas gifts around them. Both girls are quiet, each thinking her own thoughts about the time spent in Demopolis during Christmas. The train huffs, clanks, and clatters out of the station and moves on toward its destination.

# Forty-fifth Chapter

## Aucoin's Family Finds a Home

Everyone gathers at Miss Sophie's table for dinner. "Did anything exciting happen while we were in Demopolis?" asks Amanda.

"You could say that," says Sister Sarah.

"Well, are you going to tell me?"

"Miss Maggie has a new family," says Sister Sarah.

"I'll explain," says Miss Sophie. "Miss Maggie worried herself to death about Aucoin's family out in the woods all alone. I went with her to check on Ruby and Emme. What we found was just awful."

"What did you find?" asks Elizabeth.

"Ruby had burned the last stack of firewood that morning, and they had no food left to speak of. We asked when they last ate, and Ruby told us they each had a boiled potato the day before. Maggie told them they were coming to live with her. She didn't ask them. She told them."

"You brought them home with you—just like that?" says Amanda.

"No, Maggie gave them that day to pack their things. She told them to bring anything they treasured with them, even furniture. We went back the next morning with a wagon, and Mr. Michael, who helps Maggie from time to time, went with us. Ruby and

Emme were ready when we got there. It was pitiful to see how few clothes and other possessions they were bringing with them. What did impress me was the books. Ruby had quite a collection of books that she read to Emme. She had more books than she did clothes."

"That's heartbreaking," says Amanda.

"But I have a warm feeling about them," says Sister Sarah. "I predict they're going to be just fine."

"I hope so," says Elizabeth. "They deserve to be just fine after having had that Zachery Aucoin as a husband and father."

"Amanda, I made two pecan pies for dinner, and I'm taking one over to Maggie's after dinner. Do you want to go with me?"

"I'd love to."

"You two go after dinner. I'll get Elizabeth to help me with the dishes," says Sister Sarah.

"Thank you. We'll do that," says Miss Sophie.

***

Miss Sophie walks into Miss Maggie's front parlor with Amanda trailing behind her. Miss Sophie and Miss Maggie have that kind of relationship: they walk into each other's houses unannounced. A quiet fire is burning in the front parlor, and Miss Maggie and Emme are playing a game on a small table pulled up close to the fire.

Ruby jumps up when Sophie and Amanda enter the room.

"It's all right, Ruby. You know Miss Sophie, and this is her boarder, Amanda. Amanda is the schoolteacher."

Ruby, picking up the book she'd dropped, nods to both.

"Ruby, I've brought you a pecan pie. If Emme and Maggie are good, they'll get a piece of it. But it's your pie."

Ruby smiles shyly. "Thank you, Miss Sophie. I think you two ladies are trying to spoil us."

After smiling at Ruby, Amanda turns her attention to the board game Miss Maggie and Emme are playing. They are spinning a spinner and moving forward or backward, depending on the spin. "What are you playing, Miss Maggie?"

"Round the World with Nellie Bly. Have you played before?" She spins the spinner and frowns as she has to move back three spaces.

"I know Nellie Bly was a reporter for the *New York World*, who wanted to go 'round the world just like in the Jules Verne book, *Around the World in 80 Days*. I believe she made it, too."

"You're right. And I'm sure you can guess—the first one to go around the board wins."

Amanda squats down by Emme's chair. "Emme, I think you have to be smart to play this game with Miss Maggie."

Emme pipes up and says, "Mama says I'm smart." Amanda thinks she's adorable with her pigtails and tiny freckles on her nose.

"Now, Emme, don't boast," says Ruby.

"But I am smart: I can read from *Mother Goose's Melody* all by myself."

"I am impressed," says Amanda.

Maggie says, "I remember those stories. I'd love for you to read them to me. Now, I don't know about you, Emme, but I'm dying for a piece of Ruby's pecan pie. How about you?"

"Yes, I want a piece. I think I'll love pecan pie."

Sophie says, “Then come to the kitchen with me. You can help me cut the pie and serve it up on Miss Maggie’s finest dishes.”

After Sophie, Maggie, and Emme leave the room, Amanda asks, “Ruby, have you thought about school for Emme?”

“For a long time, I just thought about surviving. Now that we’re here at Miss Maggie’s, I have thought about it. Emme turned six this past Christmas. Do you think she’s ready?”

“With your permission, I’d like to put her in with our youngest students. They have been in school since October, but I’ll work with Emme. She would have almost three months in school this year, as we go into March. I think it’s an excellent idea.”

“May I bring her next week? I need some time to make her some dresses.”

“Of course, and some of us may be able to help you in the dress department.”

“You’re too kind, Miss Amanda.”

“Not at all. And, I assure you, I’ll watch over Emme and keep you updated on her schoolwork.”

At that point, Sophie sticks her head in the parlor and says, "Pie is served.”

Over pie, Ruby tells Emme that she’ll be going to school with Miss Amanda next week. Emme can’t finish her pie. “School? Me? I’m going to school, Mama?”

“And there’s more,” says Amanda. “Miss Sophie and Miss Maggie, I think we can all take Emme down to the mercantile store. I saw a perfect dress in Mr. Pitt’s store just last week, and I’ll bet it will fit Emme.”

“Of course, we can do that,” says Maggie. “And who knows what else we’ll find while we’re there.”

Amanda notices that Ruby's hands are crossed over her chest, trying to hold in some powerful emotion. Even though Ruby's head is bowed, Amanda can see a tear making its way down Ruby's leathered face. Amanda quietly tucks a handkerchief into Ruby's hands and plants a kiss on the top of Ruby's head. Amanda whispers, "You're all right now, Ruby. We've got you."

Early January 1893

# Forty-sixth Chapter

## Miss Sophie Tells a Ghost Story

Amanda and Miss Sophie are cleaning up after supper, and Amanda decides this is the perfect time to talk to Miss Sophie about Gaineswood.

"The strangest thing happened when I was home for Christmas. I saw a portrait of a lady who looked just like you—a portrait hanging at Gaineswood."

"Not so strange, Amanda. My mother's sister was married to a Whitfield. Living in Demopolis, I'm sure you know the Whitfields built Gaineswood. That would have been my Aunt Charlotte you saw in the portrait."

"I can hardly believe this. You have an aunt that married a Whitfield? An aunt who spent time at Gaineswood? I spent my childhood dreaming of living at Gaineswood!"

"I myself have never seen Gaineswood, but I've heard about it from family over the years."

"Miss Sophie, if you could see the drawing room and the library and the dining room. That's where I saw your aunt's portrait—in the dining room. The resemblance to you is amazing."

"So I've been told. Amanda, as you know so much about Gaineswood, you probably have heard the ghost stories."

"Grew up on them. I heard children hid under the bed to listen for the rustling skirts of the governess from New York who died at Gaineswood. Her body was put in a pine box and kept under the stairs until her father could come to claim her." Catching her breath, Amanda added, "And Evelyn, the housekeeper's sister, was a musician who played Scottish tunes for the family. Evelyn died, and more than one person claims to have heard Scottish music playing at Gaineswood."

"Oh, dear! I hate to ruin all those creepy, delightful stories, but no one named Evelyn ever lived at Gaineswood. The governess, Eliza Robertson, came to Gaineswood in 1856 with her sister. And died soon after. The Whitfields kept Eliza's body in the family mausoleum until someone could come from New York to collect the body."

"Miss Sophie, I love those stories. Are you sure?

"That's according to Charlotte. That's what she told Mother. But, if you love ghost stories, did you know we have a ghost right here in the house?"

"No!"

"Yes, ole Bill Parsons haunts our home. But you don't need to be afraid. He's a friendly ghost."

"Who is he?"

Bill rented a room here, and he died of a broken heart—right there in Sister Sarah's bedroom. His true love, Drusilla, married his older brother. He never recovered. From time to time, we hear sobbing."

"Aren't you afraid?"

"Lord, no! It's just Bill. And, by the way, that's why Sister Sarah lives here. She revels in living in a house with a ghost."

"I can see that. Back to Gaineswood and that portrait. It's a beautiful portrait of a beautiful lady. Just like you, Miss Sophie. And isn't this just the strangest world?"

Miss Sophie stands up and kisses Amanda on the top of her head before retiring for the night.

***

It is after Amanda is in bed that she thinks of the portrait again. She remembers the garnet necklace—the huge garnet stone that hung on Charlotte like it as made for her. She would have to ask Miss Sophie about the necklace sometime.

# Forty-seventh Chapter

## The Sheriff Pays a Visit to Grove Hill

**MURDER IN COFFEEVILLE**

---

Prominent merchant murdered on Christmas Eve

---

Grove Hill, Ala., Dec. 29---Ernest McCorquodale was shot on his front porch on Christmas Eve. He is survived by his wife, Ulrica Sophia Waite McCorquodale and seven children.

McCorquodale, prominent Coffeeville merchant, whose store is located on the bluff east of Tombigbee, was entertaining a house full of visitors on Christmas Eve. McCorquodale's wife heard a noise at the gate to the house. She called to her husband to step out on the porch with her to investigate. McCorquodale shouted, "Who's there?" He was immediately shot down by buckshot.

Sheriff W.W. "Bill" Waite, brother to Ulrica Waite McCorquodale, is investigating the murder. He is quoted as saying, "I already have a suspect, but am not ready to reveal the name at this time."

Interment was in the Coffeeville Cemetery on December 26.

Sheriff Winfield lays down the latest edition of the *Clarke County Democrat*, thinking that two unsolved murders in adjoining counties in the same month may have a connection. It's time to pay a visit to Sheriff Waite.

***

Sheriff Winfield passes the one-story, wooden courthouse and walks to the jail located behind the courthouse. Wiping his mud-crusted boots on the boot wipe, Sheriff Winfield enters the Grove Hill jail. Seated behind a worn mahogany desk is Sheriff W.W. Waite, at least that's what the nameplate on the desk indicates.

"Sheriff Waite?"

"Yes, sir. What can I do for you?" answers the fair-haired, mustached man.

Pulling aside the front of his leather jacket, Sheriff Winfield reveals his badge. "I'm Sheriff Winfield from over in Marshall County. I read about the murder of Ernest McCorquodale in the *Democrat* and thought we should talk."

"You have information for me?"

"I'm not sure. The thing is, we had a murder in Marshall in late December. Odd that there are two unsolved murders in the same area in the same month."

"I heard about Zachery Aucoin's murder. Good riddance from what I hear. Never thought about a connection between Aucoin and McCorquodale. I have a suspect in mind for the McCorquodale murder."

"Mind sharing what you know?"

"Sure. Rumor has it Kirk James murdered McCorquodale. Two stories are floating around about trouble between the two. Here's the gist of it: a farmer, Kirk James, borrowed money from

McCorquodale under the crop-lien system but was facing foreclosure. He sold his cotton in Mobile and came back that same night to pay off the debt to McCorquodale, who was closing his store just as James arrived. It was sleeting and Ulrica, who happens to be my sister, was sick. Ernest was in a hurry. He told Kirk James to go ahead and pay him. Ernest said he'd give James the papers the next day."

"The next thing you know, Kirk James receives a notice that they are foreclosing on his place. James takes the case to court, and the court rules in favor of McCorquodale. That's the Kirk James version."

"What about the McCorquodale version of the story?"

"Well, There's no mention of any late-night visit or payment by Kirk James."

"But you think James killed him? No other suspects?"

"I was standing on the courthouse steps and heard Kirk James tell Ernest, 'Well, Ernest, you have your judgment, but you'll never enjoy it.' Sounds like a threat to me."

"I can certainly see that Kirk James had the motive to kill McCorquodale—or have him killed. Now that I've heard your story, I'm finding it hard to see a connection between the two murders. As far as I know, Aucoin stuck pretty close to home. I don't know of any connection to Clarke County. Doesn't mean there wasn't one. I don't know of one."

"I'll keep you in mind, Sheriff Winfield, but I agree. By the way, what did happen in the Aucoin murder?"

"Found him dead—shot through the head. The odd thing was, someone moved his body. And even odder, they moved it to the base of Mildren Pickens statue. Mildren was a women's righter. She would have hated Aucoin."

"That's odd, for sure." Standing, Sheriff Waite offers Sheriff Winfield his hand. "Thanks for stopping by. Again, I'll keep you in mind if I see any connection at all between the two murders."

"Appreciate it, Sheriff. Thanks for your time."

***

Sheriff Winfield decides to stop by the Coffeeville Cemetery on the way back to Marshall. It's easy to spot McCorquodale's grave with the freshly dug mound of dirt. Standing and looking down at the tombstone, Sheriff Winfield reads aloud the inscription on the tombstone, just below the dates: *Sheltered and safe from sorrow.*

"Rest in peace, Ernest McCorquodale. Rest in peace," says the sheriff.

# Forty-eighth Chapter

## Sadie Leaves a Letter

Amanda, getting ready for the school day, lights the gas lanterns lining the schoolroom wall and straightens the desks. As always, she's thankful for the fathers who take turns lighting the potbellied stove so early in the morning. Moving to her desk, she immediately notices the white envelope propped up against her schoolbooks. It's out of place on a desk that Amanda keeps meticulously organized.

Amanda sits down behind the desk, opens the envelope, and reads:

*Dear Miss Amanda,*

*Harley hit me again last night because I burnt the cornbread. This time he hit me square in the face with his fist. First time he's hit me in the face so hard.*

*I'm running, Miss Amanda. Can't and won't take it anymore. By the time you read this, I'll be well on my way. Can't tell you where I'm running to. The less you know, the better.*

*I want to thank you for believing in me and believing I'm smart. My best times have been spent with you learning. I wanted you to know.*

*Your friend,*
*Sadie*

Children begin coming in for the school day. Amanda slides the letter in the white envelope and puts it in her purse before beginning the school day. Today, the middle group is diagramming sentences.

"I love diagramming sentences. You will, too," Ellen tells the students. "We are going to diagram the sentence: Tony gave Thomas new shoes." Drawing a horizontal line on the board, Amanda says, "Please draw a horizontal line like this on your slate. Draw a vertical line that crosses through the middle of the horizontal line." Amanda waits until the middle group of students finished this task. "Now draw a vertical line that meets the horizontal line but doesn't cross over it. This line is drawn about two-thirds of the way down the horizontal line.

Again, Amanda waits. "Now let me show you how we will use this form to diagram our sentence. The subject of the sentence is *Tony*. The subject is always written first on the horizontal line. *Gave* is the verb. The verb always goes to the right on the long horizontal line behind the vertical line."

"What about the shoes, Miss Amanda? Where do they go?"

"The word *shoes* is the direct object. Place it at the end of the line behind the shorter vertical line."

"But Miss Amanda, we have *Tony gave shoes.* What about the words: *Thomas* and *new*?"

"More lines, of course. *Thomas* is the indirect object. Draw a slanted L-shaped line beneath the word *gave* and write *Thomas* on the longer part of the L-shaped line."

Last of all, *new* is an adjective modifying the *shoes*. Draw a diagonal line below *shoes* and write *new* upon it."

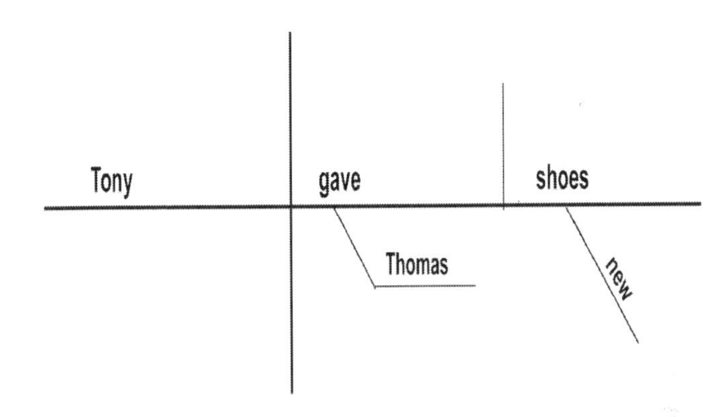


"You're right, Miss Amanda. Diagramming is fun."

"I think so, too. I'll give you practice sentences to work on, but now, I'll think we have an early recess time. Make sure you put on your coats before you go out."

The change in schedule is exciting for the students, and, putting on sweaters and coats, they hurriedly file outside into the chilly sunshine before Miss Amanda can change her mind.

Amanda walks to her desk, sits down, and re-reads Sadie's letter. Her heart breaks at the thought of Harley hitting Sadie in the face. At the thought of Sadie running. At the thought of Sadie alone. Amanda lowers her head to her desk and cries.

# Forty-ninth Chapter

## Harley Wiggins Makes an Appearance

Amanda tugs open the heavy mercantile store door and squeezes inside. Mr. Pitts is over by the cash register, placing stick candy in clear, round jars. "Amanda, what's this I hear about you organizing a womanless wedding?"

Amanda laughs. "That's right, Mr. Pitts. And what role do you want to play? The bride? The maid of honor?"

"I'll tell you what—I'll sign up to be the flower girl."

"Consider yourself signed up. You'll make a great flower…"

"Hey, you that Amanda Oglesby that's been teaching my Sadie?"

"Amanda turns to face a tall, lean man in overalls. He's dark——dark all over. Black hair in disarray on his head. Black hair sticking out from his rolled-up shirt sleeves. Black scowl on his face.

"I'm Amanda Oglesby."

"Where you hiding my Sadie?"

Taken aback, Amanda stutters, "I don't have Sadie."

"I asked. Where's my Sadie?"

"I'm not hiding Sadie, but I would. She doesn't deserve to live with a man like you, a man who hits her."

"I don't believe you, lady. You tell me where Sadie is." He is towering over her. Amanda stands firm.

"For the third time, you loathsome man, I don't know where Sadie is."

Harley Wiggins draws back his hand to hit Amanda. Before you know it, he's flat on the floor with David Henry Callander standing over him. "Don't tell me, Wiggins, that you were going to hit this lady."

"She won't tell me where my Sadie is," Wiggins whines.

"Well, I doubt if she knows where Sadie is, but I can sure tell you I'd better not hear of you even speaking to Miss Oglesby again. Is that understood?"

Harley Wiggins doesn't answer. He gets up off the floor, brushes off the back of his pants, throws Amanda a murderous look, and storms out of the store.

"My goodness, Amanda. You do know how to make friends," says David Henry as he slowly brushes the hair off Amanda's cheek and tucks it behind her ear. It's an intimate gesture that makes Amanda blush. Mr. Pitts can't help but see the gesture and the blush. He tactfully moves to the back of the store.

"I'm so glad that I ran into you, Amanda. I have an invitation for you."

Amanda shakily says, "An invitation?"

"Yes, to Callander. I have wanted you to visit for some time, and my parents would love to meet you. You are invited to Sunday dinner—right after church this Sunday. You can ride to Callander with us, and we'll see that you get home."

Still shaken and not wanting David Henry to leave, Amanda moves to the chairs by the potbellied stove and sits down. "Please stay for a moment."

David Henry sits down beside Amanda. "Are you all right?"

"Yes. Just don't leave right yet. Will you tell me about Callander?"

"Love to. Callander has been in our family forever, and I suppose I'll run it one day. It's twelve hundred acres of the best black-soil farmland you've ever seen. We've got nineteen tenant farmers and their families on the place. Besides the plantation house and the tenant houses, There's a grist mill, a commissary, a syrup mill, a sawmill, a blacksmith shop, and a cotton gin. The Linley River forms the eastern border of Callander, and on the west side is Morgan Creek.

It's dammed to furnish power to the grist mill and the cotton gin. My father makes enough cane syrup and cures enough meat from this land to feed his family and the nineteen tenant families that live on the plantation. It's a magical place! I can't wait to show you."

"Then I accept your kind invitation. Please tell your parents that I'll be delighted to come for Sunday dinner."

"Wonderful. Now I'm going to walk you to Miss Sophie's where she'll make you hot tea and hover over you for the rest of the day. You know she loves you."

# Fiftieth Chapter

## All Aboard to the Vine and Olive Colony

"All aboard," yells Amanda. All the students hop up out of their desks, all talking at once.

"Where are we going, Miss Amanda?"

"Who's the conductor?"

"I believe Randy will make a perfect conductor to the Vine and Olive Colony," says Amanda, as she locates the engineer's hat in her desk drawer.

"Here you go, Randy." Turning to the class, Amanda says, "All aboard for the Vine and Olive." The students scurry into the other classroom and find seats in the imaginary train that they love.

Amanda boards the train and faces the students. "There's a lot to tell you about the Vine and Olive, so I'll start right away. The Vine and Olive Colony was in Marengo County. The earliest people to live in Marengo County were the prehistoric mound-builders. Even though they were no longer in Marengo County by 1600 AD, we can still see hundreds of mounds they formed when they lived there."

"What were the mounds for?"

"Homes, burials, and ceremonies took place inside the mounds. One day I'll take you to Moundville where you can see actual mounds. Now, back to the Vine and Olive Colony. A Bourbon king, Louis the XVIII, replaced Napoleon, and Napoleon had to leave France. His officers and members of his court had to leave as well. Some of them came to America. They appealed to the American government for a land grant. They wanted to grow grapes and olives. In 1817, the American government granted the Frenchmen 92,000 acres in Alabama where the Tombigbee and Black Warrior Rivers join. The French started a settlement they called Demopolis."

"That's where you are from, Miss Amanda."

"Yes, it is. My family is in Demopolis. But you know, those Frenchmen made a mistake. They started building Demopolis, but they built on the wrong land. The settlers had to move a few miles to the east. There they built the town of Eagleville.

They had no luck growing the grapes or the olives. The land wasn't good for it, and the settlers weren't planters. The vines and olive seeds were imported from France. Often, the grape vines arrived in the wrong season for planting, and the olive seed would not grow. In desperation, some French settlers moved further up the river, where they founded another village named Arcola."

"Were they able to grow grapes there, Miss Amanda?

"Not really. When Napoleon died in 1821, they gave up all hope, and most of the settlers moved to Mobile, where a large number of Frenchmen lived."

"Why did they give up hope?"

"Many of the Frenchmen thought that if they were successful, Napoleon might be interested in coming to America. That was their dream. Well, I see that we've arrived. Thank you, Randy, for getting us safely to the Vine and Olive Colony." Randy grins from ear-to-ear and tips his conductor's hat to Amanda.

Moving over to the magic lantern, Amanda says, "Now, let's see what we can see of the Vine and Olive Colony."

Amanda slides in a glass plate that shows the chalk-white cliffs at Demopolis. "This is what the settlers saw when they reached Demopolis—White Bluff or Ecor Blanc, as the Frenchmen called it. The bluffs are a mile long and eighty feet high at the highest point. Quite impressive." Amanda changes the slide.

"This is a picture of Eagleville. There was one long street bordered by log houses."

"And this slide is of Colonel Nicholas Raoul and his wife. Raoul was a close friend of Napoleon and stood by him during many bloody battles. When Raoul came to Alabama, he and his wife built a cabin on French Creek.

Colonel Raoul, as you can see, is a very distinguished man in appearance. When circumstances became so bad, Raoul began a ferry, charging customers twenty-five cents to go from Eagleville to Arcola. Quite a let-down from the commander of Napoleon's soldiers to ferry operator.

Colonel Raoul's wife was from Naples, Italy, and she had been the Marchioness of Sinabaldi and a maid-in-waiting to a queen. She was a cultured, polished lady, but, when she saw the family in financial trouble, she rolled up her sleeves, baked ginger cakes, and sold them to the ferry riders.

Slide change. "And this is a picture of an olive tree growing today in Demopolis. At least, that's what most citizens believe. There has been debate though. Some say it's a plum tree, not an olive tree. I'd like to think it's from those Frenchmen who came to Alabama in 1917."

"Miss Amanda, that's a sad story."

"Yes, it is. But even though the Frenchmen failed, we have to admire their courage. Just think about leaving France, a cultured country, and moving to the wilds of Alabama. Students, I tell you, I admire those Frenchmen. Now, Mr. Engineer, will you return us to the classroom?"

Randy smiles a bashful smile and says, "Choo Choo."

***

At the end of the school day, as Amanda is walking around the schoolroom picking up a stray piece of chalk here and straightening books on her desk there, she thinks of Colonel Raoul's wife, the Marchioness of Sinabald, and her adapting to life in Alabama. Miss Sophie and Miss Maggie spring to mind. Miss Sophie, who lost her husband and opened a boarding house, and Miss Maggie, who follows in her deceased husband's footsteps by tending to the medical needs of the community. Strong women, all! Women to emulate.

Late January 1893

# Fifty-first Chapter

## Miss Sophie is Ill

"Come in, Mrs. Todd," says Amanda, as she holds the front door open at Miss Sophie's. Mable enters, holding a pecan pie in one hand and her purse in the other.

"How is she today? Poor thing!"

Amanda pauses before answering Mable Todd. Miss Sophie's loud wheezing can be heard all over the house.

"Oh!" says Mable. She lowers her voice and whispers, "Bronchial asthma. Is she going to make it, Amanda?"

"Of course. Come on in, Mrs. Todd. I'll take that delicious-looking pecan pie to the kitchen, and you're welcome to go into Mrs. Sophie's bedroom."

"Of course, I'm welcome. I am Sophie's cousin, after all."

*Her cousin? How can evil ole Mrs. Todd be Miss Sophie's cousin?*

As Amanda re-enters the bedroom, Mable is saying, "You remember the Duncan cousins? Mary Duncan died of bronchial asthma. So young. So tragic."

Amanda walks to the edge of the bed and picks up Miss Sophie's hand. "Well, I can assure you that Miss Sophie is going to be fine. She'll be making those lemon icebox pies before we know it."

"Humph!" says Mable. "You've been missing all the happenings in Marshall. Let me catch you up on the news. First, Gloria Knowles came to the circle meeting smelling of alcohol. They say she's a closet drinker—just like her daddy. And the preacher wrote a letter to the congregation saying, *your a wonderful congregation,* not *you're a wonderful congregation.*

I saved the best for last. You'll never believe this. Jim Bates, who played Joseph in the Christmas pageant, and May Barnes, who played Mary, were caught in the vestry kissing. I hear he had his hand on her behind. Imagine, Joseph and Mary, having an illicit affair of the heart. They're both married to other people. Scandalous!"

Amanda breaks up this running diatribe with an offer to serve the pecan pie. Miss Sophie smiles a tired smile. "A little piece for me, Amanda."

Amanda is thrilled to escape from Mable Todd. Coming back into the bedroom from the kitchen, Amanda serves the pie and settles down to enjoy it. Mable Todd's pecan pies are famous in Marshall. As they are finishing the pie, Mable says, "Sophie, the other day I was walking down Main Street, and this uppity colored didn't get off the sidewalk to let me pass. I tell you, colored are an abomination to society."

That's about all Amanda can take. Collecting the dessert plates, Amanda says, "I think Miss Sophie has had all the good news she can stand for one day. We are tiring her. Let's leave and let her get some rest."

Mable huffily says, "I guess I can tell if I'm tiring Sophie or not."

Amanda doesn't answer but looks Mable Todd straight in the eye. Mable gets up and stomps out of the room, yelling over her shoulder, "Don't bother seeing me out!"

"Oh, Miss Sophie, I've made her mad. I'm sorry if I misbehaved. Sorry because of your relationship with her. For me, I think she's horrid. But she is your cousin."

Sophie holds Amanda's hand and pats it. "You need to write a note to her, apologizing. I need you to do that for me."

"I will, Miss Sophie. I'll hand deliver the note. But how can you stand her? You are nothing like her."

"Take these words to heart. Treat others based on who you are, not who they are. Now, I am tired. Please close the door behind you, Amanda. I'll sleep for a while."

Amanda kisses Miss Sophie on the forehead and leaves the room. On the way down the stairs, she thinks again about what Miss Sophie told her: treat others based on who you are, not who they are. Food for thought. Deep thought.

# Fifty-second Chapter

## Bad News and Good News

### THE MITCHUM WAR

---

*Mitchum Beat Gang Behind Death of Prominent Merchant*

---

*Grove Hill, Ala., Jan. 20 - Ernest McCorquodale was shot on his front porch on Christmas Eve. It is believed that his murderer was a member of the Mitchum Beat gang called Hell-at-the-Breech.*

*Mitchum Beat is an area of Clarke County northwest of Grove Hill, southwest of Thomasville, and northeast of Coffeeville. Its population consists of approximately 368 residents who have farms in this remote section of Alabama.*

*Hell-at-the-Breech is a secret society formed in 1890. Its members are reputed to take a blood oath when entering the society. The society was formed because the rural whites of Mitchum Beat felt that the merchants, planters, and lawyers controlled the county.*

*It is speculated that the murder of Rafe Bedsole, Mitchum Beat store owner, laid the groundwork for the forming of Hell-at-the-Breech. Bedsole ran as a Republican for a seat in the state legislature against the establishment. He was poisoned shortly after a political rally and found dead by the road.*

*Sheriff W.W. "Bill" Waite continues the investigation of the murder of Ernest McCorquodale, a prominent Coffeeville merchant, but he has made no arrest at this time.*

Mr. Pitts lays down his copy of the *Democrat* as Amanda enters the store. "Hello there," he says. "I'm reading about that murder in Coffeeville. You know the sheriff went to Grove Hill to talk to Sheriff Waite—thought there might be a connection between the Coffeeville murder and our murder right here in Marshall."

"Do you think There's a connection, Mr. Pitts?"

"I can't see how there could be. I don't see Aucoin mixed up in political doings in Clarke County."

"I agree, Mr. Pitts. The two don't seem to fit."

"You know the strangest thing about the Aucoin murder is the necklace."

"The necklace?"

"Sheriff Winfield found this necklace with a huge dangling stone in Aucoin's pocket, of all places."

"That makes it even stranger. Was the necklace expensive? I can't see Aucoin having anything that expensive."

"Sheriff showed it around town. Looked priceless. You haven't seen it?"

"No, but it wouldn't mean anything to me if I did see it. Very strange."

Mr. Pitts picks up the *Democrat* and points out another story. "On a positive note, did you read about Lawyer King starting a

Knights of Pythias Lodge over in that empty lot across from the jail?"

"Miss Sophie may have mentioned that once. I don't understand what the Knights of Pythias stands for."

"Read this article first. Then I'll try to explain what you don't understand, not that I'm an expert."

## THE FRATERNAL ORDER OF THE KNIGHTS OF PYTHIAS

---

***Lawyer King is successful in bringing Knights of Pythias Lodge to Marshall***

---

*Grove Hill, Ala., Jan. 20 –The Knights of Pythias is officially established in Marshall. The Order of the Knights of Pythias, once endorsed by Abraham Lincoln, was created after the Civil War. Its purpose is to promote understanding among men of goodwill with the final objective being universal peace.*

*President Lincoln stated, "It is one of the best agencies conceived for the upholding of government, honoring the flag, for the reuniting of our brethren of the North and the South, for teaching the people to love one another, and portraying the sanctity of the home and loved ones."*

*The Order will be open to applicants from Marshall County, Clarke County, and Wilcox County. Applicants must be males in good health who believe in a Supreme Being. Contact Clifford King, Main Street, Marshall if you are interested in joining the Order.*

*Construction of the Knights of Pythias lodge is underway on the empty lot across from the jail in downtown Marshall. Lawyer King is*

> *instrumental in bringing the Lodge to Marshall; he predicts the completion of the lodge before May, as the first meeting will be held on the ninth of May—the date of the end of the Civil War.*

"This sounds like a worthy organization. Who could argue with universal peace?"

"I agree, young lady. I plan to join myself."

"I'm curious. Why the name Knights of Pythias?"

"Here's the story. The Order is named for Pythias, of Damon and Pythias fame. The two lived around four hundred years before Christ and were members of a school founded by Pythagoras, the father of Greek philosophy. Damon and Pythias went to Syracuse during the reign of Dionysus, where Pythias was accused of plotting against Dionysus, a ruthless tyrant. There, Dionysus sentenced him to death. Pythias begged Dionysus to allow him to go home to make final arrangements with his family. Of course, Dionysus thought that, if he let Pythias go, Pythias would never return.

Damon asked the king to hold him while Pythias was gone with the understanding that Damon would be killed if Pythias did not return. When Pythias returned from his home, Dionysus was so impressed with their dedication to each other that he pardoned both Damon and Pythias."

"That's a wonderful story—one that I'll share with my students. Who knows? They may grow up to be members of the Order."

"Amanda, reflect on these two stories. Both involve secret organizations. Hell-at-the-Beech was formed out of bitterness and resentment. Knights of Pythias was formed to foster understanding and peace. It will be interesting to see which one prospers."

# Fifty-third Chapter

## Amanda Goes to Callander

Amanda walks up the front steps of the plantation house at Callander and stops. The wide porch is filled with rocking chairs lined up in a precise row. The eight-foot double front doors are comprised of oddly sized panels with side lights on each side. The arched transom above the door matches the length of the door frame exactly. The louvered green shutters on the windows are so dark—they are almost black. Amanda stops to take it all in.

David Henry pulls open the door on the right, and Amanda enters a wide hall that smells of coffee, bread baking, and the lemon oil that's been used for years on Callander antiques.

Amanda looks to the left and sees the study. Bookcases line three walls. Some sections have books stored behind glass doors. Books cover all the shelves haphazardly. Whitman's *Leaves of Grass* is next to Gibbon's *History of Rome.* There are tons of books on law and engineering. In the center of the room is a huge desk made of mahogany. The desk has a wide kneehole. Amanda wonders if David Henry hid there as a child.

"Everyone's probably in the dining room. Let's walk through to the back."

Passing a staircase and a room with a closed door, they move out of the main house into the dining room and kitchen area. A tall lady has her back to them as they enter. She's arranging flowers in a vase on the sideboard. David Henry tiptoes up behind her and hugs her.

The lady—who must be David Henry's mother—screams. Turning around, she sees David Henry. "David Henry, you're going to be the death of me." Despite her harsh words, she tucks her arm through her son's and pats his arm.

"Mother, may I present Amanda Oglesby, formerly of Demopolis and currently of Marshall. Amanda, my mother, Mary Ella."

"Amanda, so nice to meet you. I've heard wonderful things about your teaching from the people in Marshall. It seems the children love you."

Smiling, Amanda says, "The feeling is mutual."

"You'll have to tell us about your Christmas pageant over dinner."

"I'd love to." They all turn as the swinging door from the kitchen to the dining room is opened by a colored woman carrying two porcelain bowls of vegetables. She's followed by a stately colored man carrying a platter of meats.

"Amanda, I want you to meet our family. Meet Lady, who is a divine cook and helps me keeps the house running smoothly. Meet Ben, who does the same. Well, he doesn't cook, but he does everything else."

"A pleasure to meet you, Miss Amanda. We've all been excited about your visit," says Lady.

"A pleasure to meet you, too. Here, let me take one of these bowls from you." Amanda takes the bowl, leans in, and sniffs. "I love the smell of cooked, fresh green beans."

David Henry says, "Just wait, Amanda. Food will cover this entire table."

David Henry was right. When Ben and Lady finished bringing in the dinner meal, there are bowls of oyster stew, porcelain bowls filled with turnips, mashed sweet potatoes, mashed Irish potatoes, carrots, squash, okra, and vegetable platters of corn fritters and sliced tomatoes. Platters of fried chicken and ham are mixed in with the vegetables. There are also hoecakes and fresh yeast rolls.

Mrs. Callander looks over the table and seems pleased before she frowns. "Where is that James William? Something must have happened."

Before Mrs. Callander can finish her sentence, an older version of David Henry pushes through the kitchen door into the dining room. "Mother, don't fash. I'm here." Mr. Callander walks over to Mrs. Callander and kisses her on the forehead, then turns to Amanda. "I'll save David Henry the trouble of an introduction, young lady. You must be Amanda. Welcome to Callander. We're delighted that you've come to dinner."

Immediately liking the man, Amanda smiles. "Thank you for having me. I'd like to hear more about your plantation over dinner."

Mrs. Callander says, "You've done it now, Amanda. That's all we'll hear during dinner. Amanda, will you sit on James William's right beside David Henry?"

After they are all seated, Mrs. Callander looks to her husband for the blessing.

"Let's bow our heads. Lord, we are grateful for your bounty. Thank you for the rain that falls on the fields, the fields that sprout crops, and the family that we hold dear. Bless this food. Amen."

Looking to Amanda, Mr. Callander says, "And you want to know about Callander, young lady?"

"Yes, sir."

"My great, great grandfather bought this land and named it after his family's home in Scotland. I've never been to the Scottish Callander—would love to. Understand it's at Loch Lomond."

"And your clan?"

"The Callander Clan. 'Mean Well' is our motto, and we're an armigerous clan—we don't have a chief."

"I'm not positive, but I think Oglesby is an ancient Scottish name. So, Scotland forever."

Mr. Callander raises his glass to Amanda; Amanda clinks it with her own. David Henry winks at his mother. He loves the interaction between Amanda and his father.

Silence as everyone eats. Amana says, "These corn fritters are wonderful. They are Lady's recipe?"

"Oh, yes. Lady is very proud of them. Calls them Corn Oysters though. I'm not sure why," says Mrs. Callander.

"Amanda, I hear Julia Tutwiler had a hand in your education, so I know you are a proponent of education. Have you heard of the Lincoln School in Marion?" asks Mr. Callander.

"I have, but I know very little about it."

"I have been contributing to the school for years. I believe education is the key to solving many of our problems as a society."

"I think that if James William didn't have this plantation to run, he'd go teach at the Lincoln School. It's his pet project," says Mrs. Callander.

"Interesting story about Lincoln School. Its conception was supposedly inspired by a Union soldier who taught colored children to read after the war. The number of students grew, and nine former slaves stepped in and made the school official back around the mid-1860s, and it has been most successful. It was one of the first school established after the Civil War for the education of the colored."

"I'm so glad to hear that, Mr. Callander. Do you know anything about the curriculum?"

"I understand that the curriculum is like any found in classical education—Greek, mathematics, history, chemistry. Probably like the curriculum you studied."

"This is exciting news for me. We can't do enough to educate our children—all our children."

"I'm proud to say that I helped establish part of the school for a teacher-training facility. In 1887, the state of Alabama focused on higher education training for colored, and the teacher-training component moved to Montgomery."

"Thank you for sharing, Mr. Callander. I'd like to learn more about the school."

"And now, young lady, I know this son of mine is dying to show you around Callander. So, if there are no objections, you are free to explore. Ben will go with you. He'll be delighted to get out of helping Lady in the kitchen."

"Thank you, Mr. and Mrs. Callander, for this most impressive meal and thank you for having me to Callander. I look forward to seeing more of it."

***

"Well, Amanda. You've seen the grist mill, the commissary, the syrup mill, the sawmill, the blacksmith shop, and the cotton gin. What's your favorite place at Callander?"

Amanda stops and thinks. "The pond with the big tree beside it and that swing hanging from the tree. I can visualize you swinging there as a child."

"Yes, I did that. Swam buck-naked in the pond as well."

"Humph! I don't want to visualize that." David Henry throws his head back and roars with laughter.

When his laughter subsides, David Henry turns to Ben. "Ben, we both know you're supposed to chaperone Amanda and me, but could you please walk over to the commissary for a Coca-Cola and leave us alone—just for a few minutes. No one will know."

"Miss Mary Ella will have my hide if she finds out, but I guess I could use something wet. Mark my words—I'll be back in a jiffy."

Waiting until Ben walks down the bumpy dirt path toward the commissary, David Henry turns to Amanda and pulls her into his arms.

He says over the top of her head, "Amanda, life with you would be fun—wonderful and fun. Do you think you could visualize yourself living with me at Callander?"

David Henry holds Amanda away from him so that he's looking into her eyes.

Amanda has no fan to court with, nothing to rest on her right cheek to give a courteous, positive answer properly. Amanda looks David Henry in the eye. "David Henry, I think that sounds very appealing. I'd love to live with you at Callander."

David Henry bows his head to Amanda and kisses her deeply, holding the kiss until he hears Ben returning.

Ben lumbers into view, Coca-Cola in hand. He's smiling—happy that all seems well with David Henry and Amanda.

"Ben, we're going to work hard to get Amanda in our family. You agree we should, don't you?"

Ben says, "Miss Amanda, you'll make a beautiful addition to Callander. We'd love to have you here."

Amanda, cheeks flushed from David Henry's kiss, smiles at Ben. "Thank you for wanting me in your family, Ben."

"You're most welcome, Miss Amanda. Now, if you two are ready, we'll get back to the house for Lady's blackberry cobbler."

# Fifty-fourth Chapter

## Sadie Returns

Amanda walks up and down the rows of school desks, checking to see that the students have left nothing behind. She is surprised to see that Willis and Eliza are still in their seats. Their mother, Pauline, has been picking them up after school since Sadie left. Hearing footsteps coming up the school steps, Amanda assumes it's Pauline.

"Miss Amanda?"

Amanda knows this is not Pauline. She recognizes the voice. She turns to face Sadie, who's standing in the doorway. The left side of her face is purple. Her lips are swollen.

"Sadie. Oh, Sadie."

"He found me, Miss Amanda. Threatened to kill me if I ran again." A defeated Sadie is standing in front of Amanda.

Amanda takes a moment to take in the shock of seeing Sadie. "When did you get home, Sadie?"

"Last night. I walked Willis and Eliza to school this morning but didn't want you to see me."

"Oh." Amanda pauses, then says, "Willis, Eliza. I have a special favor to ask of you. Will you take the erasers outside and beat them on the side of the schoolhouse until they're clean?"

Normally, Willis and Eliza would be excited about this job, but they know something is badly wrong. They pick up the erasers and move outside. As soon as they are outside, Amanda grabs Sadie and hugs her. Then, holding Sadie away from her and looking her in the eye, Amanda says, "Your husband has not won. We won't let him win."

"I think he has, Miss Amanda. He suspects something about me cleaning the schoolhouse—did before I ran away. I know he won't let me come at night anymore."

Amanda walks around the room, not talking—just thinking.

"Sadie, will you pick up Willis and Eliza after school?

"Yes. Pauline will be in the field with Harley."

"When you come tomorrow, I'll have some books for you. You can study during the day while Harley and Pauline are in the field. Sadie, you are going to have to hide these books. Harley can't find them."

"I'll do that, Miss Amanda. You're not giving up on me?"

"I'll never give up on you, Sadie. We are going to educate you whether Harley likes it or not. You won't always be with him, Sadie. God won't allow it. We'll start with Ancient World History–-the Early River Valley Civilizations, to be exact. Have you ever heard of Mesopotamia, Sadie?"

"No, ma'am."

"You remember reading the Greek myths? How Pandora loosened the evils upon the world? We're going back in time, before the Greek Civilization, to the very birthplace of civilization."

Amanda walks into the adjoining room and returns with a single book on ancient civilizations. "Sadie, this will take you away to another place and time. Speaking of time, let's organize our time.

Can you read the first chapters on Mesopotamia by this time next week?"

"Yes, ma'am. I can."

"Be prepared then. I'm going to test you. We'll have to work out something with the children that won't make Harley suspicious. You don't worry about that. I'll take care of it."

There's a light in Sadie's eyes that wasn't there before. She grabs Amanda's hands in both of hers and squeezes. "Thank you so much, Miss Amanda. I think I can thank you, instead of Pandora, for the hope in my world."

# Fifty-fifth Chapter

## The Law and Domestic Violence

Amanda is on a mission. To see Sheriff Winfield. Someone has to do something about the way Harley Wiggins treats Sadie. Walking into the sheriff's office, Amanda finds Sheriff Winfield seated behind his desk. She can't help but notice the necklace on his desk—a very expensive- looking necklace with a large dangling stone.

"That necklace is stunning. Is that large stone a garnet?"

"I'm not sure," answers the sheriff. "I've been showing this around town. I haven't shown it to you?"

"No. I would remember, but there's something familiar about it."

"This is the necklace found in Aucoin's pocket—the murdered Aucoin."

"Oh, I've heard folks talking about it. It's stunning."

"I'd appreciate you letting me know if you remember anything about this necklace. I'm no closer to solving Aucoin's murder."

"I'll be sure to let you know if I remember anything. But I need to talk to you about Sadie Wiggins. Do you know her, sheriff?"

"Yes, I know who she is. Married to that Harley Wiggins, right?"

"Yes, but did you know he beats her? Did you know he's brought another woman into their home—a woman and her three children?"

"No, I didn't know that Harley beats Sadie, though Harley doesn't appear to be an upstanding Marshall citizen."

"Can you, as the law in Marshall, do anything about the beatings?"

"Yes, I'll go talk to Harley Wiggins. It's interesting, Amanda. From ancient times up 'til about twenty years ago, a woman was considered to be a man's property. He could do with her whatever he wanted, including beating her. Legally, all that changed right here in the state of Alabama. Fulgham vs. the State of Alabama. The court ruled that women have the same protection under the law as men."

"I always thought men that hit their wives for any reason were nothing but low-life. Certainly, I've never heard of a male in our family hitting a female."

"I agree with you on the low-life part. I'll talk to Harley. I need to see evidence though. Not just she said, he said."

"That's not a problem. Make sure you get a good look at Sadie's face. That's all the proof you need."

"I will. Thank you for coming in. I'll run out there before it gets dark. Oh, and Amanda, don't forget about the necklace. If you remember anything, let me know."

"Yes, sir. And thank you for looking after Sadie."

***

Sheriff Winfield steps up onto the porch of the Wiggins' house. It's a typical sharecropper's house of unpainted clapboard, tin roof, and two chimneys made of river stones. Ladderback chairs line the porch, their cane bottoms sagging halfway to the floor. This house stands out from the row of sharecropper houses because the yard is swept clean, and two cast-iron pots sit on each side of the steps. The pots are overflowing with petunias and something that looks like herbs. Very attractive.

Before the sheriff can knock on the door, Harley comes around the house. He looks up, surprised to see the sheriff at his house. "Help you, sheriff?"

"Hello, Mr. Wiggins. It's you and Sadie that I want to see. Is she inside?"

"Yes, sir."

"Will you ask her to come out?"

"What you need her for?"

"Please ask her to come out."

Standing in place, Harley yells, "Sadie, come out in the yard."

Sheriff Winfield returns down the steps and waits for Sadie. Harley yells again, a decibel higher, "Woman, I told you to come out in the yard."

Slowly, the front door opens, and Sadie steps out onto the porch. She stops when she sees the sheriff. Sheriff Winfield smiles up at her. "It's all right, Sadie. I want to talk to you."

Sadie comes down the steps and stands before Sheriff Winfield. He's shocked to see the bruise on the left side of her face. "Sadie, how did you hurt your face?"

Silence.

"Sadie, I need to know about your face." Sadie hangs her head and does not answer.

Confronting Harley, Sheriff says, "She looks like someone hit her. Did you hit her, Wiggins?"

"What if I did? She's my property."

"No, she's not. She has the same protection under the law that you do as a man." The sheriff sneers when he says the word, man. "I tell you what, Wiggins. I am coming out here at least once a week to check on Sadie. I'd better not find any bruises on her in the future, or you're going to jail. So, you better see to it that she takes good care of herself, no bruises."

After the sheriff has walked away, Harley turns on Sadie. "You go complain on me, woman?"

"No," answers Sadie.

"I don't believe you. You're gonna be sorry that sheriff set foot on our land."

Watching Harley walk away, Sadie thinks maybe Harley will be the sorry one. For the first time in their married life, she feels Harley will be held accountable.

February 1893

# Fifty-sixth Chapter

## "Valentine's Day"

"Happy Valentine's Day, class. And I have a surprise for you. We're going to have a visitor today. While we're waiting for him to come, I'll tell you about Valentine's Day."

"Who's the visitor?"

"Why's he coming today?"

"Is it a good surprise?"

"Patience. Now about Valentine's Day. Near the time of Christ, so way back in history, an emperor named Claudius ruled in the Roman Empire. The story goes that a young priest named Valentine disobeyed Claudius and performed marriages for young couples. Emperor Claudius heard of this and put the priest in prison. Claudius wanted the young men for military service and didn't want them married.

Valentine, the priest, fell in love with the jailer's daughter and, before they executed him, he sent the daughter a note signed, 'from your Valentine.' That may have been the first valentine. Keep in mind, students, we don't know if this story is true."

"Randy, would you look out the door and see if anyone is walking toward the school?"

Randy scoots out of his desk and runs to the door. "Not a soul in sight, Miss Amanda."

"Thank you, Randy. Hum, let me think about another story." Amanda walks slowly around the classroom. "Aha! I have one. Some scholars think that Valentine's Day started in the Middle Ages when the people believed that birds select their mates on February fourteenth. Lovers would recite—"

"Hello, everyone. Have you been waiting for me?" All heads turned toward the front door where Mr. Pitts stood just inside the classroom with a huge basket in his hands.

"Mr. Pitts. So glad you've come. I told the students that we have a surprise today. Do you want to tell them?"

"Why, yes. I do. Happy Valentine's Day, students. To make this day special, I've brought each of you a valentine."

Eyes pop open. Bodies squirm with anticipation. Mouths split into grins.

Mr. Pitts walks down the rows handing valentines to each student. Each valentine features a character on a background covered in paper lace. Inside each valentine is a tiny pocket just large enough to hold a penny. Ann is the first to find the penny.

"Look, I have a penny in my Valentine." Ann holds the penny high in the air for all to see. All the students start searching their valentines for the pocket holding a penny.

"Careful, students don't tear your valentines." Mr. Pitts is looking on with great satisfaction at the excitement he's caused in the classroom.

"Oh, and Mr. Pitts, we have a gift for you." Amanda has had the students make valentines. Amanda has pasted the valentines into a notebook for Mr. Pitts.

"I can't thank you enough. Hum, let see." Mr. Pitts read aloud as he turns the pages.

"Be Mine."

"You're my valentine."

"I love school."

Looking up at Amanda, Mr. Pitts swallows to keep from laughing. "Class, you have made my Valentine's Day most special."

Surprising Amanda, Burt stands up and says, "And Mr. Pitts, you have made our day special, too."

***

Amanda is sitting at her desk after all have left for the day. Sitting in the glow of love shared in the schoolroom that day, she hears footsteps coming up the steps and looks up as David Henry walks into the classroom. A disheveled, tired-looking David Henry.

"What on earth, David Henry?"

"I just got back in town. I apologize for my appearance."

"I did not know that you had been out of town."

"Yes, I just got back from Demopolis."

Before Amanda can react, David Henry kneels on the schoolroom floor at Amanda's side. "Amanda Oglesby, will you be my bride?"

Amanda looks David Henry in the eye and nods.

David Henry takes a piece of blue velvet fabric out of his pocket, unfolds it. Resting in the center of the velvet fabric is a platinum ring with one pear-shaped diamond and one pear-shaped sapphire nestled together on top. David Henry reaches for Amanda's hand and slides the ring on her finger. He then pulls her to her feet, takes her face in his two hands, and kisses her. When he stops kissing her, she grabs his lapels with both hands and pulls him back to her.

Finally, Amanda says, "I know. Let's show Miss Sophie. I've just got to tell someone."

"I agree. Let's show Miss Sophie."

Gathering up her things, Amanda closes the school door before walking down the steps with David Henry.

"Oh, one more thing," says Amanda. "I assume my father said, 'Yes.'"

***

Miss Sophie opens the front door to David Henry and Amanda.

"What a surprise! Come in, children. Come in."

David Henry raises Miss Sophie's right hand to his lips before saying, "I had heard that you were ill, Miss Sophie. I don't believe that was true at all. Look at you. You look delightfully well."

"Oh, go on, David Henry. I'm proud to say that I am recovered. Of course, I knew that I would recover because Sister Sarah predicted it." Her grin shows that she may or may not have had much faith in Sister Sarah's predictions. "Enough about me. Come in and have tea with me and tell me what you two are about."

Following Miss Sophie into the parlor, Amanda and David Henry sit together on the settee and wait for Miss Sophie to return with tea. "You tell her, Amanda. She'll want to hear it from you."

"I think I'll just show her."

As the parlor door opens, David Henry gets up to help Miss Sophie bring the tea service into the parlor. Once they settle, tea in hand, Miss Sophie takes a long look at the couple. Her eyes crinkle as she smiles. "Do you two have something to tell me?"

Amanda gets up, walks to Miss Sophie's chair, and extends her ring finger.

"Oh. Would you look at that? I'm tickled pink for you both. When is the wedding?"

"I just got the ring this afternoon. You're the very first to congratulate us."

David Henry says, "And we haven't had time to make wedding plans yet. Doesn't society dictate that you wait six months after the engagement to wed?"

"Pooh on society," says Sophie. "I'm sure that you'll work out what's best for you. And won't this be exciting? Planning a wedding?"

"I can hardly take it all in. Yes, it will be wonderful. Think of the dinners, dances, and rehearsals. We'll have to pick out our china pattern and our crystal pattern and a silver pattern. And think of living at Callander."

David Henry appears to love Amanda's excitement. "Miss Sophie, your tea is delightful, but do you have anything stronger? Our engagement deserves a real toast."

"Why, David Henry. You know I keep a bottle of sherry in the liquor cabinet. I'll go get it."

Returning to the parlor with sherry and glasses on a silver tray, Sophie says, "David Henry, will you do the honors?"

Once they all three have a glass of sherry, Sophie says, "I want to drink to the happiness of a young pair whose future welfare is near and dear to my heart, Amanda and David Henry."

# Fifty-seventh Chapter

## Teaching Mesopotamia

Sadie bounces Mildred on her lap as she talks with Amanda about the Callander's trip to Demopolis to meet Amanda's parents.

"Did they all get along?" asks Sadie.

"Oh, goodness, yes. I was afraid David Henry's parents would be overwhelmed; all the Ellards and Oglesbys turned out for the occasion. We're a pretty daunting group when we're all together."

"But all went well?"

"Absolutely. David Henry's parents fit right in, and my family has already taken David Henry under its collective wings."

"That's good. So, are you planning the wedding? When will it be?"

"We discussed this when we were all together in Demopolis. We think in early July."

"Miss Amanda, I'm so happy for you. The Callanders have always seemed like the best folks around. So good that you're going to be one of them."

"I think so, too. Now about Mesopotamia. You enjoyed this look at ancient times?"

"I love what I've read so far."

"When we studied Mesopotamia earlier this year, we talked about the Tigris and Euphrates Rivers. You know the word

*Mesopotamia* is Greek for land between rivers. I asked the students if they knew of any place in Alabama that is between rivers."

"Did they? Did anyone know?"

"Before you came to class, Sadie, the class took an imaginary trip to Cahawba—the first capital of Alabama. Cahawba was situated between the Alabama and Cahawba Rivers."

"If I were teaching, they'd have to locate Mesopotamia on the map of the ancient world."

"Good. And we'd have to talk about the peoples' lives. Even comparing them to ours. Just like Harley and the other sharecroppers around Marshall, the Mesopotamians were planters."

"Yes, and we could talk about the Mesopotamians inventing the wheel and the plow. Doesn't that amaze you that they plowed just like we do? I even read that they invented something that attached to the plow and spread seed. Now, that's clever."

"You're clever, Sadie. I asked you before if you have ever dreamed of teaching. You'd be a good teacher, Sadie."

Sadie lowers her head to rest on Mildred's head. "Look at me. Taking care of another woman's child. No decent clothes to wear. Living with an abusive husband and sharing my home with another woman. Who would let me teach?"

"It's not hopeless. Educating you, Sadie, is one of the most rewarding things I do. Who knows where it will lead?"

"I'm giving it my all. It's like I can't learn enough. I want to know more about the ancient people and the people that came after them. I want to improve in mathematics. And what about science? I have so much to learn before I can teach.

"You're getting there, Sadie. One day at a time. Now, back to Mesopotamia. Isn't it fascinating that they invented a number system of math based on the number sixty? Today we divide an hour into sixty seconds. Amazing!"

"And don't forget the Mesopotamians developed the first written language. And their religion. They built temples called Ziggurats to honor the gods. Only the High Priest was allowed to speak to the gods. That's like the temple Solomon built. Only the High Priest could enter the Holy of Holies in Solomon's temple."

Amanda is amazed at Sadie's thought processes. She had taught this unit on Mesopotamia earlier in the year. The similarity between the Ziggurats and the temple in Jerusalem had never occurred to Amanda.

Amanda explains that it's time for Sadie's first test on Ancient History. "Sadie, I've worked out with Miss Sophie for you to take your tests at the boarding house during the day when Harley and Pauline are in the field, and Willis and Eliza are in school. Miss Sophie has agreed to take care of Mildred while you take your tests. That way, we don't have to explain to the children what you are doing. They'll never know. That way Harley won't know either."

"I'm ready to take the test. Do you want me to take it tomorrow?"

"Tomorrow will be fine. I'll leave the test with Miss Sophie. Plan on being there after lunch when Harley and Pauline are back in the fields. Oh, and besides the Ancient History book, here's a textbook on photosynthesis. You can begin this textbook while you continue with the one on Ancient History."

Sadie juggles Mildred and the textbook on photosynthesis until they are comfortably situated. Smiling at Amanda, Sadie quips, "I'm certainly glad that you like educating Sadie, Miss Amanda. And for the record, the scribes—that's the teachers—of Mesopotamia could have learned from you."

Leaving Amanda astounded, Sadie hurries down the steps of the schoolhouse and heads home.

# Fifty-eighth Chapter

## Ruby and the Arcadians

Amanda walks into the mercantile store to find three of the local sharecroppers' wives have backed Ruby up against a store counter and are harassing her.

"We're glad yor husband is dead. He was sure mean."

"Yeah, we figure some of his meanness had to rub off on you."

"Sright. And we don't want ya ' round our town."

"Don't want yor child here neither. Why don't y'all just skedaddle from Marshall?"

Before Amanda can react, Miss Maggie crosses the store in five giant steps. "Morning, ladies. So nice of you to be so welcoming to Ruby and Emme."

The "ladies" in questions, mostly hang their heads. All except for Betty Smith. "Mornin' Miss Maggie. You defending this trash?"

"Well, I guess I am since they're a part of my family."

"Part of yor family?"

"You heard right. Ruby and Emme are living with me. So, you insult them; you insult me. You really want to do that?" Miss Maggie shifts her purse so that the ladies can see inside her purse and be reminded of the revolver Miss Maggie never fails to carry.

"Well, Miss Maggie, we didn't know they wuz living with you."

Looking at the clock on the store wall, Betty says, "Lord, look at the time. I was to be home ten minutes ago." That said, she turns and leaves the store as fast as her two legs will carry her. The other wives hustle along after Betty.

Amanda laughs out loud. "Miss Maggie, you are spectacular."

"Humph! I don't know about that. I can't stand that trash! Ruby, you are to let me know if they ever bother you again."

"Yes, ma'am. I will."

"And Amanda, what brings you to the store today?"

"I was going to ask Mr. Pitts if he knew of any historical locations in Alabama that my schoolchildren and I could visit."

"You taking those children on field trips?"

Amanda grins. "Imaginary ones. I call the exercise 'All Aboard.' We get on an imaginary train and ride to different locations in the state. We've been to Cahawba and near Demopolis to the location of the Vine and Olive Colony."

"I'd love to be in your class. Your class sounds fun."

"Come visit anytime, Miss Maggie."

"Now, let me think. A place in Alabama that the children need to study. Umm."

Ruby softly says, "How about Arcadia? It's not in Alabama—not even in these United States—but children could learn about the Arcadians that came to Louisiana and became Cajuns."

"Are you Cajun, Ruby?"

"Yes, ma'am. Mr. Aucoin was, too."

Amanda takes in this stocky woman with the crossed eye—a woman proud of her heritage despite the poverty that surrounded her most of her life.

"Do you know the poem, "Evangeline?" asks Ruby.

"My goodness, yes," replies Amanda. "One of my favorites. Henry Wadsworth Longfellow—what a poet!"

"Growing up, I heard Evangeline was a real woman named Emmeline. That's who I named Emme for—Emmeline Labiche. So romantic—an Arcadian like me roaming around looking for her lost love."

"Thank you so much, Ruby. I like this idea. My students can learn about the Arcadians in Canada and how they became the Cajuns in Louisiana," says Amanda. The older students can learn about Mr. Longfellow and his poem."

"It would make Emme proud: the class could learn about her history."

"Well, that settles it," says Miss Maggie. "I think you've solved your problem, Amanda."

"Me, too," says Amanda. As Amanda leaves the store, she shouts over her shoulder, "All aboard to Arcadia."

March 1893

# Fifty-ninth Chapter

## Sadie Has Plans

"I've been studying photosynthesis, Miss Amanda," says Sadie. I know just how I'd teach a lesson on photosynthesis."

"Yes?" Amanda is curious to see what Sadie has planned, always enjoying how Sadie's mind works.

"Well, first I'd make sure the students can say photosynthesis. It's a mouthful. Then I'd review what they're supposed to know. Each student would get to plant a plant in a cup or bucket they bring from home. I'd bring the plants and the soil. We'd talk about the parts of a plant while we're planting, making sure each student could independently name the parts. Students would understand that the plant is their responsibility to take care of for the rest of the school year."

"I like your idea. So far, so good."

"I'd have a diagram of photosynthesis up on the wall so all the students can see it. Students would learn that plants need water, carbon dioxide, and sunlight to make food. Carbon Dioxide passes through small pores in the plant leaves. Water is absorbed through the plant roots and passes up the stem to the leaves. Sunlight is absorbed by a green chemical in the leaves."

"Photosynthesis happens in the leaves of the plant," Sadie continues. "Leaves are made of small cells that have even smaller things called chloroplasts in them. Chloroplasts contain a green chemical called chlorophyll—that's what makes leaves green."

"Sadie, I think I'll just let you teach this lesson to the students."

"Oh, but there's more," says Sadie. "Chlorophyll absorbs the energy of the sun, and this energy splits the water molecules into hydrogen and oxygen. Leaves release the oxygen that we breathe. Hydrogen and Carbon Dioxide make food for the plants. So, you see, we couldn't live without photosynthesis and the plants couldn't either."

Amanda applauds loudly, and Sadie's mouth splits into a wide grin.

"What do you think, Miss Amanda? Do I understand photosynthesis?"

"I think so. Without a doubt."

Amanda rummages around in the drawer of her teacher's desk and brings out a folded paper—Sadie's test on Mesopotamia. Handing the paper to Sadie, Amanda says, "Congratulations, Sadie. You made a hundred."

Sadie takes the paper from Amanda and reads down each line to see that there are no marked mistakes. Looking up at Amanda, Sadie has tears pooling in the inner corners of her eyes. She hands the paper back to Amanda.

"Would you keep my papers here at the schoolhouse? Can't have Harley finding them. I promise you I won't need to hide anything from him much longer. I have a plan."

Sadie refuses to say more and leaves the schoolroom, leaving a puzzled Amanda behind.

***

Walking into the mercantile store later in the week, Amanda is surprised to see Sadie helping a customer. Gone is the sack dress Sadie usually wears. She's now wearing a green and brown plaid dress. The top of the dress has a row of buttons up the front that end at a high-necked collar trimmed in tiny black lace. Sadie has scrubbed her face and pulled her hair back in a tight chignon. Amanda takes pleasure in watching this new Sadie complete the transaction with the customer and wish her good day.

Turning, Sadie sees Amanda. Sadie smiles broadly and, gathering the skirt of her dress up in two hands, does a little bow. Sadie laughs out loud at Amanda's expression.

"Miss Amanda, I told you I wouldn't have to hide my schoolwork from Harley much longer. I've left—left him and Pauline and Willis and Eliza and Mildred. I'm never going back."

"What happened? How have you been able to leave?"

"I made up my mind. I wasn't going to stay with Harley anymore. I came to see Mr. Pitts and asked if I could work in the store."

"Obviously, he said yes."

"Not only am I helping out with customers, but Mr. Pitts is also letting me stay in a room above the store. I have my own room with a bathroom down the hall. It's heaven. I can study without worrying about Harley, and I don't have to be around Pauline."

"I'm stunned. Living here is the answer to every prayer I've sent to heaven for you—for you to be away from Harley."

"I'll never be beaten by a man again; never as long as I live. And the learning—I'm just going to keep on learning."

Amanda's eyes fill with tears. Here's Sadie, bright and shining Sadie, all on her own. Who knows how far this new Sadie will travel or what she will become? Amanda's heart is full as she hugs Sadie, holding her close for a moment.

Breaking the mood, Sadie proclaims with pride, "I'm a liberated woman, Miss Amanda."

# Sixtieth Chapter

## The Callanders Hold a Ball

"Callander has never looked lovelier," says James William Callander to his wife, Mary Ella. Looking around the ballroom with its fourteen-foot high ceiling decorated with three large chandelier medallions, a Waterford chandelier hanging from each, Mary Ella agrees. Mary Ella can see her reflection in the heartwood pine floors. Wrought iron candle holders that stand six feet tall line the ballroom. The glass chimneys sparkle around the tapers lit inside. Mary Ella, with Lady and Ben's help, has added shiny magnolia leaves to the base of each chimney. Simple but classy!

Amanda and her parents, Rebecca and Milton Oglesby, walk off the porch through one of the open floor-to-ceiling windows. The bottom window is fully opened to form a door. David Henry is first to reach the Oglesby family.

"Welcome to Callander," says David Henry, bowing to Amanda's parents.

Returning the bow, Amanda's father says, "I love this ballroom—a room not always found in homes today. If this is representative of Callander, I can't wait to see the rest of your plantation."

Walking up to the group, James William says, "Then I'll look forward to sharing Callander with you tomorrow. Welcome."

Turning to Rebecca Oglesby, James William bows. "Welcome to Callander. And I want to be the first to thank you for sharing your beautiful daughter with us."

"She is a treasure, isn't she? Though I can say the same for your son. We're both fortunate."

"I couldn't agree more."

An orchestra plays softly at the far end of the ballroom as the citizens of Marshall come into the ballroom to meet Amanda's parents. Amanda notices the parents of many of her schoolchildren are in the room and is touched. Amanda also notices Sadie standing against the wall—an educated Sadie wearing a beautiful lawn dress that floats around her ankles. Amanda tears up, thinking of Sadie's struggles. Miss Maggie notices Sadie as well and walks over to join her.

David Henry's parents have taken Amanda's parents in hand and are making introductions around the ballroom. David Henry steps behind Amanda and says, for her ears only, "Miss Amanda Oglesby, I am the most fortunate man in the world to be with you in this ballroom, knowing that we'll be married soon."

Turning to look up at David Henry, Amanda says, "I love you; you know."

"I love you, too."

"Enough of that, children," says Mr. Pitts, smiling. "What a grand gathering! I think everyone is Marshall is here."

"I think so, too. Mr. Pitts, I haven't had an opportunity to thank you for taking in Sadie."

"The pleasure is all mine, and Mrs. Pitts loves Sadie being at the store. I have more time to be at home. You know, Mrs. Pitts and I have been married forty years. I wish the same for you two."

Before they can talk further, the clinking of a spoon again crystal is heard. James William clears his throat. "Friends, we are gathered tonight to celebrate the engagement of Amanda Oglesby to my son, David Henry Callander. I propose a toast to the future bride and groom. To my David Henry and his Amanda." It is very quiet as all in the room, except David Henry and Amanda, raise a glass to toast. "Now, I am proud to say that Callander offers one of the best buffets in four counties. Please help yourselves."

David Henry and Amanda are first to serve themselves with beef, goose, ham, turkey, and oysters accompanied by corn pudding, creamed onions, sweet potatoes, and collards. Balancing their plates, David Henry and Amanda are making their way to the front of the room when they come face-to-face with Miss Sophie.

Amanda is excited to see her friend, who looks quite refined wearing a beautiful, low-cut velvet gown with the most amazing garnet earrings that dangle alongside Miss Sophie's chin. Amanda opens her mouth to greet Miss Sophie but quickly closes it. She remembers! The dining room at Gaineswood. The portrait of the lady who looks just like Miss Sophie. The lady who is wearing a low-cut velvet gown, a pair of dangling garnet earrings, and a large garnet necklace that hangs on the lady like it was made for her—the same garnet necklace that Sheriff Winfield has over at the jail.

"Amanda, you look like you've seen a ghost. Aren't you going to speak to Miss Sophie?"

Amanda places a quick kiss on Miss Sophie's cheek. "Hello, Miss Sophie. You are stunning."

"Oh, No. You are the stunning one, Amanda." Her smile takes in both David Henry and Amanda. "I'm so proud of you two. I feel that you're my children, too."

"We'd be honored. What if I call you Aunt Sophie?"

"You are a charmer, David Henry." Taking a quick look at Amanda, Sophie moves off to circulate the room.

"Amanda, what's wrong?"

"Oh, nothing. Nothing I can't work out. Come with me. I want you to meet more of my students' parents."

***

"She knows, Maggie. I could see it on her face." Maggie and Sophie are sitting at Miss Maggie's kitchen table with their shoes off, having a late-night cup of tea.

"She can't know. She can't know everything. All she may know is that the necklace found on Aucoin's body is yours."

"That's enough. Amanda's a bright girl. You know she'll think that I had something to do with his death."

"Why are you worried? I shot the son of a bitch."

"Maggie, we're in this together. Now, what should I do?"

"Nothing. You do nothing. Can we agree on that? Will you promise me you won't approach Amanda with this?"

"OK. I promise. But you know I'll worry."

"I know, Sophie. I know you will."

***

Amanda pulls her gown over her head, slides into bed, and pulls the quilt up to her chin. She won't be sleeping anytime soon. How could Miss Sophie's garnet necklace end up in Aucoin's pocket? Did Miss Sophie have anything to do with Aucoin's death?

Should she tell Sheriff Winfield what she knows? It will be a long night for Amanda.

# Sixty-first Chapter

## Amanda Hears a Confession

Ending a long school day, Amanda looks forward to a cup of tea at Miss Sophie's. After placing her things on a chair in the hall, Amanda walks into the kitchen and is surprised to see Miss Sophie and Miss Maggie already seated at the kitchen table. She is even more surprised to see the large garnet necklace coiled on the kitchen table.

"Oh, there you are. Come sit down. I'll fix you a cup of tea." Sophie bustles around, removing the tea cozy off the teapot and pouring tea into a rose-patterned teacup. Sophie places the cup in front of Amanda and offers her a small bowl filled with orange marmalade, which is delicious stirred in tea. Silence fills the room while Amanda prepares her tea. The necklace lies on the table in front of the three of them like an unwelcome guest with a story to tell.

"Was I right? Last night, did you compare me to the painting hanging in the dining room at Gaineswood?" Miss Sophie looks at Amanda intently but does not wait for her reply. "Did you realize the earrings I wore matched the garnet necklace worn in the portrait at Gaineswood? The same garnet necklace that Sheriff Winfield was showing around town—the one taken from Aucoin's pocket after he was found murdered?"

"Yes," says Amanda softly.

"I knew it! I knew you made the connection and, knowing you, I'm sure you spent a sleepless night deciding what you should do with what you knew."

"Yes."

"Stop worrying, child," says Miss Maggie. "Sophie and I went to the sheriff's office this morning and confessed."

"I don't understand—what did you confess?"

"Well, we killed Aucoin or rather I did. Shot him in the head."

"But why?"

"Well, for one thing, he was in Sophie's bedroom going through her jewelry. Aucoin picked the garnet necklace for Sophie to wear—while she had sex with him."

Amanda sucks in her breath. Freezes. Forgets how to breathe out. Sophie's voice fades in and out, "Amanda. Amanda, are you all right?"

Then Maggie. "Breathe, Amanda."

Amanda feels Maggie's touch on her arm. With a whoosh, Amanda breathes out.

"I think we'd better start at the beginning," says Sophie. "In late October, Aucoin came to my house and informed me he wasn't satisfied with his sex life at home, and he had chosen me to take Ruby's place. You can imagine how repulsed I was."

Amanda, still stunned, nods her head.

"That December day Aucoin died, Maggie and I were coming home from the community vegetable garden. Maggie agreed to come to my house for lunch but went home first to put up her vegetables. When I entered my house, I heard a noise upstairs and investigated. Aucoin was standing in my bedroom, holding the garnet necklace. He put the necklace in his pocket and came forward to attack me. Thank goodness Maggie came in for lunch and heard the noise."

Maggie picks up the story. "Well, I shot Aucoin—square in the forehead. We waited 'til we were sure everyone was asleep and, using a flatbed cart, moved Aucoin's body to the base of Mildren Pickens's statue. We thought that was funny, at the time."

Sophie says, "We forgot all about the necklace in Aucoin's pocket until Sheriff Winfield started showing it around town."

Gradually Amanda is beginning to absorb what the ladies are telling her. Sadly, she says, "And you went to the sheriff because of me. So I wouldn't have to decide about telling what I know."

"Now, child. It was the thing to do. We're both relieved it's over."

"Is it over?"

"I think so. The sheriff quoted Job 4: 8. 'According to what I have seen, those who plow iniquity and those who sow trouble harvest it.' Then he thanked Miss Maggie for ridding the town of Aucoin, saying, in his lifetime, the only time he'd come across pure evil was when he encountered Aucoin."

"And he gave Sophie back the garnet necklace. He did warn her that she'd never be able to wear it again."

Amanda says to Maggie, "And you took in Ruby and Emme. Oh, Maggie!"

"I had to. As evil as Aucoin was, he provided for Ruby and Emme. I took that away from them."

"Will they ever know what happened?" asks Amanda.

"Never. We'll never tell. The sheriff won't, and I'm sure you won't tell."

"No. I'll never speak of Aucoin's death to a single soul. Not even David Henry."

"Then I think it's over," says Sophie.

But Amanda has the last word. "You need to know something. I had decided to keep everything to myself. I didn't know how you were involved, but I would have kept what I knew about the necklace to myself. The sheriff is right. Aucoin was pure evil."

# Sixty-second Chapter

## The Last Day of School

The last school day is almost over. To Amanda's relief, none of her students are graduating this year. All will be back in October to begin another school year. Next year will be the last year for at least two of the older students, but Amanda will cross that bridge when she comes to it. It's a long time before all of them will be gathered together again, and Amanda worries that they will forget so much during the long break.

"Students, I know that you're excited about the upcoming months, but I can't let you go. We are going to do a couple of things to stay in touch. First, a review. What are the five parts of a letter?"

Ann raises her hand and answers when Amanda nods to her. "Heading, Greeting, Body…"

Before Ann can finish, Burt jumps in. "Closing and signature."

"Yes," says Amanda, as she begins handing out envelopes to the students. Each of the envelopes has Amanda's address at Miss Sophie's on it. "Once a month, you are to write a letter to me, telling me about your life, and—you advanced students—I have an additional assignment for you. Try to write at least two Donald stories to include with your letters. Know I will be so excited to hear from each of you. Make sure that you take the letter to the post office. Miss Elizabeth will make sure I get it. I need to receive it before the end of each month. So how many letters will I receive from each of you with school starting back in October?"

Silence. To Amanda's surprise, Emme holds up six fingers.

"Very good, Emme. I will receive six letters from each of you between now and October."

Randy seems very concerned. "You're coming back, aren't you, Miss Amanda?"

"Of course. Why do you ask?"

"My daddy says most counties don't let teachers teach after they get married. I have been so scared you wouldn't be back," answers Randy.

"Me, too."

"I was worried, too, Miss Amanda."

"But we're so lucky to have people like Mr. Pitts and Mr. King on our school board. They know how much I love and need to teach and are willing to let me do so. Speaking of Mr. Pitts, he's coming up the steps right now."

Walking to the front of the schoolroom, Mr. Pitts says, "I couldn't let the school year end without wishing you all well before we come back together in October. And I'm stealing Miss Amanda's thunder, but we have a surprise for you: each of you will take home a library book to read over the summer. Someone will be at the schoolhouse every Friday afternoon beginning in May so that you may return your book and check out a new one. Some Fridays Miss Amanda will be here. Some Fridays I'll be here. We're excited to have you reading when you're not in school."

"Thank you, Mr. Pitts, for sharing this exciting news with the students. Now, students, follow me into the library, and I'll help you check out your first book for the break. Mr. Pitts, may they bring their cards to you? Students, remember to sign the card in the book and take the card to Mr. Pitts."

Chaos ensues as Amanda tries to help all twenty-eight students choose the best book to take home. When each student has a book in hand and Mr. Pitts has all the library cards, the school day is over. But not quite. Looking out the window, Amanda sees a stream of parents coming up the walk to the school. The parents file into the room and stand around the wall.

Mr. Pitts clears his throat. "Amanda, we couldn't let the school year end without showing you how much you mean to all of us. We couldn't ask for a better teacher and are so relieved you will be back with us next year. Now, before next year starts, we understand that you have an important event coming up in your life—marriage. To celebrate your marriage to our own David Henry, each of the ladies has copied down her favorite recipe for you. I know Lady does most of the cooking at Callander, but you won't always live there. Besides, every bride needs to know how to cook. It's a gesture of love and appreciation, Amanda, for all you've done for our students this year."

Tears flow freely down Amanda's face as each of the mothers passes by Amanda and hand her a recipe card. The parents file silently out the door of the schoolroom, children in tow, after they give Amanda their recipe cards. Amanda is left standing in the middle of the schoolroom holding the cards and crying. Mr. Pitts pats Amanda on the shoulder, turns, and walks out of the school, leaving Amanda alone.

July 1893

# Sixty-third Chapter

## The Peddler Comes to Town

"And how are the wedding plans progressing?" asks Sophie.

"Beautifully," says Amanda. "I had the final fitting for my wedding dress when I was in Demopolis last week. The strangest and most wonderful thing happened—as I slipped the wedding dress on the bells of the Presbyterian Church started ringing."

"An omen. What a splendid omen!"

"I thought so, too." Amanda pauses to listen. "Miss Sophie, what is that racket outside?"

They both walk to the window facing the street. A horse-drawn wooden cart, bells jingling, is making its way down Main Street. Canvas drops are rolled up to the top of the cart and tied so that everyone can see the notions inside the cart.

"That's the peddler, Amos Levy. He usually makes his way through Marshall in late spring after most of the spring floods are over. He's late this year."

"What an interesting concept. We don't have peddlers in Demopolis."

"Peddlers make their way through the rural areas, selling farm supplies for the men and thread, needles, pots, lace, buttons, fabrics as well as dress patterns for the women. Some peddlers even measure their customers for clothes and shoes. They bring everything back on their next trip."

"What a sad job!"

"Not at all. Most peddlers in this area are Jewish men who speak several languages—they have to so they can communicate with all their customers. The peddlers bring news of the outside world to families living in isolation, so the peddlers are usually highly welcomed into the homes along their way."

"But what about Mr. Pitts? Aren't the peddlers competing with the mercantile store?"

"Mr. Pitts doesn't see it that way. He's the one who gives Amos most of the supplies he sells. Amos will pay Mr. Pitts for the supplies he sold and pick up more goods while he's in town."

"Look, there's Sadie."

As Amanda and Miss Sophie walk up to the peddler's wagon, Sadie is completing a purchase. It appears that she's buying a decorative tin. As soon as she spots Amanda, she hides the tin behind her back.

"Sadie," says Miss Sophie. "What treasure have you found?"

Sadie's face turns bright red. Embarrassed, she says, "No treasure. Nothing you'd be interested in. But look at this lace. Isn't it beautiful?"

Amanda is puzzled by Sadie's behavior and impressed by the way Sadie steers Miss Sophie's attention away from the mysterious purchase.

Sadie turns back to Amanda. "What's new with the wedding plans?"

"We have posted our bans—me at my home church in Demopolis and David Henry in the Methodist church here. It's still important to have your intention to marry announced by your minister. And I was just telling Miss Sophie that I've had the final fitting for my wedding dress."

"It's so romantic. You and Mr. David Henry are like Perseus and Andromeda."

Impressed as always by Sadie's knowledge, Amanda replies, "Our love for each other, yes, but there's no Medusa in our story. Thank goodness!"

# Sixty-fourth Chapter

## David Henry Gives an Unusual Wedding Gift

Amanda finds Mr. Pitts behind the cash register at the mercantile store. "Mr. Pitts, I treasure the recipes the parents gave me. It wouldn't surprise me if you didn't have something to do with that."

"No, ma'am. It was not my idea. You don't know how much you mean to the schoolchildren and their parents."

"Thank you for that. The feeling is mutual. But I came in to talk to you about the most unusual wedding gift that I received from David Henry."

"Oh, really?"

"Yes and as a matter of fact, it involves you."

"That's curious. Well, don't keep me in suspense. What is it?"

"David Henry knows how much teaching means to me. He is encouraging me to continue. He also knows that Sadie Wiggins is important to me—that I want to see her teach at Marshall School. So, David Henry has proposed that he pay Sadie's salary. I'll teach the older students, and Sadie can teach the younger students. We'll both be able to teach at Marshall."

Silence. Mr. Pitts is thinking. Finally, he says, "Two teachers for the price of one?"

"Yes, sir."

"Well, Amanda, I have to run it by the other two trustees. I don't see them objecting. But Sadie has to be certified."

"Where does she stand?" asks Amanda.

"Sadie has taken tests in reading, geography, English grammar, mental arithmetic, written arithmetic, and physiology."

"Did she pass?"

"I don't know. I administered the tests, but Lawyer King is grading the tests."

"When will we know?"

"Any day now. I'll run your idea by the trustees and will let you know as soon as I have an answer. Oh, Sadie will have to take the course on Theory and Art of Teaching. It's a course held at Troy State Normal School this month—happens to be the same week of your wedding. If she passes all her tests, the trustees will pay for Sadie to take this course. All the hotels in Troy offer free room and board to future teachers taking the class. Sadie will not have expenses. I see no roadblocks for her, except she has to pass the tests."

"Thank you, Mr. Pitts. If you allow us both to teach, you won't regret it."

"Yes, I think it's a winning situation for Marshall, but I do have to say—it's the most unusual wedding gift."

# Sixty-fifth Chapter

## The Wedding

Amanda is in her old room at home. Sitting at her dresser, she looks in the mirror and makes a tiny adjustment to her hair. It's almost time to put on her veil and let her father walk her into the parlor where the wedding will be held.

There's a knock at the door. Amanda opens the door, expecting to see her father. Instead, it's her mother. "Mr. Pitts, Miss Sophie, and Miss Maggie have just arrived for the wedding. Mr. Pitts asks that I bring this to you." Amanda's mother hands Amanda a tin box. She recognizes the box. It's the one Sadie purchased from the peddler earlier this month.

Amanda's mother kisses her on the forehead. "It's almost time for the wedding to begin. You know how happy we are for you. Your father and I agree David Henry is the perfect man for you. Bless you, my dear child."

Amanda's mother has barely left the room when Amanda raises the lid of the tin box. Inside are six different tests with Sadie's name written at the top. Each of the tests is scored. Each test is scored 100.

***

Amanda walks into the parlor on her father's arm. The sweet smell of the phlox in her bridal bouquet floats in the air along with the strains of Mendelssohn's "Wedding March." Amanda's dress of silk mist taffeta has a bell-shaped skirt trimmed in seed pearls. Handmade roses mark the waist in the back where the skirt extends into a chapel length train.

Amanda smiles when she sees Elizabeth, her maid of honor, in place at the front of the drawing room. Passing by the Corinthian columns halfway into the drawing room, Amanda spots Mr. Pitts, Miss Sophie, and Miss Maggie—the latter two in their wedding finery. Seated in front of the Marshall trio is the assortment of aunts, uncles, cousins, and, to Amanda's amusement, Donald, dressed in dress pants, a white shirt, and a tie, which hangs lopsided on his chest.

Amanda looks at David Henry, the tall, distinguished man who will walk through this life with her. Her smile widens. David Henry smiles back and, of course, winks.

"Who will give this woman to marry this man?" asks the pastor.

"Her mother and I do," answers Amanda's father, as he raises Amanda's right hand to his lips and kisses it.

Amanda takes her place by David Henry as they turn to face the pastor.

# Sixty-sixth Chapter

## Early October 1893

### Open House at Marshall School

A feminine hand forms letters on the old blackboard over the ghost of words written there before and erased. It's open house at Marshall School. Sadie Wiggins writes on the board.

Amanda walks up the schoolhouse steps and sees that Sadie has arrived before her. Amanda takes in the new Sadie, dressed in a bell-shaped skirt and long-sleeved white blouse.

She smiles as she remembers the open house just one year ago when she was a first-year teacher. At that open house, she met a willowy, tall woman dressed in a flour-sack dress, a woman with an evident yearning for learning and an ugly purple bruise on her upper arm. Sadie has journeyed far.

Amanda looks at the quote Sadie wrote on the blackboard: "Education is not preparation for life. Education is life itself. John Dewey."

Amanda and Sadie turn to face the first parents coming up the schoolhouse steps.

## About the Author

Alayne Smith is a retired broadcast journalism teacher who earned M. Ed and Ed. S degrees in Instructional Technology from the University of Georgia. She taught broadcast journalism for fifteen years in Gwinnett County, Ga., where she developed the first broadcast journalism course at the high school level. With other Gwinnett County broadcast journalism teachers, she contributed to the development of an eight-course continuum of courses in broadcast journalism and video production. Two of Alayne's students won the 1999 Southern Regional Student Emmy Award from the National Academy of Arts and Sciences. Sixty students produced documentaries and feature stories, advancing to International Media Festivals held in New Orleans, Dallas, Houston, Indianapolis, and Denver. She served as a committee member for the International Student Media Festival, 1995-1998, and as a CNN Student Bureau Advisor, 1999 – 2001.

While working at the Broadcast and Learning Department of Gwinnett County Public Schools, Alayne designed classes, developed manuals, and developed a cluster training approach for media specialists, K-8, to maximize the use of each school's broadcast equipment. She co-taught sessions in each of the county's seventeen clusters, reaching media specialists from over ninety-six schools. Media Specialists were offered hands-on instruction to assist them with creating informative, curricula-based, attention-getting broadcasts.

*Ellen and the Three Predictions,* published in March 2017 by Cactus Moon Publications, is Alayne's first novel. *Ellen and the Three Predictions* is a historical fiction novel written for young adults. It is set in the late 1950s and early 1960s and details the life of aspiring broadcast journalist, Ellen Jones, and the predictions made for Ellen's life by Old Luella, a local soothsayer. *Ellen and the Three Predictions* was a semi-finalist in the William Faulkner – William Wisdom Creative Writing Competition 2016.

Alayne is a member of the Atlanta Writers Club, the Georgia Association for Instructional Technology, the Georgia Writers Association, Gwinnett County Retired Educators Association, and the Society of Children's Book Writers and Illustrators. She currently lives in Lawrenceville, Georgia, with her husband.

# More by Alayne Smith

I look down at her predictions for me. There are three:

She will be an advocate for the beauty. . .

She will find the soldier. . .

She will foil a dictator. . .

*Ellen and the Three Predictions* details the life of eighteen-year-old Ellen Jones and the predictions of Old Luella, a seer in the small town of Marshall, Alabama whose predictions Ellen reads after her mother's unexpected death. The predictions seem far-fetched to young Ellen but throughout this book, the reader will learn far before Ellen, just how significant her role in the lives of those she loves will be.

Through the political and social changes of the early 1960s, Ellen, a budding journalist, comes to terms with her role in the world as she encounters each of Old Luella's predictions. These encounters take her through the social taboos of Callendar Plantation, Alabama - to the promise of love and a career in Miami - and finally, to a daring rescue in Castro's Cuba.

Ellen's Notebook is carefully prepared as she becomes more passionate about the career and responsibility of journalism. Introducing readers to life in the early 1960's mirroring much of today's complex social climate.

77126334R00212

Made in the USA
Columbia, SC
29 September 2019